Praise for Barbara

Something Unpredictable

"[A] heartwarming tale of romance that presents humanity in all its eccentric glory."

—*Abilene Reporter-News*

"Chepaitis creates characters and situations that will entrance readers."

—*The Tampa Tribune*

These Dreams

"[A] must read."

—*More* magazine

"Heartfelt and moving. . . . Chepaitis endows her characters with genuinely human warmth, and her challenging contemporary themes make the story more interesting than the average romance."

—*Publishers Weekly*

Both available from Washington Square Press

Something Unpredictable

a novel

barbara chepaitis

WASHINGTON SQUARE PRESS
new york london toronto sydney

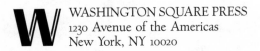
WASHINGTON SQUARE PRESS
1230 Avenue of the Americas
New York, NY 10020

ISBN: 978-0-7434-3753-0

First Washington Square Press trade paperback edition July 2005

10 9 8 7 6 5 4 3 2 1

WASHINGTON SQUARE PRESS and colophon are
registered trademarks of Simon & Schuster, Inc.

Manufactured in the United States of America

For information regarding special discounts for bulk purchases,
please contact Simon & Schuster Special Sales at 1-800-456-6798 or
business@simonandschuster.com

to the Old One, with thanks and love,
and Veronica Cruz, who has allowed me to steal so much

acknowledgments

This book is (of course) imaginary, but many real people acted as guides and resources throughout the journey. Therefore, I'd like to offer my sincere thanks, first of all, to Susan Derda, who gave me the most up-to-date information on diabetes and caring for the diabetic. She also makes incredible cakes, and offers the kind of hospitality Carla would be proud of. If you ever need medical research or a good Easter dinner, Susan's the one to call.

My thanks also go to the Mohawk community of Kanatsiohareke, for their generosity in sharing wisdom, especially with the Thanksgiving Address. Terry Bach sat with me in a train station in Chicago and told me stories about old women that were invaluable. I learned a great deal from Professor John Delano, who teaches with eloquence about both the beauty and limits of science, and from Blue Diamond Septic, which provided me with more information on septic systems than I ever thought I'd want to know.

Acknowledgments

Two Amandas helped me out: Amanda Geldard, whose high-spirited nature and love of weather helped breathe life into Delilah, and Amanda Trotter, the truest kind of friend to me, and to rocks and mountains everywhere. And there is Matthew Ryan, whose superman complex—and I say this with the highest regard—informed my understanding of Jack. Thank you all for being who you are. Keep up the good work.

Then, of course, there is the land of Settles Hill, which took up residence in my imagination before this writing, and has lodged there well beyond the limits of this book. May the sky there stay big, and the people authentic, and may I always be grateful for that.

*something
unpredictable*

the hill

The old woman stood at the top of the hill, at the edge between the clearing and the trees, and listened to the land breathe in and breathe out. It did this slowly, she thought, and you had to listen slowly in order to hear it.

She listened, and in the breathing discerned the echo of other voices. Old voices. Voices of friends who had stayed in the house at the bottom of the hill with her. Family voices, long dead, and some buried under fallen headstones in the small plot that still remained beyond the trees. Voices of the circus crowd that followed her here whenever she came back for a respite from travel. The voice of her brother, and the voice of a baby girl, crying for the comfort of warm arms. Voices she didn't know except through stories her grandmother told her long ago.

She closed her eyes and listened, letting the sound flow through her, unimpeded by any thought. In the breath of old voices and the land was at least some of the knowledge she would need.

When she opened her eyes again, she saw that in the west, the sun was washing the sky in a bath of red and gold. It had been a decent spring, and promised to be a good summer. Just enough rain, and warmth enough even for an old woman's bones.

She bent and picked up a smooth white stone from the grass. It looked like a beach pebble, out of place in this land of grass and trees and hard, gray rocks. It felt good in her hand, rounded and cool. She put it in the pocket of her pants. Later, when she got undressed, she would find it there, and smooth it in her hand to help her find sleep.

Sleep wouldn't come easily, she thought, if what Kootch told her was right. She had too much to think about. She needed time to prepare, and she was still too excited to do that. His news created a deep jangling of anticipation in her, a sense of newness and possibility, a feeling she hadn't known for some time.

She scanned the ridge, the pond, the house, and beyond to the mountains, where the sun was almost completely down now. She'd been standing for some time, and her feet were tingling, her eyes fuzzy, and the world a little too blurred. She spit out an expletive, to chase away a soft sorrow this caused her. Sorrow was the emotion of helplessness. She wasn't helpless. Not yet. And there was no need for sorrow, regardless of the outcome. After all, it would be an adventure, no matter what happened. No matter what she chose to do. Who knew what might happen next? Who could say it would be bad? Nobody could, because it was a great unknown. And it was the mystery of that, the not knowing, that created adventure.

The first time she put her hand on the rippling muscles of a tiger's back, she felt that way. It was an animal that could, and might, crush her skull with its jaws, even though it purred at her touch. She'd heard all the stories about the men who'd worked with the big animals for years, and then, one day, for no apparent reason, the animal would turn on them, maul or kill them for reasons nobody could explain. Some trainers said that wouldn't happen if you kept control. Others said it wouldn't happen if you knew your animals and treated them well. She didn't kid herself. The big cats were a mystery, and working with them was risky. But to be able to feel that fur, the motion of that muscle with the palm of her hand, was worth it. An adventure.

She sniffed at the air, smelling the night coming on. She didn't know exactly when things would happen. Kootch wasn't sure about that. But it could be any time at all, so she wanted to be ready. She wanted to know the right things to do and say.

She knelt as if in supplication, and pressed a hand to the earth, felt its warmth, its soft, slow, generous life tingling against her palm.

She breathed with it, slowly and with careful intent, as if one of them were focusing on the act of labor and birth, though it would be impossible to say which one. Occasionally, she mumbled to herself. Mostly, she listened.

When the light disappeared, and the crescent moon became visible above the horizon, she stood up, her knees creaking and stiff.

She made her way down the ridge and toward the house, and went inside.

The hill breathed in, and breathed out, and was silent.

w a t e r

 Delilah stared at the bathtub, which was three-quarters filled with blue Jell-O cubes.

"So get in," Thomas said.

"Get in?" she asked.

When she didn't move, he briefly stopped fiddling with his camera equipment and blinked at her.

"You'll want to take your clothes off first," he noted. "Otherwise they'll get stained."

"And I won't?"

"You'll wash," he said, and went back to his camera.

She sighed, and started to undress. She'd helped Thomas with other art projects, such as his ten-foot-tall pasta tower, and it was fun enough, but this was different. She wasn't sure it would be fun to model for a series of photos on the human body immersed in Jell-O, which Thomas wanted for an upcoming photo show.

Still, she knew Thomas. When he was into one of his projects, he occupied a world composed entirely of his own visions, and no discomfort mattered. Especially not her own. She didn't take it personally. Besides, he made her life a lot less dull than it would be otherwise. At thirty-one, still living with her parents, with no career to speak of, she didn't have much to brag about beyond her willingness to slip into a tub full of Jell-O for the sake of art.

Not that she was complaining. After all, living with her parents meant occupying a room in a sweet little three-thousand-square-foot Spanish contemporary on two acres of prime land in Key West. The house itself was, as her mother frequently pointed out, big enough to house two families of Guatemalans, which it had done occasionally, so they didn't really get in each other's way.

If she were the beach bunny type, her life would have been a blast, but she didn't think she was built for that. She was too normal looking, with brown eyes, medium-length brown hair, medium height, and medium build, though she'd be the first to admit that it would be accurate to say she had hips.

And while Key West was known as a party town, she was not much of a party girl. She could hold her liquor too well and it took an inordinate amount of money to get her drunk. The party life being out, and in the absence of anything she could generously call a career, she still wanted something to get her up in the morning. Some anticipation of surprise, or adventure. Something that said she mattered on the planet—aside from her mother's periodic demands that she participate in an activist event like a Vegan Supper to Save the World.

"This isn't going to feel good," she said when her clothes were off and she had one foot poised over the tub.

"Sure it will," Thomas said. "Kind of like a very cool lotion, or—or like sex."

She raised an eyebrow at him. "How do you know?" she asked.

"I did a trial run. It seemed only fair."

She contemplated the thought of Thomas naked, in a tub of Jell-O. It did not make her think of sex. But to Thomas, art definitely took precedence over sex. In fact, that was her only complaint about him, besides the fact that he couldn't cook, didn't have a job to speak of, and was living in the caretaker's house on her parents' land for free, without any indication that he ever intended to move out. Still, he had one distinct advantage over a lot of men she knew. He was there.

She closed her eyes and plunged a foot into the Jell-O. It made a squishing sound.

"God," she ejaculated.

"All the way in," Thomas encouraged her. "Unless you want naked bits to show."

She put her other foot in and stood there, shin deep. "They'll show anyway," she said. "This stuff isn't opaque."

"It'll all be decently blurred. Slide down."

She shuddered and lowered herself slowly. "Ewww," she said. "This doesn't feel like sex. It feels like—like goo. Gooey worms and—and goo."

"Beautiful," Thomas purred when she was fully immersed. "Now, let one hand dangle over the side and close your eyes. Good. Let your head kind of loll, like you're dead."

"Am I?" she asked.

"Metaphorically," he said. "The series is about how popular culture sucks us in and kills us all in the end. Turn left a little. Good." She heard his camera clicking away.

After a while, he had her roll over on her stomach, splayed out, eyes open and staring blankly. "Wow," he said. "I wish you could see yourself. That cellulite is perfect."

"Cellulite?" she squeaked. "What cellulite? I don't have cellulite."

"Don't move," he said.

Out of the corner of her eye she saw him approaching her with a yellow rubber duckie, which he put on her back, but she was beginning to lose sensation by then. It was a defense mechanism, she was sure, to avoid feeling like a piece of canned fruit cocktail. To avoid feeling slimy, and riddled with cellulite.

It was about that time that she heard the insistent chirping coming from the region of her pants pocket. Her cell phone. She'd resisted getting one, but her father thought it would be a good idea, and it had proved handy—to bail her mother out of jail after a civil disobedience moment, or rescue her when she treated a diner full of homeless people to lunch and then realized she didn't have her credit card with her.

"Delilah," Thomas said reprovingly, "I told you, no cell phone when we're working."

She rolled over, slid under the Jell-O and came up sputtering, pulled herself upright and choked out, "Get it."

"In a minute," Thomas murmured, snapping away with his camera.

"*Get* it," she insisted, splattering Jell-O around as she tried to pull herself out of the tub. She slipped back under and was briefly terrified that she'd drown. Death by Jell-O. Thomas would never be able to explain, and her parents would be terribly embarrassed at his subsequent murder trial.

She made an effort and pulled herself up.

"Mm," Thomas said. "Keep doing that. That's good."

"Get it," she demanded, "or I'll smear Jell-O on your camera. It'll be ruined and my parents won't necessarily buy you another one."

Thomas made a face at her, but put his camera down and got the phone out, opened it, and held it to her ear.

"Delilah?" a voice said. Then, with more urgency, "Delilah?" Her mother.

"Yes, Mom. It's me."

"I'm so glad. Are you busy? Because if you're not I really, *really* need to see you for just a few moments. Well, actually, for more than a few moments."

"What is it? Is Dad okay?" She was accustomed to the sound of her mother's voice in incipient hysteria, and it didn't really worry her, but she did worry about her father. Someday his patience would just give, and he'd self-combust.

"Your father's fine," she said, sounding a little miffed. "This isn't about him."

"Then what's wrong?" Delilah asked.

"Nothing's wrong. Just—disturbing in a way. I mean, not in a bad way, but in a way."

"In what way?"

She drew in breath and released it in little sputters. "I found my mother," she said.

"Lemme clean up," Delilah said. "I'll meet you in the kitchen."

Two

air

Her parents' kitchen was big and cluttered. The round pine table at the center was usually covered with flyers for upcoming political events, or a grant her mother was writing to feed the hungry and clothe the naked, or educate the naked and clothe the hungry, while making sure no more cats were euthanized. Her mother liked to keep busy trying to save the world, and encouraged Delilah to do the same. The problem was, Delilah had seen how futile it was, and thought maybe she should hold out until she thought of something more effective. She imagined it might take a while.

Her father kept his papers—which traced the rise and fall of money in the world and were more about saving his family—in his study, which was full of dark wood and books and had a fireplace, just as if he lived someplace that actually had a winter. He retreated into it when things got to be a bit much around the house—a not infrequent occurrence, since her mother not only worked the activist circuit, she frequently housed it.

Delilah was aware that her family wasn't particularly normal, but she hadn't ever met one that was. She was just grateful that her family's abnormalities were mostly benign.

When she entered the kitchen, her mother and father were sitting at the table with an older man with a gray walrus mustache and a woman who looked like an ex-nun—the bowl-on-the-head haircut, navy blazer, and little gold cross were dead giveaways, Delilah thought.

"Lilah," her mother said, blinking at her, "you're a Smurf."

She grinned stiffly. Thomas had been wrong about the Jell-O washing off. She was tinged all over in a vaguely unhealthy shade of blue. "Just a science experiment," she said. "Don't worry about it."

She went over to her father and patted his shoulder. He patted her hand in return, and gave her a little concerned smile, then turned back to her mother, whose hand he was holding. The man with the mustache was shaking his head.

"Hi," she said to him. "I'm Delilah."

"Oh," her mother said, waving her free hand at them. "Lilah, dear, this is Henry and Sister Bernadette. They're staying for a bit. School of the Americas protest."

"Nice to meet you," she said, and they smiled. Then Sister Bernadette—not ex yet, after all—touched Henry's arm.

"We should give them some privacy," she said. "It's a family matter." They rose, nodded solemnly, and left the room.

Delilah was about to open her mouth to speak to the issue at hand, when she heard her sister's voice calling from the hall.

"Mom? Dad? Where are you?"

"In the kitchen, Margo," her mother called, and her sister appeared, stood a moment to take in the scene, then came to the table and sat. Delilah noticed that she was using a new lipstick. A nice bright coral that went with the splashes of coral in the flowers on her Ann Taylor skirt. Probably called Coral Delight. Probably Chanel. She liked Chanel.

Margo turned to Delilah, and raised her eyebrows. "Smurf party?" she asked.

"I'm auditioning for the feature film," Delilah said.

She didn't want to get into it. Not with Margo, who liked to lecture her about the misspent nature of her life. When that happened, Delilah liked to resent it. It was part of the family dynamics, as was Margo's view of herself and her mother as the ones who took positive action, while Delilah and her father were the dreamers, slightly out of touch. Delilah wasn't sure how this happened, when it was invariably either she or her father who did things like change the oil in the car, get the cat to the vet, or bail Mom out of jail.

Of course, Margo had a mainstream kind of life—husband, career as an interior decorator, mortgage, and so on—but Delilah couldn't see how being an interior decorator gave her a more valid perspective on reality than, for instance, her job, which was waiting tables for tourists. And her mother's penchant for political fringes didn't qualify her for normalcy, though she claimed it kept her in touch with what was Really Happening. Perhaps, Delilah thought, she and her father encouraged them in subtle ways, like not arguing with them. Or maybe she preferred the role she was in because it relieved her of the responsibility of getting a life. At any rate, since she was blue, she didn't think she could argue the point right now.

"Delilah," Margo said with reproach in her voice.

"Don't worry. It'll wash. So I'm told."

Margo made a clucking noise, shrugged, and turned back to their mother. "So tell me about it. What's wrong."

"Nothing," she said, "Not wrong. I just need a consultation."
She sighed, and continued. "You know I've been researching my
genealogy—my adoptive parents' genealogy, that is."

Margo nodded. She and Delilah both knew, and thought it was
odd, since their mother was adopted. What did the genealogy of
her adoptive parents matter? It wasn't her history. But she claimed
their history had more influence on her than her birth parents' history, since her adoptive parents raised her. She believed in the
power of nurture over nature. Delilah thought it was her social science background.

"Anyway," she continued, "the agency I was using sent me
some material, and it had the wrong names. Somebody named
Carla Diamond. I called and asked them about it, and they said
yes, of course, Carla Diamond. My mother. Who lives in upstate
New York."

"Lives?" Margo asked. "Present tense?"

"Very present. Very tense. I told them, no, no. My mother died
ten years ago, meaning my adoptive mother, of course. And her
name wasn't Carla Diamond. Obviously they'd made a mistake.
But the only mistake they made was finding my birth mother."

"Jesus," Delilah said. "Aren't those kinds of records sealed or
something?"

"Not then," my mother said. "Or not in this case. I don't know.
It was—well, over fifty years ago."

"Did they tell you anything about her?" Delilah asked.

Her mother whispered something that sounded like a yes, and
squeezed her father's hand.

"Like?" Delilah continued.

"Don't push her," Margo said. "This can't be easy."

"But it's a good thing, isn't it? Now you'll know your mother.
People spend years trying to find that kind of thing out, and it was
handed to you, like a gift."

Her mother made a sound like she was gargling, and put her hands over her face.

"It's okay, Lana," her father said. "Really it is. You don't have to do anything about her, after all. She doesn't even know you exist."

"Will somebody tell me what it is?" Delilah demanded. Just then a young man with a shaved head wandered in and opened the refrigerator. He got out a carton of milk, poured himself a glass, and left with it.

"Who?" Delilah asked her father.

"I'm not sure," he said. "Lana?"

"School of the Americas," she mumbled. "I told you. They're staying until the rally tomorrow, then the trip to Georgia."

Delilah's father nodded, then looked at her. "She's a circus woman," he said.

Delilah let the words bounce around, waiting to see if they'd attach to anyone in the room. The young man with no hair? Gender was often nonspecific with friends of her mother, but he didn't look like a woman. After a while, she just shook her head.

"Your grandmother," her father said, and her mother groaned. "This woman. She's a circus woman."

"Bearded lady?" Delilah asked. "Contortionist? Fat woman?"

"Delilah," Margo exclaimed, using all the syllables with forced accent.

"Tiger trainer, I think. Yes, Lana? Yes. Tigers, and horses. She did things with horses. Not anymore, of course. She's very old now."

Personally, Delilah thought it made sense. Her mother's adoptive parents were ordinary people—an accountant and a secretary—but her mother lived as if all the misfits of the world were her kin. Her real mother a circus woman? No surprise there.

"That's kind of cool, Mom," she said.

Her mother gaped at her. "Cool? I led a protest against the circus last month. The way they treat the animals is disgraceful. And you have no idea what else I'm finding out about my birth family. It's very disturbing. Colonizers. Presbyterian ministers. One of them was eaten by pigs. Another one slaughtered a Mohawk family. They owned slaves. Slaves, for God's sake."

She turned to Margo, who clucked her tongue obligingly. Delilah thought, not for the first time, how odd it was that in spite of the fact that Margo was as suburban Florida as they come, she and their mother connected in a way that was never true for Delilah.

She'd always blamed that on the fact that Margo was four years older and the firstborn, while Delilah was more attached to her twin brother, Joshua. Her mother told her she made a special effort to see that Margo didn't feel displaced by all the attention "the twins" were getting. It helped them bond, she said. And she figured Delilah had Joshua, which she did. For a while, anyway.

"What will you do?" Margo asked sympathetically.

"That's the question, isn't it?" she replied. They nodded at each other knowingly. Again, Delilah was left out.

"Do nothing," Delilah said. "Mom, you don't have to do anything. Right, Dad?"

"Well," her father said, "I looked into it a little bit on my own. Apparently the woman's living alone, in an old house in a town called Brentville. It's not too far from where you went to college, from the map."

"That's right. I know Brentville," she said. "It's about fifteen miles from the University, near the Helderberg Escarpment."

"What?" her mother asked.

"Helderberg Escarpment. Younger late Silurian and Devonian marine sequences, bordered by the collision of northeastern Proto North America with a volcanic island arc during the Middle Ordovician Taconic Orogeny."

"She's talking geology again," Margo said.

That, Delilah supposed, was another difference between them. In a family of liberal arts graduates, she was the one who wanted a microscope for Christmas. Her mother said she got it from her father, whose interest in economics was the closest thing she knew to science, though both Delilah and her father kept explaining that economy wasn't science, it was magic.

"We went there for fieldwork when I was at school," Delilah explained further. "I used to go there for picnics. It's really nice, Mom."

"Where she lives may not be so nice," her mother said portentously.

Delilah looked at her father, who shrugged. "We don't know. We know she's on social security. She's alone. The property has apparently been in the family for over two hundred years, so we can assume an old house."

Delilah wondered which part of "we" he was included in. It sounded more like her mother's campaign, though of course it was her father's money, the ill-gotten gains of capitalist investment and an unexpected instinct for the flow of money through the world, that would finance it. He never complained, but he was more a participant than an agitator. Always had been. Delilah's mother said that's where she got her passivity from.

"Why not just leave her?" Delilah asked. "She left you."

Her mother and sister cried out a chorus of protest.

"Well," Delilah said, "she did."

"She may have had a good reason to," Margo pointed out. "She was very young, maybe. A teenage pregnancy."

"She was thirty," her mother said. "She's eighty-one now."

"Oh, well then. There you go. She was obviously too young. I mean, I'm thirty-one, and I don't feel ready for a baby. Of course, you were—what, Mom, twenty-one?—when you had Margo, but you were different."

"She saw to it that Mom was adopted," Margo pointed out. "She went through the pregnancy and gave her life. That's worth something, isn't it?"

Delilah raised her hand in a gesture of surrender. "Okay. You have to do something. So send money and a card. I'm sure Hallmark has something appropriate."

"I don't feel right about that. It seems—cold," her mother said.

"In other words, you need to torture yourself," Delilah said. Another chorus of protest.

"You're being very harsh," Margo said. "It's your worst trait."

"Look," Delilah said, "I spent all afternoon in a tub of Jell-O, and I'm still blue. For all I know, I'll remain blue forever, and it doesn't go with my waitress uniform, which is orange and says Sunshine Palace on it. So you'll have to cut me some slack."

"For being blue?" Margo said.

"For being honest," she replied. "You expect it of me, then you yell at me for it."

Margo and Delilah glared at each other. It was a recurring argument between them. Whenever a skeptical opinion was wanted, her name got called. Then she got yelled at for being what they expected her to be. Somehow, Delilah was supposed to provide the voice of clarity in the family, while everyone else got to play Nice People.

"Let's not," her father suggested. "You and Margo can take it up later if you need to. Right now, we have a situation to deal with." He pulled in breath and let it out slowly, then turned to Delilah. "Your mother thinks someone should go visit the woman."

A long silence followed his words.

"Someone?" Delilah asked at last. Mumblings that didn't resolve into sentences rolled around the table like distant thunder. Vague understandings began to coalesce in her thoughts.

"Mom, when did you find out all this?"

"Just today," she said.

"Just now?"

"Today. Well, last night but it was late so it might as well have been this morning."

"But Dad said he looked into it."

"Yes, and he told me what he found out this morning. Last night. Late."

"Oh," she said. "But you actually got the information from the genealogy people . . . sometime last week?"

Her mother mumbled something about not believing it, the power of denial.

Right, Delilah thought. Of course. Everything was perfectly clear. Her mother had long since made up her mind how to handle this. Get Delilah to do it. What else does she have to do, anyway? She pressed the heels of her hands against her eyes. When she removed them, everyone was looking at her.

"No," she said.

"Delilah," her mother said, speaking in her quiet voice. "You know the area. It seems to me . . ."

"No," she said. "I'm not going to meet my grandmother the circus woman. I'm not going with a basket of fruit, or money, or a Hallmark best-wishes-from-the-daughter-you-abandoned card. I'm not going to upstate New York. I'm not going."

They were all still staring at her. She did the only thing she could under the circumstances. She left the kitchen.

water

Delilah went back to the caretaker's cottage, where Thomas had cleaned the tub and was working his photos on the computer. He'd taken shots on both digital and regular film, but would have to take the film to a lab downtown for developing because her mother had drawn the line on setting up a color lab in the cottage. Or at least she'd drawn the line on financing it. She wanted to save the world, not Thomas's artistic career.

Thomas met Delilah's mother at a meeting on garbage and sewage issues where he was taking photos for an alternative newspaper. He talked his way into residence in the caretaker's cottage by bartering photos of activist events and promising to do the occasional odd job around the yard. He was true to his word about the photos, but any other work he did was more odd than job. Once in a while, Thomas would get on the rider mower and take it around the place for as long as his attention held, which meant they had some grass that was long and wild, and some that was cropped short. And occasionally, he would clean out the pool.

Other than that, he wasn't one for yard work, unless you called it landscaping when he put a statue of Madonna in an upended tub, with figures of Elvis and the Beatles standing around, worshipping. Delilah's mother didn't call it landscaping, though Thomas had been very proud of it. He even rigged up a little cassette that would play "Like a Virgin" when you pressed a button.

And Delilah's mother didn't count the inflatable sex dolls he scattered over the lawn for a photo shoot, doing things like serving cocktails to the Buddha statue out in back, or hunting lawn deer statuary. He had a long discussion with Lana about them, Thomas saying lawn statuary was one more indication that they were going to hell in a handbasket, while Lana said it was the just Art of the People, and they had a right to it. Her father solved the argument by telling Thomas to take his photos and get rid of the damn things. It was the closest Delilah had ever seen him come to losing his temper. He was a tolerant man, or had learned to be after years of marriage.

Delilah leaned over his shoulder and looked at the photo of herself, which no longer looked like her since he'd done things to her face and hair.

"What do you think?" he asked.

"Interesting," she said.

"That's a cop-out," he noted.

She nodded. Interesting was a word that could work just about any way you wanted it to. She liked it, and used it a lot. "My mother wants me to go to upstate New York."

"Oh?" he asked, squinting at the screen. "What for?"

Thomas was that rare species, a Keys native, and saw very little reason to go anywhere else, except possibly to Manhattan. He often teased her about her background, which included a few years in Chicago, a year in Northern California, a semester in Westchester County, two years in Denver, and quite a few years in Syracuse, New York. All these moves were about her father seeking tenure as a professor of Marxist theory and economy. For some reason Syracuse was the most amenable to Marxists, so they stayed there the longest. But they still didn't give him tenure, and when it was clear nobody would, he discovered the stock market, which was kinder to him than academia.

"I was thinking of adding some pink," Thomas said, tapping on the screen.

"Sure," Delilah said. "If I go to upstate New York, will you come with me?"

"What for?" he asked. "Need help tipping cows?"

"Ha," she said. "Ha ha ha."

"Anyway," he added. "I can't. I've got to finish this for the show. Lots to do, not much time."

"Michael is there," she mentioned.

"Michael," he said, then repeated it. "Michael. Michael. That would be . . ."

Her jaw tightened. "Michael, about whom I have told you so much. Michael, the legislative assistant who broke my heart in upstate New York. Michael, my ex-fiancé who will someday be governor. President. God."

"Oh," Thomas said. "That Michael. I wasn't sure which one you meant. Well, you don't have to see him. I get the impression he wouldn't want to see you anyway, right?"

Thomas was definitely not getting it. She had a sinking feeling that he never would, and that might be why she was with him. He had so little chance of ever getting any of it that she was perfectly safe. He would never look up from his art projects long enough to notice her, much less another woman.

He'd already been in residence in the caretaker's cottage when she returned home, and after they spent a night of talking and laughing over a bottle of red wine and a few independent films, they fell in bed together. He had the distinct advantage of being available, without asking a lot of her.

In many ways, it was the ideal relationship. It was certainly different than her last one, because where Thomas didn't get it, Michael got it all, and could recite it correctly at the drop of a hat. Even when Delilah found out about the other women he was sleeping with, he said all the right things. It wasn't anything wrong with her. He just didn't think he was inherently monogamous, and maybe no man was. Maybe only women were. It was a purely biological thing, and she shouldn't feel rejected, or demeaned. Blah blah, she thought. Blah blah blah.

"I might run into him," she said now. "Michael, I mean. Or I might call him just to torture myself. I am my mother's daughter after all."

"Yeah," he noted. "You do that kind of thing." He stopped manipulating the mouse and looked up at her. "You never answered my question. Why does your mother want you to go to New York?"

"To see her mother, whom she just discovered. My grandmother, the circus woman."

"Oh," he said. "That should be fun."

"You ever been to upstate New York?" she asked.

"No, but I don't worry about it the way I worry about Omaha."

"Omaha?"

"I went there once. I was in a bar, and they gave me my drink in a Flintstone jelly glass. I worry about Omaha. At least you're not going there."

"You still should come with me. You can get good photos of circus things."

"It's been done. Besides," he waved a hand at the computer, "too much to do."

He turned back to it. She lingered a little longer, then left the room, and the cottage. She doubted that he noticed. They weren't locked into formalities like hellos and good-byes.

She walked across some of the acreage that comprised her parents' property, past somebody she didn't know who was mowing the lawn. Her mother didn't hire people. She counted on a constant stream of guilt-ridden activists to work for her.

Delilah avoided the kitchen, heading straight for her room, which was upstairs. She went in and sat down on her bed, contemplating her hands, asking herself what she felt. The first word that came to mind was guilty. She had seen the look her father gave her before she left the kitchen. He was counting on her, maybe more than her mother. And that was the problem. Everyone had gotten used to counting on her. Delilah will cook for the activists. Delilah will sit in a tub of Jell-O. Delilah will go see the circus woman. It was no wonder, she thought, that she couldn't figure out how to save the world. She didn't have time.

What really bothered her now, though, was that she minded. Usually she didn't. Not much. Doing things for people gave her the illusion that she was needed. But today, something in her said no, and she wasn't sure why. Maybe she was just aggravated because the whole scene followed so quickly on the blue Jell-O, and she'd reached overload.

Maybe, in her aggravation, it occurred to her that she might have more luck finding what she wanted if she just briefly stopped doing what everyone else needed. Or it occurred to her that doing things for people was a way of not looking for what she needed. Some people used drugs. She was helpful.

Or maybe it was just that she didn't want to go back there, and resented that nobody in her family took that seriously enough to notice, much less protect her from it.

Probably it was all of the above combining to reach a turbulent state, the way water did moving along in a steady, complexly patterned flow until some unknown factor shook it one notch more, into too much. Then the pattern disappeared in turbulence, and there was no determining what it would do next. That was chaos theory, which she'd learned about in college. It often seemed to apply directly to her life.

She didn't get any farther than that in her thoughts before there was a knock on the door. She closed her eyes and didn't say a word.

"Delilah?" a voice asked. It was Margo's voice. "I saw you come in. You can't pretend you're not there."

"Yeah," she said. "I can. It just won't get me anywhere."

Delilah didn't say anything else. After a while, Margo spoke. "Then can I come in?"

"What happens if I say no?" she asked.

Another silence, this one longer. "I ask you again," she said.

Delilah was about to say come in, when she heard another voice, deeper and lower. Her father. Margo's voice whispered back, and then her door was knocked on again.

She sighed. "Come in," she said.

The door opened, and her father hovered in the doorway. "It's okay," she said. "You can come in all the way. Margo, too."

"She went downstairs," he said. "Your—um—mother wanted her."

"Thanks," she said, meaning it. If she had to talk to anyone, her father would be the first choice. He'd talk to her, but he wouldn't bug the hell out of her.

He came into the room and closed the door. He hooked his thumbs in his belt, rocked back and forth on his heels as if about to give a lecture in Marxist theory, then cleared his throat. Delilah looked at him expectantly, waiting to hear what he'd say.

He frowned, went to the window, and looked out.

"It's nice out," he said. "Not too muggy."

"Yeah," she agreed.

"Won't last long, though. Summer soon."

"Yup," she said. She sighed. He sighed.

"Dad," she said.

"Delilah," he said at the same time. Then they were both silent.

"You go," she suggested.

He pulled a roll of Tums from his pocket, extricated one, and chewed on it. "I don't want you to go if you're strongly against it," he said, "but it would be a help. You know that."

"I know," she said dully.

"Is there maybe some very important reason why you *don't* want to go?" he asked.

"Besides that it's weird? I mean, it's weird, Dad. I'm supposed to go there and say, 'You don't know me but I'm your granddaughter by this woman you gave up for adoption over fifty years ago and probably don't want to think about. Just thought I'd stop by to say howdy.' It'll be weird."

"Yes," her father said. "It will be."

Her father never denied her reality. It made disagreeing with him very difficult, but also made him comforting to be around. She might feel bad, but she wouldn't feel crazy as well.

"Are there other reasons?" he asked.

She could tell he really wanted to know, not just to convince her that she should go, but to weigh the reasons she had for not wanting to, and see if hers were actually better than his.

"Michael lives there," she said.

"Oh. I'm sorry. I'd forgotten that. But you don't have to see him, do you?"

"No," she said hesitantly, because the truth was, it wasn't just Michael. It was what he stood for. Her failure. Her failures, plural. No career. No husband. Nothing much to say about herself that was important or valuable. And worst of all, no connection to anything. Humans need to be connected to something. A cause, a God, an interest in reality TV. Something outside themselves. And she hadn't gotten it right. Upstate New York was her geography of failure to connect. She didn't want to go back to it. But explaining that to her father was difficult, because to explain it was to name it out loud, and to name it out loud was to feel it. Not feeling it was the whole point.

"You have other friends there, don't you? Monica still lives there?"

She nodded. Her father liked Monica, an old friend and ex-roommate who had come to visit last year. Monica, a social welfare specialist, talked Marxist theory with him at the dinner table, and her father had beamed at the two of them as if they were his prize pupils.

"But it's hard to go back," he noted sympathetically. "Memories you'd rather not revisit?"

She nodded again, but said nothing.

"You're like a cat," he noted. "They don't walk in reverse. After Joshua died, you wouldn't say his name, and when you walked past his room, you turned your head away. Do you remember that?"

She did, vaguely, though she couldn't call up any feelings to go with the memory. Just a quick flash of her face turning from his door, like a photo, with its emotions all held in check within the image. She was surprised that her father brought it up now. He rarely talked about Joshua, and when her mother did, he often grew quiet.

"I remember you sent me to a therapist," she said, keeping it light. "I hated his ties, and he had bad breath."

"We were worried," he said apologetically. "And I guess I'm worried now."

She stared down at her hands, then stole a glance up at her father. He was still looking out the window, and she had a moment to contemplate his profile. He would probably be considered homely by most people. Too tall at six feet five inches, his face long and narrow, bags under his large dark eyes, and ears that could kindly be said to stick out. This was in contrast to her mother's well-groomed good looks. Her liberal leanings never kept her out of the beauty shop, which was another place where she and Margo connected. Delilah's idea of styling was pulling her hair back into a ponytail.

She'd often wondered about her mother and father as a couple. That they loved each other was obvious. That they were unlike each other was just as obvious. Even their wedding picture looked like Abe Lincoln marries Gwyneth Paltrow, because in her youth her mother was slim as a reed, fair and wispy as a summer day. And while she had a hummingbird energy that kept her flitting from one cause to the next, her father had a stillness and compassion with which he'd contemplate the foibles of the world.

He turned to his youngest foible now, and contemplated her with compassion. "I think," he said, "it might be good for you to get away from here for a while."

She was again surprised, but her father wasn't any good at dissembling, or manipulating, so she knew he meant it.

"Why?" she asked, trying to stay bright and perky. "More Guatemalans moving in?"

He smiled back, but sadly. "Sometimes I think we make it too easy for our kids to stay home. Not enough generation gap to push you out of the nest. When you came back, I thought you needed time, you'd been hurt. And I've rather selfishly enjoyed having you here, so I haven't said anything before now. But Delilah, I don't want you to wake up twenty years from now and wish you'd made different choices. Or made *any* choices, because right now, I see you absolutely refusing to make them, though I don't know why. Please don't take that the wrong way," he added. "I don't want to offend you."

That was her father. Hitting nails on the head with a hammer through a pillow. A rather complicated task, but he was good at it. Good enough, at least, for Delilah to be made uncomfortable in the way you are when someone says a truth you'd rather not hear.

"Maybe," she suggested, "I'll never wake up, and then it won't bother me."

"If you were a different kind of person, I'd say that was possible. Unfortunately, I think you're just intelligent enough to be a burden to yourself."

"I don't think going to see Grandma will help any of that."

"Maybe not. I just—I can only say I have a parental instinct that it would be good for you to get away."

"Then maybe I should do a European tour or something," she suggested. "It might work out better. Less family involvement."

"Fine," he said, "if you'll do it. Will you?"

"Probably not," she said. "I can come up with too many reasons not to. You'd have to finance it, and Thomas would want to come and how do I tell him no. Like that."

"That's what I thought. Then I'm voting for the trip to New York, and I wish you'd give it a shot."

No doubt about it. He was good. And in all likelihood, he was also right. She felt the only way to hang on to some illusion of control was to delay saying yes.

"I'll think about it," she said.

He put a hand on her shoulder, leaned down, and kissed the top of her head. It was a gesture he reserved for important moments, and she was touched by it. As if she were young enough to need that. As if she always would be.

"Try to think about it for what *you* need," he said. "See if that helps."

He left her alone, knowing that she was the best person to talk herself into this the rest of the way. Her mother wasn't that subtle, or that patient. In a very few moments, there was another knock on her door. When Delilah said "come in," her mother poured herself into the room and engulfed her in a hug.

"Oh, I knew you would. I can always count on you, Lilah."

"Jesus, Mom," she said, pulling away. "Were you eavesdropping?"

"Of course not," she said. "I just happened to be passing by. We'll have to decide what you'll say, and what you'll bring. I'll take you shopping. You'll need clothes."

"I didn't say I'd go. I said I'd think about it."

"Oh. Of course. That's what I meant. I knew you'd think about it."

"Right," she said. Then she sighed. "When do I leave?"

Four

earth

Delilah always preferred driving to flying. Having her feet that far off the ground left her feeling anxious and slightly depressed. And flying gave her no time to transition from one landscape to the next. First she was here, and then somewhere else. But when she drove up from the Keys, she got to see how the land moved from long, flat roads surrounded by water, to the long, flat roads of Jacksonville, surrounded by strip malls, which she thought of as its own peculiar ecosystem. Then there were the swamps and wetlands, the pines and Spanish moss of the South, and the winding mountain passes that led her into the North. She liked noting the slow changes that signaled her entry into each new kind of land, which she would greet as she passed, as if each were a friend.

And in many ways, each one was. Her family moved from place to place so frequently when she was growing up it was difficult to make long-term friends. Each move had become the opportunity to learn about a different landscape, the chance to learn the wordless language of this river, or that lakeshore forest, this kind of plant life, that kind of stone and dirt.

She especially liked mountains as a species of geology. They had a protective presence, watchful and considerate. Though they were made by great smashings of landmasses into each other, each one had its own rocks and formations, traces of how and when that smashing occurred. Those traces told the story of millions of years of motion, because the smashing took that long, and was, she knew, still taking place, even though most people thought of mountains as still and immovable. Humans, being a brief species, couldn't perceive the Himalayas growing at a rate of about a centimeter a year.

Then, there was the landscape she was headed for, a Taconic formation near the Helderberg Escarpment. She'd studied them in geology at the University, where she learned to obsess about the way land shapes itself. Of course, she was also obsessed with what kind of weather patterns moved across it, so she studied atmospheric science, too. And with what kinds of things live on it, so she took courses in ecosystem life cycles. And with the way humans interact with that, so she took courses in human waste and garbology. Somehow it all got her a degree, and as a result, she was an amusing and competent waitress.

She could have gone on in her studies, but at a certain point she'd discovered that science had some fatal flaws. She'd read about a Harvard study on the use of estrogen to prevent middle-age heart disease. The study concluded that estrogen was ineffective, and had bad side effects like increasing breast size and lowering sex drive. For twenty years, that was accepted as scientific truth. Then, a woman saw the study, and spotted their error.

They only tested the estrogen on men.

Apparently science would never make knowledge more powerful than the unfathomable workings of the human heart, with all its prejudices. And though the words of science seemed like magic that might someday open up an understanding she longed for, in fact they were just descriptions. She could say a mountain was Taconic orogeny, or she could say it was a soft rolling green, like the back of some large furred beast at rest. Which one told more, she wasn't sure.

Maybe she just expected too much. Idealists, she thought, generally end up bitter and disappointed, with a tendency to drink too much.

Still, what she'd learned wasn't useless. It kept her amused for the thirty hours of driving between Key West and Brentville, which kept her from thinking too much about her own life, or what might happen at the end of the trip.

Much family discussion preceded her leaving. Should she invite the old lady to lunch and hand her a check, or should she go to her house and see what she needed first? Should she plan on being there a week, or two days? And how was she to explain the fact that she was there, and not her mother?

The last question was hotly debated. Delilah wanted to tell the truth—that her mother was too chickenshit. That was universally voted down. Even Thomas was against it.

"What do you suggest?" she'd asked. "That I say you have some terrible disease?"

"We-ell," her mother replied, contemplating.

"No," Delilah said. "Absolutely not. Bad juju. No way."

In the end, they'd settled on saying that her mother thought Carla might be uncomfortable if suddenly confronted by a daughter she'd given away, and so Delilah came instead. Delilah didn't see much sense in it, but agreed to end the discussion.

It had also been decided that she wouldn't phone her grandmother until she got to town, based on the theory that it would be harder to refuse to see her if she'd driven all that way. The question of how long she'd stay, and what she'd do about offering her money would be resolved in the moment. She packed for two weeks, just in case.

She also made two decisions for her own sanity. First, she didn't take the cell phone. She had visions of it chirping almost constantly, at the worst moments. Her mother offered to buy her a laptop so she could stay connected by e-mail or instant messenger, but Delilah said no. She'd be where she was, and call when she could.

She also made her own arrangements about where she'd stay. She called Monica and asked if she was up for company. She was.

She arrived at Monica's apartment at around ten in the evening, road weary and befuddled by the sudden absence of motion. Monica was about fifteen miles from Brentville, within the city limits of the capital of New York State. She'd made her way out of the area lovingly called the student ghetto, and into one of the blocks occupied by state workers, professors, and Double Income No Children professionals. It was a political and collegiate city, small enough to be manageable, not so small as to be totally without museums or music or good restaurants. Monica's apartment was in an old Victorian, with a turret.

She buzzed the apartment and Monica's voice came on the intercom, sounding happy and excited, which was normal for Monica.

"Delilah?" she asked. "Is it you?"

"Me, in the flesh," she replied.

"Oh, how exciting. Come up. Third floor."

Delilah dragged her bags up the three flights of dark, polished wood stairs, and saw Monica standing in the door and beaming, a bottle of Jack Daniel's in her hand. Delilah noted that she not only had a drink, she had the right one. Champagne for celebrating, red wine for romance, tequila for damage, Jack Daniels for conferring.

"Monica," she said. "You haven't forgotten."

"How could I?" she said, ushering Delilah inside. "I'm still seeking revenge."

That was in reference to a night they'd drunk a bottle of tequila to do damage over the demise of Monica's relationship with a man named Monty, who used to climb up the side of the house and onto the second story porch in order to prove his love for her, but wouldn't stop seeing his other girlfriends. Monica ended up in the bathroom groaning all night, while Delilah slept like a baby rock and never even got a headache.

"Never," she said. "Not in a zillion." She grabbed the bottle and took a swig.

"I put you in the turret room," Monica said. "You'll like it."

"Turret room? Ooh. I'm impressed."

Margo would have approved of it, Delilah thought. What looked like Pottery Barn curtains wafted in the window, and an Eddie Bauer duvet covered the futon they'd purchased years ago, when Monica graduated and got a real job. At the time they decided Monica needed everything, so Delilah's memory of the end of her failed graduate school days was a massive spending spree, of Monica's money. Delilah was dead broke at the time, and considered it a testimony to their friendship that economic shifts never made a difference between them. Nor did distance, or a rapid turnover in boyfriends.

They'd been thrown together as roommates in the top flat of a student ghetto house by the totally random process of off-campus housing. Monica was getting a Master's in public administration. Delilah had finished her undergraduate degree, and decided to go on for a Master's in business administration. It seemed like a good idea at the time. A geology major and business should equal a good-paying job with an oil company. It probably would have, if she stayed. But she didn't. The intensity of competition made her laugh. People took themselves so seriously. And then, she didn't like the clothes. Suits. Skirts. High heels. They made her worry about what was showing that shouldn't. Besides, she couldn't hike a mountain or explore the woods wearing high heels.

She left the MBA program and worked as a pet groomer for a year, which had its points. When its points began to need sharpening, she decided to try for a Master's in elementary education, which seemed benign and interesting, and involved working with people who wore sneakers instead of suits. She was two semesters into it, going part-time while she waitressed to earn her keep, when Michael dumped her. Or, technically, she dumped him, with extenuating circumstances.

She went to his apartment to help him pack for moving in with her, and found him in bed with another woman. She hated him for being so predictable, and herself for not predicting it anyway. Mostly, she felt all the usual betrayal, rage, loss, and inevitable failure of that kind of moment.

She left school, left the apartment, and made her way back to Key West, where her parents had moved the year before, to lick her wounds and decide what to do next. If she had to be a miserable failure, she thought, she might as well do it in the sun.

Monica, on the other hand, got an appointed position in the governor's office, with a long title Delilah could never remember, though she knew Monica was responsible for things like human service legislation. She had a life. And they were still friends. The only change Delilah noted was that when she came to visit Key West, she had upped the ante on her sunscreen from fifteen to forty. They were in their thirties now, she said, and had to be respectful of their skin.

After Delilah had her bags settled into her room and found the bathroom, they made their way to the kitchen table with the Jack Daniel's and some leftover *arroz con pollo* and cheese and crackers, to begin discussion of current events.

"So," Delilah said, passing her the bottle, "tell me everything."

"No," Monica replied, taking a sip and passing it back. "Oh no. You're having all the excitement. Tell *me* everything."

"Everything? Thomas? The tub of blue Jell-O?"

"Jell-O?"

"It's kind of a long story," Delilah said.

"Start with your grandmother. Your *abuelita*. So sweet."

"My *abuelita*. Well, it seems I have one."

"Yes. How did you find her? What's she like? How is your mother taking it?"

"Mom found her by mistake, she's a circus woman, and I'm here but my mother's not, which tells you how she's taking it."

"Well, your mother has issues," Monica noted mildly.

Delilah laughed. Monica strived to be kind and nonjudgmental, though having survived being raised in the South Bronx as a black Puerto Rican female, she was tough as nails. Still, you'd never know it because she had all the social grace Delilah felt lacking in herself. She thought it was odd that Monica had somehow gotten all that tact and diplomacy, while Delilah, a daughter of privilege raised among academics and liberal activists, spent a lot of time pulling her foot out of her mouth.

She and Monica had speculated about that. Delilah thought it was determined by Heaven—she was Sagittarian, a sign of notorious tactlessness, and Monica a Virgo, which is a considerate and thoughtful sign. Monica thought it was reaction to social context. But then, Sagittarians believed in the random workings of fate, while Virgos like to plan.

"Apparently," Delilah said, "my mother's issues are genetic. Her great-grandfather was eaten by pigs, and his father kept slaves, and God knows what his father did with turkeys."

Monica shuddered lightly. "Thanksgiving is ruined for me since you told me about the turkeys. Just ruined." She raised the bottle and took a sip.

That was a bit of trivia Delilah picked up in a Literature of Puritan America class, where the professor told the students that the early Puritans lacked female partners, so they turned to their domestic animals for companionship. Unfortunately, the biblical punishment for that behavior was death. So they hung the animals. Even more unfortunately, the behavior was so widespread they started running out of domestic animals. After a while, the elders saw some merit in punishing the humans instead of the animals. Delilah told Monica that the last man hanged for bestiality in the United States was caught enjoying his turkeys.

"I'm just speculating about him and the turkeys," Delilah amended, "except that he had opportunity and probably motive. But the pig thing is true, and so are the slaves. I think they slaughtered some Mohawks, too. Mom is horrified, and Dad is suffering from status inconsistency. A Marxist immigrant Jew married to landed gentry, sort of."

Delilah raised the bottle to drink to that. "But it's funny to think that my family was keeping slaves, and your family were slaves. What if my family owned yours?"

Monica shook her head. "By the time they got to New York, slavery was illegal here. But your family may have befriended them."

"I don't think they'd want my forebothers as friends. Anyway, I have to go see Grandma tomorrow. Your turn now. What about this guy you're seeing—Marshall?"

"Him? Oh, he's gone. He got terribly drunk at a restaurant he took me to—not a very good one, either—and I left him at the curb."

"You what?"

"You know. After dinner when he was very rude and obnoxious to me, I told him I'd get the car—my car, of course—and he was standing at the curb waiting, and I just drove away. I waved to him."

"Nice of you."

"I thought so. Oh, listen. You won't believe this—guess who I'm working with."

"Who?" I asked.

"Guess," she said.

"I don't know. Mahatma Gandhi."

"Michael Swerton."

Delilah had just taken a swig from the bottle, and now she choked and sputtered. Interesting, she thought, that his name still had that effect on her. Interesting in a not good kind of way. "Oh, God," she said. "You work with him?"

"Occasionally. There's some legislation I'm trying to push through, and he's involved. Politics makes for strange bedfellows. Isn't that the saying?"

"Yeah. You're not, though, are you? Bedfellows, I mean. With Michael."

"God no," Monica said. "My mother had another saying—you sleep with babies, you wake up in shit."

"You should've told me that years ago."

"I did. You didn't listen."

"I never listen. Is he married yet? Did he get ugly? Fat? Maybe going bald?"

"Honey, he looks like a million dollars. Not married, either."

"Who *is* he sleeping with?" Delilah asked.

"Everybody, as far as I can tell. Every time he shows up at a function, he's got a different one on his arm. I could arrange for you to sort of casually bump into him, if you want."

"I don't want."

"But here you are also looking like a million dollars. It'd hurt him to see you."

Delilah thought it would be nice to hurt him. But if they had to talk, what would she say? It's so good to see you, Michael. Of course I'll vote for you in your gubernatorial campaign. Me? Why, I'm a personal service worker in the for-profit sector. That's right. I waitress. In Key West, on a beautiful estate. Well, yes, my parents' estate.

No, she thought. Definitely not.

"When I get married, I'll come back and torture him," she said.

"Are you getting married?" Monica gasped, then clapped her hands. "Oh, a wedding would be so much fun. Dresses and decorations. Cake and guest lists."

Delilah eyed her. Large portions of Monica's days were consumed getting funding for battered women's shelters, for AIDS programs, for drug-treatment programs. She met with advocates for these causes on a daily basis, and heard stories that made Delilah's hair curl. And then, she turned her thoughts to coordinating linens.

"Monica, I think you spend way too much time dealing with the wounded people of the world. Weddings aren't actually fun, you know."

"I think humans are at their best when they're planning weddings. Linens, and flowers. Lovely evening receptions."

"Did I tell you about Thomas and the Jell-O?"

Monica's smile disappeared. "Is that—something I want to know?"

"Probably not. Anyway, I don't think weddings should be planned around him yet."

"Not the type you'd marry?" she asked. "Drinks too much? Bad temper?"

"He's really nice," Delilah said. "Really, he is."

"Uh-oh. Kiss of death. Though I do think it's time to get over the bad-boy phase, don't you? I mean, you're thirty-one. I'm twenty-nine."

"You're thirty-two," Delilah corrected. Monica was six months older than she.

"That's what I said. And I think we need to reevaluate."

"Call a meeting of the Foundation?"

"Precisely," she agreed.

Delilah grinned. At some point in their time together, they started referring to themselves as the Foundation. They dated so many losers, Monica said, it was only right to think of themselves as a charitable operation. Periodically, when important issues like "Do I sleep with him?" or "Is this color good for my skin tones?" or "Have I finally gone mad?" had to be resolved, they'd call a meeting of the Foundation to render a decision.

"It's been a while," Delilah said.

"Too long," Monica agreed. "It's time."

"Then, this meeting is officially called to order. What's on the agenda?"

"The shifting of our mission statement to meet the current needs of the Foundation."

"Okay," Delilah said. "Any suggestions on the table?"

Monica reached across the table and got a napkin. "Pen?" she asked. Delilah grubbed through her purse, and got one.

"Red ink," Delilah said.

"Never be afraid of color," Monica replied. "Let's see. As we approach our thirties . . ."

"As we are both now in our thirties," Delilah corrected.

"What I said. The Foundation hereby states that its mission is . . ."

"Death to all bad boys?" Delilah suggested.

"Lilah, we're a charitable foundation."

"It would be a charity to other women."

"You've got a point. But very messy. What would we wear?"

"Okay then," Delilah said. "We'll devastate them by our absence."

"Very nice," Monica agreed. "Devastation to bad boys, through our absence." She wrote it down. "And . . . what else?"

"Pursuit of personal happiness through . . ."

"Shopping," she wrote down. "Lots of shopping."

"Need money for that. And we're a nonprofit. At least I am."

"It's time to change that, too, girl," she noted. "You know, there's a time to turn inward, and look to the health of the Foundation itself. An increased focus on career, leading to an increase in discretionary funds. Ultimately, it'll be part of our contribution to the world."

"It goes against everything my mother ever taught me," Delilah noted. "I think I'm supposed to be saving the world."

"Let's start on saving your wardrobe and go from there," Monica suggested. "And your mother is doing just fine, in case you haven't noticed. She found support for her charitable organization in a cozy little mansion in Key West. And here you are, doing her work for her. Maybe your problem is you've been working for *her* foundation so long, you forgot about your own."

Delilah fidgeted. Monica was beginning to sound like her father, and if two people she loved and trusted saw the same thing, the odds increased that they were right. "She did okay," Delilah granted. "But she also spent a lot of years chasing my father's academic career, which wasn't incredibly lucrative."

"We're focusing on the present," Monica said. "A new era."

"Okay," Delilah said. "A new era. No more bad boys. Thoughtful reflection on our capacity to contribute to the world, and collect contributions from it. How's that?"

"You have a way with words. And Thomas? Is he part of the new era?"

"Sort of," she said. "At least he's not a bad boy."

"But," Monica asked, "is he a boy?"

Delilah shrugged. "Everybody has to grow up sooner or later."

"I hope you're not banking on that."

"Not at all."

"Good girl," Monica said, and handed over the bottle.

"No more," Delilah said. "I have to call Grandma in the morning. I'd rather not be hungover."

"I'd rather you were," Monica said, grinning, and from under the table, she pulled up another bottle.

FIVE

air

In spite of Monica's best efforts, Delilah was not hungover when she called her grandmother's just before noon. She spoke to somebody who was not her grandmother, unless she'd done a gender switch. He was just Sam, he said.

"Is Carla there?" Delilah asked.

"Nope. She's out. This is just Sam. Who're you?"

"Um—Delilah. From Key West. I'm visiting and I—um—wanted to come see her."

There was a long pause. "Delilah?" Sam asked.

"Yes. Are you—um—her husband?" Delilah asked when it continued.

He laughed. "Carla wouldn't know what to do with a husband if he came with a user's manual. Come on up. She'll be back soon enough."

He gave her directions, and hung up without asking who she was or what she wanted.

The directions were easy. Get on Route 12 and drive out about ten miles. It was a nice drive, and once she was a mile or two past the city, she would never guess she was near the state capital. It was all country, with a little gas station, a shop for a guy who carved bears out of old logs, and fruit and vegetable stands from the nearby farms.

At Settles Hill Road, Sam said take a left, and go up a hill, which she did. Then she drove up some more. Then she kept driving up. At a certain point, the trees parted, and the sky revealed itself as big. It was a good blue one, with a few puffy cirrocumulus clouds, and some altostratus thrown in for contrast. They were innocent. Not there to make trouble. Just there to make the sky look more blue. The day was warm, with a soft breeze.

Just as Sam said, about three miles up the hill she saw a white house on a knoll, and in the back a pond nestled under a ridge of land that climbed up to pine trees. It wasn't fancy, but it wasn't an unheated shack with no plumbing, which gave her a sense of immense relief. She pulled into the driveway and sat in her car, rehearsing what she might say.

She thought of saying, "Hi. I'm Delilah. You don't know me, but I'd like to talk to you." She tried it out a few times and liked it. It was slow, and could go anywhere it needed to at a moment's notice, depending on what the old woman was like.

Delilah had her trepidations about that. What if she was frail, and barely cognizant? What if she smelled? She'd noticed from serving old people that sometimes they had a faint odor of urine, medicines, and baby powder about them, and she didn't like it. And they spent a lot of time talking about all the ways their bodies were falling apart, and imminent death. It made her simultaneously nervous and impatient.

But she didn't know if this was the norm, because her experience with old people was limited. She saw her grandparents maybe once a year when she was growing up, and they were all dead now. In college she was surrounded by people her own age, isolated from old people except for some of her professors who were nearing retirement age, which wasn't nearly as old as this woman. And Key West attracted young gay men and beach bunnies more than it did retirees, so her experience there was no help.

Maybe, she thought, it was a conspiracy. Old people were kept invisible, shunted off to nursing homes, stashed away in enclaves of Florida that nobody else visited, used for CIA experiments to prevent or induce aging, depending on governmental needs. She would have to talk to Monica about that. Have a meeting of the Foundation. In the meantime, she had to deal with the problem more immediately, which was made more difficult by the fact that it all seemed so surreal. She wasn't connected emotionally to any of the events she was taking part in. The only real feeling she had was a fear of embarrassment, and a lack of confidence about how to proceed.

While she sat thinking, she felt a thump against the side of her car. She looked out the window and down and saw a tiger cat with no tail. It meowed in a rusty, aggressive way as it wound itself around a pair of legs, which were very white with blue veins running through them. They were wearing sneakers and white socks. She raised her focus up from the legs to the rest of the body that went with it, which was neither fat nor skinny, short nor tall.

The face on top was an old woman's face, wrinkled, but not deeply, and the skin was rosy. Her mouth was tightly shut, held in place by a square jaw that looked as if it worked hard. Her eyes were dark and sharp, with hardly any lashes. The hair on top of the head was a combination of blond and gray, as if attempts had been made to work with the bottle, and they'd not quite worked. It stuck out in little tufts here and there. Where it was white, it was almost translucent, and the light made little halos around it.

"Who're you?" the woman asked. Delilah noticed when she opened her mouth that she had almost all her teeth, and one of the front ones was gold.

She smiled and got ready with her little speech.

"Well?" the old woman asked, her voice as sharp as her eyes.

"I'm Delilah," she said. "Your granddaughter."

She didn't mean to say that. It just slipped out. She waited for her grandmother to choke, or go pale. She didn't. She waited for her to smile or tear up or ask questions. She didn't. Delilah waited for her to say something. She didn't.

She squinted at Delilah, reached down to pet the cat, grunted, and straightened back up. She put a hand on her hip and shook her head slightly.

"You better go on inside," she said. "I've got errands, but you can wait in the kitchen until I get back."

The old woman turned away and walked to a white car—an old Dodge—and got in. Delilah sat in her car and watched while she started it up and wound her way in reverse down the driveway. She drove down the road very slowly, and Delilah thought of all the old ladies she'd gotten behind who drove like that, and how she'd cursed them soundly. She was irritated that a relative of hers should be doing that to other drivers.

After she was gone from view, Delilah got out of the car and went to the door, knocking softly on it. Nobody answered. She put a hand on the doorknob and turned it, opened the door, and went inside.

The first thing she noticed was that her parents were right. It was an old house.

The narrow hallway she walked down had an interesting slope, and the wide pine boards on the floor were long worn of varnish and stain in a clearly discernible path. The hallway opened up into a big kitchen with old industrial-strength carpet that may have once been a discernible color, but that was long ago. There was one cupboard by the sink, and a big old table surrounded by mismatched chairs in the center. The refrigerator and stove were vintage from maybe the '60s, but so was the fireplace—from the 1760s, by the look of it.

Margo would have called it an interesting mix of pre- and postindustrial style, with not much to offer beyond curiosity. She would have put in track lighting and a central island, while trying to maintain the feel of Days Gone By. From the hallway Delilah could see into the living room to the left, also big, with another fireplace and a worn couch facing it. And she saw doors. A lot of doors. There seemed to be doors everywhere, some open and some closed, as if the place were more of a labyrinth to be conquered than a house to be lived in. She was curious about where they went, but not curious enough to open any.

She went to the kitchen and sat at the table, waiting for whatever might happen next. For a while, nothing did, so she got up and started scouting around for coffee. There was a bag of ground in the freezer, and she opened it, inhaling deeply. Dunkin' Donuts. Nice. She wondered if her grandmother had one of those old metal percolators, since she didn't see a coffeemaker, then became concerned that maybe she'd have to do the camping trick of heating water in a pot and putting the coffee in.

"Use the machine," a voice behind her said.

She turned, and at first saw nobody. Then, she looked down a notch. A very small man was regarding her. He was perhaps three and a half feet tall, deeply wrinkled, his hair thick and wavy and gray. He had it tied back in a ponytail, and he wore a T-shirt that said I DO WHAT THE VOICES TELL ME TO DO.

"Hi," she said. "I'm Delilah."

"Use the espresso maker," he said, pointing to the counter

where she saw that there actually was one. A good one, too, she noticed.

She frowned at him, then transferred the frown to the coffee. "It's not espresso."

"Oh," he said. "Well, the espresso's in the fridge." He went to it, opened it, and got out a bag. Then, he dragged a chair over to the counter, stood on it, and started the machine going.

As he worked, Delilah had a flashback of herself and her brother making fun of Mr. Thompson, a neighbor who was a dwarf. They were imitating the clumsy way he tried to jump for an intercom button that was a little too high when their father came out and caught them at it. She didn't know how long he had been there. Long enough, apparently, to know what they were doing.

He wrinkled his eyebrows and asked quietly, "Has Mr. Thompson been by?"

They nodded.

"Did you say the blessing?" he asked.

They made fidgety motions and said nothing.

"There's a blessing," he said. "In Hebrew." He said it in Hebrew, and when he was done, he waited. He was always good with placement of dramatic pauses.

"What's that mean?" Joshua asked at last.

"It says, 'Praised are you, Creator of the Universe, who varies the forms of your creatures.' It's the blessing for seeing dwarves and giants."

"Giants?" Delilah had asked.

"Or anything made in a unique way. Next time you see something like that, say the blessing. English will do."

For weeks, she and Joshua went around saying the blessing for squiggly worms, for odd-looking bugs, for Mr. Thompson, for really fat people. Then, they forgot all about it. But the damage had been done. The idea had gotten into Delilah that there were many strange creatures in the world, each one worth celebrating. That, she told her father years later, explained her love of the Discovery Channel, and weirdly formed rocks.

"Thanks," she said now to Sam. "Espresso'll be nice. Do you—um—live here?"

"Sometimes." He jerked his head toward the living room. "Back part of the house."

"Oh. Does anyone else live here?"

"Sometimes," he repeated. "It's a big house. I'm Sam. I talked to you this morning."

"Oh. Yes. Of course. So . . . She . . . um . . . doesn't live alone?" That would be good. Her mother would be relieved to know that.

"Carla? Not all the time. There you go," Sam said. He hopped off the chair, and he left the room, disappearing through one of the doors.

"Oh my," Delilah murmured. "People come and go so quickly around here."

She sat at the table with her espresso, wondering what would happen next. Elephants, perhaps? Trapeze artists?

As she wondered, a voice yoo-hooed from the door she'd entered.

"Carla?" the voice asked. "Whose car is that? Did something happen to yours?"

The voice was soon joined by the presence of a middle-aged woman in a white polyester pantsuit, who smelled of the hairdresser's. Her hair was puffed and shaped, so Delilah assumed she had just come from there. She stood in the kitchen staring at Delilah, her mouth stuck in the shape of the letter "O."

"Hi," Delilah said. "I'm Delilah. It's my car."

The woman smiled, regaining her composure. "I'm Eleanor," she said. "A neighbor." She blinked around the room as if expecting someone else to be there.

"Sam's around," Delilah said. She pointed toward a door. "He went that way."

"Sam?"

"Sam. He said his name was Sam. The—um—small man?"

"Oh," Eleanor laughed. "You mean Kootch. You must be new, or he'd never tell you he was Sam. Nobody calls him that. You said—Delilah?"

"Carla's granddaughter," Delilah said, then, when she saw the look on Eleanor's face, wished she hadn't. What was she thinking, blurting it out like that to someone she'd never met, whose relationship to her grandmother she didn't have a clue about. For all she knew, Eleanor was a Mary Kay representative, come to collect on a bill, though Carla didn't look like the makeup type.

Eleanor put her hand on the back of a chair, and held on. "Her—what?"

"Granddaughter," Delilah muttered. "Have a seat?"

She pulled the chair out and sat, continuing to stare as if Delilah might suddenly transmogrify into something even more frightening.

"But—Carla doesn't have any children."

"She did. Fifty-six years ago. My mother. She gave her up for adoption."

"Oh my," Eleanor said. "Oh my."

"Look," Delilah said, "I'm sorry. I shouldn't have said anything. Maybe Carla won't want people to know. I mean, I just got here, and she left, said I should wait for her, so I don't really know what I'm doing here. I mean, it's a funny situation, right?"

"It most certainly is," Eleanor agreed, nodding vigorously. "Well, now. This is news. Did you—I mean, she knows, doesn't she?"

"I told her. Then, like I said, she left."

Eleanor pressed two nicely manicured and polished fingernails against her temples. "Left? I'll bet she went shopping. She's so stubborn. I try to take her, but she runs off on her own any chance she gets. You said you told her?"

"Yes," Delilah repeated patiently. "I told her. Then she left."

"Oh yes. Of course. I'm sorry. This is a bit of a surprise. I'm—I've been Carla's neighbor for many years—thirty years, I'd say—and she never mentioned a daughter. You think you know someone, and then you find out . . . well, you find out things."

"I guess that's how my mother felt when she found out."

"And she sent you?"

"She was nervous about coming. Can you tell me about Carla? My family sent me because they're worried that she needs help. But it seems like there's people around."

"Well, there's Kootch. He comes in the summer, to get away from the Florida heat, but then goes to see the penguins, and then it's back to Florida. He's been trying to get Carla to move there for years, but she won't go. Stubborn, like I said."

Delilah cleared her throat. "Penguins?" she asked.

Eleanor laughed lightly. "Kootch has a thing about penguins. He goes to New York and makes money on the stock market, then he takes a trip to Antarctica to see the penguins. But his home is in Florida, really."

"Oh. I . . . see. He, um, said other people live here?"

She tapped a finger against her chin and mused. "Well, there was Harry Ed, but he died last winter. He used to stay in the cold months, help out. Then he'd go spend the summer in Alaska."

"More penguins?" Delilah asked.

"Oh no. There's no penguins in Alaska. Grizzly bears. He studied them. And there's Big Bertha, but she went into an assisted-living place, so she won't be here except to visit. Not that she could ever help much, with her arm and all. Of course, everyone used to stay when the circus was in town, and then for years after her uncle sold it—gosh, that's twenty-five years ago now—they'd still show up. In fact, this'll be the first winter she's really been on her own. So I guess Kootch *was* right, but he isn't anymore. Of course, I stop by, and so does Jack—such a helpful young man—but neither of us lives here."

Eleanor broke off her musings, and smiled at Delilah. "But how nice. She has a granddaughter. Will you stay?"

"For a little while," Delilah said, feeling as if she were about to be recruited. A replacement for Harry Ed.

"That's good," Eleanor said. "I'm so glad. I have to go see my daughter for a while. She had a baby, and it was a difficult birth. But I've been worried about Carla, leaving her and all. You'll stay how long?"

"I don't know," Delilah said. "I hadn't made definite plans."

"Then you can stay a while. Your folks want you to, right? At least a month?"

"I hadn't planned on it," she said. "Not really. I just wanted to see what she needed."

"She needs someone to be here," Eleanor said. "So now you know."

The door opened, and Eleanor pressed a finger to her lips as if they'd been sharing a secret Delilah wasn't to give away. "Carla?" she called. "Is that you?"

"Yeah," a voice called back without enthusiasm.

"Well, how nice," Eleanor said, as Carla shuffled into the room. She cast an ugly glance at Eleanor, as if viewing a butcher's case where a cut of meat had gone bad.

"I've been talking with your granddaughter. How lovely for you to have her visit," Eleanor said enthusiastically.

Carla squinted at Delilah. "You told her that?" she asked.

Delilah nodded dejectedly.

"Big mouth," Carla muttered. Then, she lifted her head and sniffed. "Somebody making espresso?"

"I am. I mean, Sam—Kootch was."

"Well," Carla said. "You made it. You drink it. Don't help me," she added, when Delilah started to rise. "I don't need it."

Eleanor nodded knowingly and mouthed the word "stubborn" while Carla unpacked her groceries. Eggs. Milk. Orange juice. Bread. Dietetic cookies. Groceries of the single woman, any age.

"It's so good Delilah will be here while I'm away," Eleanor noted.

"Yeah," Carla said flatly. "Great."

"And she can stay here. Maybe in Big Bertha's old room? I could air it out for her."

Carla stopped and looked at Delilah. "You staying here?"

"I—don't know," she said. "I've got a friend I can stay with if it's trouble for you."

"Stay here," Carla sighed. "Everybody does."

At least, Delilah thought, her mother came by it honestly.

SIX

fire

Eleanor spent some more time fussing over Carla and then left. Carla muttered something about busybodies, and said she was going to take a nap. She didn't seem inclined to talk, and Delilah wasn't inclined to make her. She went over to Monica's and got her things, left a note explaining where she was, and said she'd be calling her for emergency shopping. Monica always said there was nothing like it in times of stress.

When she returned to Carla's, late afternoon was becoming early evening, and Carla was awake, sitting in the kitchen, staring out the sliding glass doors at the pond in back.

She turned around and stared at Delilah a minute, as if remembering who she was, then said, "Look at that." She pointed out the sliders.

Delilah looked first at Carla's finger, and noticed there was dirt under the nail, then followed where she pointed. Standing at the edge of the pond was a great blue heron, female, gracefully lifting her legs and placing them back down as she scanned the water for food. She strolled the shallow of the pond, unlikely in her size and grace. Periodically she would stop and meditate, while golden slants of light brushed the back of her neck.

Delilah, who was a sucker for predation, watched for some time as the heron stood still as a rooted tree, meditating on water and fish, then pierced the water with her beak and came up with her supper, lifting her head back to swallow what she caught. Then, she lifted her great wings, moving them like a woman shaking out sheets before hanging them on the line, and somehow she was airborne, her long legs trailing behind her.

"Praised are you, Creator of the Universe," Delilah murmured, "who varies the forms of your creatures."

Carla tapped a finger on the table. "What?" she asked.

"Something my father taught me. Did you know that the wingspan of the great blue heron is six feet? That's bigger than I'm tall by half a foot. They pierce fish with their beaks to catch them. And they'll eat other birds, too. You wouldn't think something that beautiful would be a cannibal, would you?"

Delilah knew many people who romanticized nature, and saw it as something to strive for rather than something they were already a part of. As if humans weren't made out of the same stuff as the stars and the earth, filled with the same water that flowed in the rivers, breathing in concert with the trees, and running the complexity of a nervous system with the same electric charge as lightning. As if humans weren't also predators, and sometimes cannibals as well.

Carla's mouth twisted into something that was not a smile. Then, she said, "I don't know what you eat."

It took Delilah a minute to pick up the thread. "What I eat?" she asked.

"For dinner. Are you one of those vegetable eaters? Do you like hamburgers? I don't know what you eat."

"Oh," she said. "Well, food, I guess. I'm not really fussy."

"Good," Carla said. "There's some cans in the pantry. Make yourself something."

She pushed herself up from the table, and started to make her way out of the room.

"Do you want anything?" Delilah called after her.

Carla stopped and stood still a long time, a golden slant of light resting on the fuzzy white hair at the back of her head, reminding Delilah of the heron in the pond. She half expected her to dive for the floor and come up with a fish. "What?" she asked.

Delilah made her voice louder. "Do you want any supper?" she asked, speaking clearly and slowly.

Carla rotated her head around. "I'm not deaf," she said.

"Oh. Well, do you then?"

"I ate. Your room is upstairs. First door on the left. You want me to show you?"

"No. I'll find it. And if I don't, I'll let you know."

Carla shuffled out of the room, and in a little while Delilah heard the sound of a TV going somewhere beyond the living room. The theme music for *Homicide* played.

In the pantry, she found cans of tuna and boxes of macaroni and cheese and made herself at home with them. She thought of joining Carla in the TV room, since she liked *Homicide*, too, but then she'd have to talk to her, and she didn't feel up to it. She grabbed an old *National Geographic* and read about "The Mysteries of the Human Mind" while she ate.

After a while, the TV went off, and she heard Carla shuffling around, ascending a set of creaky stairs. Shortly after, she heard the sound of water running in a bathtub upstairs. She wandered toward where she'd heard the TV and found a sort of sitting room, with yet another fireplace, toward the front of the house. She turned the TV on, surfed channels until she found the Discovery Channel, and sat down to watch.

On the screen, a warthog jogged spryly through tall grasses, while a very cultured female voice with a British accent narrated its day. The warthog likes to keep busy, grubbing around for warthog food and snuffling at other warthogs, the narrator informed Delilah. It all looked like a pretty good warthog kind of life, but then the camera panned beyond the tall grass, to where three cheetahs lay on the ground, sniffing the air. Trouble in warthog land.

"Ooh," the British woman said as the cheetah leapt. "An *unfortunate* day for the warthog."

Yes, Delilah thought. It was.

After the carnage was over and the program changed to something about UFOs, she turned the TV off.

The house was suddenly dipped into a silence that was more complete than Delilah ever heard inside human habitation. It was not just an absence of sound, but a thickness that the world descended into, a resonant depth that included aloneness as well as quiet.

There was not a sound of a car going by, or a siren, or a human voice. The sun shed its last light on the great northeast as this part of the world turned away from it to give other parts a turn at daytime. Then it was both quiet and dark.

Delilah started turning on lights.

She thought of calling her mother, but the sound of her voice would be so loud in the quiet of the house, it didn't seem right. She didn't know if Carla was asleep, and if she was, Delilah didn't want to wake her. If she was awake, Delilah didn't want her to listen.

She went to the kitchen and stood by the sliding glass doors.

She slid one open a crack, and now could hear the crickets, singing their songs in the night. This was, somehow, an immense relief. She wasn't alone. Insects still occupied the planet. She gazed out past the pond and thought what a fine place this would be during firefly season. She could imagine the ridge behind the pond thick with their silent blinking lights.

She was very fond of phosphorescing creatures of all kinds, especially fireflies. They seemed to her to be part of the mystery of the world—a biological entity that glows to attract a mate. In parts of tropical Asia they gathered in trees in great numbers, creating synchronous flashing that went up and down and from tree to tree, like a stadium of people doing The Wave with lights. Praised are you, Creator of the Universe, she thought.

Somewhere in the distance, she heard a rumble, and thought this would also be a great place to watch a storm. Looking up, she could make out stars directly over the house, but to the west the sky was darkened by a thick blanket of cumulonimbus moving in fast.

"Show time," she murmured, and just to prove her right, there was an explosion of light and sound, almost simultaneous, and all the lights in the house went out.

She gasped, and leapt back from the glass door but went no further because she couldn't see a damn thing, between the explosion of light and the sudden, absolute darkness. There was never this much darkness in Key West, with all the ambient light around. And except for camping, she'd never been in a place without streetlights.

More thunder rumbled, and thick drops of rain splattered against the roof intermittently. She looked out the sliders again, and up toward the sky. Dark clouds had erased the stars, and within their thick layers lightning curled and danced like electric snakes twisting to a music she couldn't hear. Spider lightning it was called, and it crawled horizontally through the clouds for stretches of ninety miles across the sky.

"Oh my," she murmured appreciatively.

She'd seen lightning in the Southwest, where it dropped down through a curtain of sheer clouds that walked across the plains. Vertical dancers, they seem to be making their way with determination toward some undefined destination. And she'd seen lightning cover the sky in a sheet, or descend in quick forks tossed down to the earth. But though she'd read about spider lightning in class, she'd never seen it until tonight. It was a real treat.

She walked closer to the sliders and opened them, but stayed inside. Twice in her life, she had narrowly avoided being hit by lightning. Both times, the place where she had been standing ten seconds previously was hit. She knew that once someone was hit by lightning, the odds of being hit again rose exponentially, leading to speculation that there are people who attract lightning. Though her father always said she was highly charged, and she did tend to set off store alarms, she hoped that since she'd been missed by lightning twice, odds of being missed again rose exponentially as well. Besides, she thought, spider lightning doesn't come out of the clouds.

With the assurance of these rationalizations, she stepped onto the deck and stood, listening to the storm.

Lightning, she knew, was still a mystery. Though the nature of the charge was understood, much about where it moved and why was unknown. She liked that. Humans move electricity along paths from one end of the continent to the other, and lightning was still a mystery. One of the tasks of lightning, it seemed, was to keep scientists humble, reminding them that they didn't necessarily understand the drama of attraction and repulsion. But anyone who had ever been in love could have told them that.

A crack, and a fork of light made her jump back toward the

sliders. Mysteries were fun, but they could also be dangerous. Spider lightning could become regular old kill-you-quick lightning. Weather, a complex, dynamic system, could reach turbulence from small atmospheric shifts. And lightning would cause that same turbulence in the motion of her muscles, nerves, and heart, if it hit her. Humans were also chaotic systems.

The spider lightning moved away and sheets began to flash on and off at the horizon. She was fascinated by its motion, and its lack of intent. People tended to associate motion with intent, and get angry at the movement of natural forces, as if lightning or tornadoes or disease had a motive to cause harm. It was a form of consolation, Delilah thought, necessary for creatures that had too highly evolved nervous systems to accommodate the notion of a lack of control. At the same time, she had to admit that she'd probably resent it if she were hit by lightning. She'd take it personally, since it was her personal existence that was at stake.

But if she was hit, what then? The world would go on. There would be the tiniest blip of absence in it, and then the vacuum would fill itself. Maybe Margo would have a baby, and name it Delilah if it was a girl. She would be remembered, but not for long or by many because after all, she hadn't gotten around to that saving-the-world thing yet.

This thought was disconcerting, and oddly comforting. Disconcerting for the obvious reasons. Comforting because there was something right about being swallowed into the continuity of the earth so completely. If she disappeared in a puff of lightning-induced smoke, at least she would have done little harm. To make a big imprint is often to also make a mess.

But the lightning did not find her that night. It moved toward the east, and the rumbles of thunder grew as harmless as the complaints of an old man.

She went back into the kitchen, where she considered whether or not she should see if Carla was okay. She decided against it. She had a feeling that if Carla wasn't okay, she'd let somebody know.

Then, she crinkled her nose. She smelled something. Smoke.

Brief fear, and then she recognized it. Cigarette smoke. "I'll be damned," she muttered. "Carla's a smoker."

She wasn't upset by this. Merely jealous. She'd given up smoking a few months ago, but the smell still spurred her body to remember the pleasures of addiction. Quitting was one of the hardest things she ever did, and she often hated herself for doing it, even though she knew it was the right thing.

Right now, though, a cigarette seemed like something she'd really enjoy having. That, and some of Monica's tequila.

She decided it was time to go to sleep, partly out of lack of anything better to do, and partly to escape her own urge to smoke and drink heavily. She groped her way through the dark of the house toward the stairs, and toward her room, which she found mostly by feel. She opened the door, discerned the outline of a bed, and made her way toward it slowly and carefully. She was about halfway there when her foot landed on something soft that made a horrible sound not unlike the death cry of the warthogs.

"Jesus H.," she expostulated, and jumped, stumbled against the wall, and stayed still.

As she did, the lights came back on, casting pools of white into the shadows of her room. In one of them, she saw a black cat, staring at her with large eyes and its ears laid back. It was a big cat. It made itself bigger, hissed, and backed out of the room.

She let her heartbeat settle back down to normal, wondering if all her experiences here would be of adrenaline surges caused by creatures that came and went rapidly and mysteriously. She found the light switch for her room, flicked it on, and looked around.

The room had the same slope as the other parts of the house. It was small, painted a dull green, which had grown duller with age, had a slightly musty odor, a tall oak bureau, a window, two doors, and a bed with a nightstand next to it. On the wall that she would face as she lay in bed, there was a fireplace with a large oil painting hung over the mantel. It was of a giant orange glowing moon, with a face that leered at her ominously. She turned the light back off.

Suddenly, she was exhausted. She left the lights on in the rest of the house, and hit the bed hard. Before she knew it, she was asleep.

Carla, who had been watching the storm, felt the blink of light returning when the power came back on. She lit another cigarette and sat in her room, which was dark because she'd turned the light out before the storm.

It was a good storm, and she spent a moment deliberately appreciating it. She knew that one of the problems of being old was the despair that rose when familiar experiences no longer brought pleasure, and new experiences were resisted. Old people especially, who needed to tend their physical safety, would sit in their rooms and rot slowly, rather than try the one thing that might brighten their minds and heart. Carla knew the danger of that, and wouldn't let it happen.

She'd had more than her share of thrills, between the tigers and the travel, the lovers she'd taken and the ones she'd refused. She'd known good people, and she missed them, but on nights like this they felt not so far from her, and that was good. Still, it would be a mistake to spend her days reliving what was and resenting its passing, rather than enjoying what she had all around her. She didn't want to be that kind of old.

Not that she wasn't just plain old now, though somehow, this still surprised her. Old age itself had come as a shock. One day she looked in the mirror and she was young. The next, it seemed, flesh sagged at her jaw, and there were lines and bags around her eyes. She had panicked. She went out and bought expensive lotions and creams and patted them on obsessively to try to make her skin go back to where it used to be.

Of course, they didn't work, and this only deepened her panic. She was used to not having control over events in her life, but not accustomed to relinquishing control of her body. Her horror at this was profound. It went into her as if she'd swallowed something poisonous that she could feel moving through her cells, eating away at her. She began noticing that her friends were getting old, too. Kootch went gray. Bertha got even bigger, developed yet another chin. Her uncle struggled with a heart condition that made his face turn red and blue, and that eventually made him give up the circus.

When he left, the new owner looked at her as if she were used up, and in circus terms, she was. They'd long since stopped letting her perform, relegating her to office work and teaching the younger women how to look good with the horses. When she stopped working in the ring, the tigers went to a zoo, because nobody else wanted to take the risk of dealing with them.

That was the hardest part. The day she said good-bye to Benna and Bella, she thought the best part of her life was over. She hung on at the circus only out of a clinging lethargy that wouldn't let her see any other options.

Then, her brother died, and she came home, thinking she would do nothing here except get older, more useless, more sad. She was wrong.

Coming home began a new adventure for her, right here in this house she'd grown up in, on this most familiar piece of earth, breaking her and making her over again. It gave her muscles in places she didn't know you could have them, aches in joints she never thought about before, and pleasures she hadn't imagined.

She'd had to see it new, learn it all over, in a different way than when she was a child.

One of the first things she did when she came home was take down the mirrors. She did this not to deny her age, but to teach herself not to care. In the circus, she'd developed a performer's interest in her own looks. Being without mirrors was an uncomfortable discipline at first. Her biggest fear about not having mirrors was that she'd act on a younger image of herself that still lived in her head, and make herself ridiculous.

But she was too busy with the house and the land for that kind of nonsense. She found that in the absence of focus on her self-image, she listened closely to what was around her. The pulse of the earth beat all around her, and its rhythm became the pulse of her body. She felt the wind carving lines into her flesh. When she looked at her hands, they seemed to have absorbed the dirt she gardened in. Then, one day, as she stood on the ridge between the clearing and the trees, she felt the breath of the leaves at the back of her neck. She turned, and became aware of a soft rustling, a chorus of whispers and small laughter. Chidings and concerns.

Like the moment when letters become words and you can read what before were only marks, something in her shifted from hearing to listening, from listening to understanding. The land was speaking to her. She could hear it. She stood for a long time, lost in wonder. She asked herself if it was madness, but it felt normal enough. And she wasn't hearing anything grand. No voices told her to save the world, or rule it. Mostly it was a felt language that described a sense of friendship, of kinship.

What she heard it say was that she was not alone.

After that, mirrors didn't matter anymore. Being old wasn't quite as frightening. Being seen as no longer sexy wasn't as sad. She wouldn't be alone in her oldness. The earth was older.

She stamped out her cigarette and stuck her head out the window, breathing in deeply. The air was fresh with the washing of the storm. Lightning made the earth richer, more ready for growth. Fire burned the old trees, and opened their seeds to bring on the new. The air, full of ozone and water, smelled both new and old. It reminded her of the baby scent of her own daughter, scent of flesh that was brand new, and as old as the species itself, elusive and subtle and unmistakable.

That baby had been sent away, but another daughter returned, and she was a mystery Carla would have to unravel before she decided what to do next. So far she seemed merely young. Carla didn't necessarily love her, or like her. She just recognized an attachment as old as lightning, old as the species, and new as any storm. She was relieved to find that she didn't actively hate her, though. The girl seemed bright enough, if a little spoiled. But most young people were spoiled. They couldn't help it. Maybe it was even good. Life shouldn't be hard if it didn't have to be. Often when her friends said young people were spoiled they were just expressing jealousy, because their own lives had been hard.

But whether she could learn what Carla wanted her to learn, what she needed to learn, remained undetermined. She would have to watch, and listen, and wait to learn.

In the meantime, there was the pleasure of the storm, and the darkness, and a little more nicotine.

She lit another cigarette, breathing out to send ribbons of smoke out to greet the night, and thank the spirits of the storm.

SEVEN

combined elements:
earth and water

The room didn't look any better to Delilah in the morning, though the Orange Moon Face seemed more perky than leering. She went to one of the doors that she assumed was a closet and opened it. Clothes still hung on the rack, and there were suitcases, purses, shoes on the floor. The other door was either locked, jammed, or led somewhere she probably didn't want to go. But the bed had been comfortable, and the pillows were down, covered with real cotton pillow-cases that matched real cotton sheets. All of it smelled of clothes hung out on the line, though she didn't imagine Carla had cleaned up just for her. Perhaps Big Bertha liked her room kept fresh for visits.

She grabbed her toothbrush and other bathroom things and made her way down the hall to find a bathroom. She opened one door that was an empty, unfinished room, with no Sheetrock covering the studs. She opened another one that was a sort of den, with books lining the shelves on the walls. A large, intricate spiderweb hung in the doorway, and she decided not to go through it to investigate. It looked like someone went through a lot of trouble to put it there, and she didn't feel right about messing it up.

The third door she opened was a bathroom, with a sink and large old claw-foot tub, but no shower. The wallpaper was roses and leaves, yellowing and peeling. She ran the water in the sink and got her toothbrush ready. When she looked up, she saw that there was no mirror above the sink.

She turned around, thinking maybe it was on another wall, but there was no mirror in the room. She lowered her toothbrush, and opened the bathroom door, thinking she'd have to get a mirror from some other room.

Carla was standing in the doorway, fully dressed, as if she were waiting, awake for hours. Unless, Delilah thought, she never actually slept but wandered the night in the shape of a black cat, making lightning appear in the sky.

"Hey," Delilah yelped, and then cleared her throat to cover her surprise. "Good morning," she said more calmly. "I was just—brushing." She waved her toothbrush. "But there's no mirror in here. Did it break?"

Carla scowled and shook her head. "I haven't had a mirror here in twenty-five years. Not since the circus went under and I didn't have to anymore."

"No mirrors?" Delilah asked, a little shocked at the notion.

"Not in this house," Carla replied.

Delilah stared at her toothbrush. For all her life, she'd brushed her teeth in front of a mirror. That's how she was taught. That seemed to be how she found her teeth in the morning. "How'll I brush my teeth?" she asked.

"You know where your mouth is, don't you?"

"I—never thought about it."

"People think too much about how they look, and forget how they feel," Carla said.

"Why's it more important to know how you feel?"

"To stay alive," Carla said.

Delilah considered this. "But if you feel like crap and you look at yourself and you happen to look okay, that could make you feel better."

Carla snorted. "How often does that happen?" she asked.

Delilah chewed thoughtfully on her lip. Carla was right. If she felt like crap, the mirror usually confirmed her opinion. "Okay," she said. "No mirrors."

"When you're done, come outside," Carla said. "I need some help."

"Yes, sir," she replied. "I mean, ma'am. I mean, Grandma."

Carla stopped, her back still turned. "Don't call me that," she said sharply.

"Don't call you—sir?"

"Grandma. Don't call me that."

"Oh," Delilah said. "Okay. Then, what should I call you? *Abuelita?*"

"What?"

"Never mind. What should I call you?"

"Call me Carla. It's my name." She shuffled out, and Delilah went back to her teeth, which she found even without the mirror. She had learned something new. That was a good thing, she supposed.

When she was done, she went outside. She didn't see Carla, so she wandered over to the pond, which she hadn't yet had a chance to investigate close up. It was a good size, with a marshy area at one end, full of rushes and reeds. She stopped at the edge, and looked into the green water. As if she'd invoked it, a baby mud turtle floated up from the bottom and popped its head out of its shell, regarding her blandly.

Soon it was joined by another baby turtle, and another. They floated, and she began to suspect their blandness was a form of turtle happiness, or at least contentment, from the way they blinked their eyes in the sun, and continued to float. A larger turtle appeared and floated among them. It was a regular herd. Delilah wondered how many of the turtles got eaten by the heron in a given week.

One of them reversed its balance and stuck its head in the water, its little turtle butt sticking up in the air. Two more followed suit. Synchronized swimming, for turtles. An Olympic moment if ever there was one.

"Hey," a voice said behind her. She jumped, and the turtles dove back for the bottom, their baby turtle butts bobbing briefly on the surface before they disappeared.

"Oh. It's you. I was just watching the ecosystem do its thing," Delilah said, waving a hand toward the pond. One by one, the turtles began to reappear.

"Those are turtles," Carla said.

"So I suspected," she said.

"Leave 'em be."

"I wasn't bothering them," Delilah said a little sharply.

"Well, don't. This is their home."

"I see that," she said. "What kind are they? I know you have wood turtles around here. They're on the state list of special-concern animals, but I don't know what kind these are."

"They're turtles," Carla said. "The kind with shells. Come with me."

Delilah was hoping for more information, but Carla was, as usual, a font of critical silence. She walked away, and Delilah followed. A gray cat, narrow and long, appeared from somewhere and trailed along behind. Carla led Delilah around to the back of the pole barn, where she stopped at a pile of what looked like garbage, mixed with leaves and dirt. The cat curled around her ankles. She reached down to stroke its head.

"Compost heap needs turning," she said. "Kootch forgot to do it before he left. Jack'll be here later, but he's got other stuff to do."

Delilah shuffled from foot to foot, suddenly feeling rather young. She knew about compost, of course, from Human Waste 102 and Garbology 123. She knew how much landfill space would be saved for every kitchen that composted its refuse. And her mother had a compost tumbler in the yard. She'd spent a lot of money on it, as she reminded Delilah whenever she forgot to take kitchen scraps out to it. But with the tumbler, you just moved the handle. Delilah had never turned a compost heap by hand. Not that it grossed her out or anything. Not after tubs of blue Jell-O. But she was a little nervous about doing it right, especially with Carla watching.

"What do I do?" she asked.

She made a motion with her hand. "Turn it," she said.

"With my hands?"

"With your hands on the pitchfork," she said, and pointed to the one stuck by the side. "When you're done, the garden needs weeding."

Then, of course, she left. Delilah was getting used to that.

The cat stayed at the compost pile, sitting to stare at whatever it is cats see, as Delilah lifted the pitchfork, plunged it into the pile, and started turning. Eggshells emerged and disappeared under the crunchy loam of old leaves and earth made black and rich by rotting things. Corncobs appeared and disappeared. She saw an old potato and an unidentified bone, which she resisted picking up to see what kind it was. The compost didn't smell bad. In fact, it had a thick, clean scent. Here was garbage, agreeably turning itself into dirt. Every day another miracle.

With the sun strong on her back, and a doable task to complete, everything seemed right and good. She hummed to herself as she worked. She heard the cat purring softly right behind her.

Then, gunshots rang out. Three shots in rapid succession.

She whirled, her pitchfork held out in front of her, her only weapon, and was facing a man with a black patch over one eye, his hands in fists at the side of his hips. Christ, she thought. Pirates.

"Hey," he barked out. There were two more shots. The cat scooted away.

Delilah looked at him, beyond him, and at him again. Clearly he was not doing the shooting.

"Who are you, and what the hell are you doing?" he asked.

"I could ask you the same thing," she said, "but you'll probably say your name is Funky Frank, except that everybody calls you the boogie-woogie washer man, and then you'll turn around and walk away."

He frowned. "What?" he said.

"Nothing," she said. "Who's shooting things?"

"Shooting?" He looked around, and another shot was heard. "Oh. That. It's just old man Bower. Got a thing about rabbits in his garden."

"Bunnies?" she said, lowering the pitchfork, but not putting it down. "He's shooting bunnies?"

"Don't worry," the man said. "He's got cataracts. Can't see worth a damn. I don't think he's ever actually hit one. Who *are* you?"

"Delilah Karov. Who are you?"

"I'm Jack," he said. "Jack Brown."

Jack. That was a familiar name. Carla said something about Jack. So did Eleanor.

"The helpful young man?" she asked.

"What?" he asked again.

"Carla knows you?"

"Of course," he replied. "Does she know you?"

She stuck the pitchfork in the pile and looked him over. He wasn't bad-looking, for a pirate, and since he was a known entity she no longer felt obligated to kill him.

"I'm here visiting," she said. "She asked me to turn the compost."

"Oh," he said. "Oh." He ran a hand through his hair, which was dark and thick and long, then shrugged his broad shoulders. He was big, all muscle, and looked as if he spent a lot of time in the sun. His face was all angles and the one eye she could see was dark brown and almond shaped. "Sorry," he said. "I didn't mean to be rude or anything. I just—when I went inside, Carla said to check around the pole barn. She thought somebody was poking around. I guess she meant—well, something else—but when I saw you standing there . . ."

"What—you thought I was raiding the compost heap for buried treasure?"

"Sometimes Carla has odd folks around," he said.

"Yeah," Delilah said. "I noticed."

He approached with his hand out, and she shook it.

"You're a friend of Carla's?"

"A—relative," she said, not getting into particulars this time. "And you're . . . a neighbor?"

"A friend. My apartment's in the city. You're not from around here, are you?"

"Key West, actually," she said.

"Oh. You came a ways, then."

"Anything for family."

"Bone Island," he said, as if completing a thought.

"What?"

"Key West. From the word "cayo." It means bones. They thought it was made of bones. And I guess it was, really. Coral, right? Dead coral everywhere. What's it like living there? Besides hot, I mean."

"Oh, it's great. Makes you feel like you're constantly on vacation."

Jack rubbed thoughtfully at the back of his neck. "Feel guilty about that?"

Delilah was impressed. When she said she lived on Key West, most people went immediately to envy. She wondered what it said about his psyche that he stopped at guilt, but of course he was right. She did often feel guilty. A too-abundant human presence on Key West was making the reef literally drown in shit. Though the problem was mostly exacerbated by cruise ships that dropped off thousands of people in an area that couldn't handle the sewage, Delilah was still there, still human, and inevitably added to the load.

"Sometimes I feel guilty," she admitted. "It's—kind of a funny place. I guess it was mostly hippies and sailors for a long time, but then it got chichi."

"Chichi?" he asked.

"Elitist. Rich people."

"Which are you?" Jack asked. "Sailor, hippie, or rich person?"

She grinned. "Guardian of the compost heap."

He grinned back She liked his grin. It had a touch of wickedness in it. "I'll accept that," he said. "Will you be staying a while?"

"I don't know. It kind of looks that way."

"That's good," Jack said.

"Is it?"

"Well, sure. I mean, with Harry Ed gone, and Kootch heading for his penguins, it'd be good for Carla to have someone around."

"She seems to do just fine. At least, she's great at delegating."

"That's for sure. Speaking of which, I better get inside. The upstairs toilet needs work."

"Oh," she said. "Are you—like a handyman?"

"Sort of like," he said, with that grin showing up on his face again. "I fix broken things. I'll see you, okay? Delilah, right?"

"Delilah," she agreed.

"Nice name," he said. "I like your name." Then, like everyone else, he turned around and walked away.

"Okay," she said. "Okay."

She turned the pile a little more, and then wandered over to the vegetable garden and did a quick survey. Tomatoes. Peppers. Beans. Squash. And plenty of weeds in between. She began having at them, and continued the assault until she was aware that the angle of light had shifted, telling her it was the noon hour, and it was hot, and she was thirsty.

She went inside and found Carla in the kitchen, doing something inexplicable with a bowl and a spoon. When Delilah entered, she lifted her head from her task and actually smiled. It was a coy smile. Or maybe, Delilah thought, sly would be a better word.

"What's up?" Delilah asked.

"Nothing. Old man Bower scare you?" she asked cheerfully.

"No," Delilah lied. "As long as he doesn't think I'm a bunny, I guess I'm safe."

Carla chuckled. "Don't be too sure."

Delilah went to the sink to wash her hands and get a glass of water. "Done weeding," she said.

"That's nice," Carla cooed.

"I met Jack. Did you tell him I was a prowler?" she asked.

"What? Me?" she said, all of her expressing large shock. "Why would I do that?"

"He said you sent him out there looking for prowlers."

"I told him something's been prowling by the garden. Wanted to see if it was a raccoon or a fox. He knows tracks."

"Oh. I guess he got it wrong."

"Huh," she said brightly, "He's usually smarter than that. Must be tired. Go on upstairs and see if he's done. Tell him I want him down here. I got something for him."

Delilah finished her water and moved toward the living room, but Carla stopped her.

"Not that way," she said. "You want the other part of the house. Back stairs."

Delilah turned around and looked at her. She pointed toward a door on the other side of the fireplace, then bent her head over the bowl, muttering. *Abuelita* my ass, Delilah thought. The loving term Monica used for grandmother did not apply. *Bruja,* meaning witch, might be more like it.

Delilah found herself going down a hall she didn't know existed, toward a set of steep and narrow stairs, which she ascended. When she got to the top, she heard sounds emanating from down the hall. This must be Carla's area of the house, she thought. Where she disappeared to at night when the rest of the circus people or unacknowledged grandchildren were being chased by black cats in the rest of the house.

She followed the noises she heard to a bathroom, also without mirrors, where Jack was standing at a sink washing something dark and suspicious-looking off his arm.

"What's that?" she asked.

He turned to her, then back to his scrubbing. "You really wanna know?"

"Maybe not," she said.

He laughed. His laugh was like his grin, with enough wicked intent to make it fun. "It's tar," he said. "From the roof."

"Oh. I thought—well, you mentioned the toilet."

"And the roof. The toilet was just a float replacement. Of course, it won't help the leach field. We found sludge bubbling up there last week."

"That's bad. Think it needs new lines, or more fill?"

His eyebrows went up a notch.

"It *is* a fill system, right?"

His eyebrows ascended a little higher up his forehead. "She tell you about that?"

"No," Delilah said.

"Then how'd you know?" he asked suspiciously.

"Well, first I called the FBI and got the classified report. Then, in the middle of the night, I went out and dug around a little. . . ."

He laughed again, and reached for a towel. "No, really. How'd you know that?"

"There's a big mound of sand left of the house, but this land is Taconic orogeny. Shale and clay. Not much else you can do here, with that kind of soil."

Now his eyebrows knit down hard over his eyes, and he regarded her suspiciously.

"Human Waste 102," she said at last. Then added, "I was a geology major. We studied this area."

"Interesting," he muttered.

"Whenever I say that," she noted, "it's because I'm either bored or clueless."

"Neither," he said. "It's just—well, I guess I didn't figure you for a geology person." He put the towel back on the rack, folding it neatly. "You look more like liberal arts."

"I was raised badly," she said. "What're you? Conservative arts?"

He put his nose up toward the ceiling and considered. "I like Frederick Church," he said. "Monet. Georgia O'Keeffe. What's that make me?"

"Overeducated?" she guessed.

He laughed again. "How's the compost?"

"Turned. Garden weeded. Bunnies shot. At least, he stopped shooting. Is that legal—for him to just sit there shooting?"

Jack shrugged. "After enough generations on the same piece of land, people feel entitled to do things their own way."

This was a new thought to Delilah. She was accustomed to transition. To be upwardly mobile, you had to keep moving, and her family had done so. There was no place on the planet that she actually called home, and this thought gave her an unexpected twinge of sorrow. Key West was the epitome of that for her. So many people were there just for a cruise stop, or a week, or maybe a month at most.

She saw Jack considering her face, his gaze equally as thoughtful. "It takes a little getting used to," he said quietly.

She grinned. "There's free-range roosters and spring-break kids on Key West. Can't be much worse here. Oh, hey. Carla wants you in the kitchen. Says she has something for you."

"Oh no," he said, and put a hand on her arm. He looked truly frightened. "Was the oven on?"

"I don't know. Why? Will she cook us?"

He sniffed at the air. "I don't smell burning. It could be okay."

"What?" she asked. "What could be okay?"

He shook his head, still looking deeply concerned. "Carla doesn't eat sugar, but once in a while she'll bake something. Cookies or," he shuddered, "a pie. Whatever it is, don't eat too much of it. You got pockets?"

He looked her up and down. She was wearing a loose-fitting pair of shorts, nice soft cotton with deep pockets. She thought he might be insane.

"You got pockets," he said. "Use them. Let's go."

When they got downstairs, Jack looking grim, Carla was standing at the table, icing a cake.

"Carla," Jack said, nudging Delilah with his toe, "you shouldn't have."

"It's no bother," she said, with that cooing voice again. "You do so much for me. Delilah, get some plates. In the cupboard."

She did, with forks, and when Carla was done icing, she started slicing. "Now you go ahead and enjoy," she said, and stood at the table, watching them.

"Ha," Jack said. "ha ha. I'll bet it's—oh, chocolate. It's chocolate, right?"

"Devil's food," Carla said.

He cut a piece off with his fork and lifted it to his mouth, put it in, and started to chew. When it was clear that he wasn't going to die immediately, Delilah did the same.

No, they wouldn't die. They would just wish they had. Because while it looked innocently like a chocolate cake, it tasted like brown crayons melted with old girdles, salted liberally.

"Wow," Delilah said, chewing hard. "That's—interesting."

"Interesting?" Carla asked sharply. "Interesting?"

"I mean, I never had cake with this much—flavor in it. And texture."

"Oh. Well, it's my mother's recipe. Lots of flavor. Not like those box cakes."

"Mmm," she said, nodding at Jack, who nodded back.

"Would you like some milk to go with it?" Carla asked.

"Oh yes," Delilah said. "That'd be great."

As soon as Carla's back was turned, Delilah cut off a big piece and got it into her pocket. She noticed Jack was doing the same. He stopped her before she put the whole thing in her pocket, shaking his head at her. Carla brought them milk, and they gulped it down, with the rest of the cake.

"Ooh," Carla said. "You two must've been hungry. You ate so fast. More?"

"Not for me," Jack said, patting his belly. "Gotta watch my figure."

"Me, too," Delilah agreed.

Jack rose from his seat, and patted his belly again. "Thanks, Carla. I guess I'll be going for today, then."

"There's just one more thing," Carla said, smiling at him. "I want you two to go get something for me."

"Get something?" he asked.

"Yeah," she said. They waited.

"What?" Delilah asked at last.

"Something I want," she said. "It's at that place."

"That place," Jack said. He looked at Delilah, who shrugged. "Carla, are you okay?"

"You know that place. Something—um—for the cat. The medicine you get for the cat's ears. I'm out."

"You mean the pet store at the mall?" Jack asked.

"Yeah," she said, looking relieved. "That place. I need more of the medicine. You know what it is, Jack."

"Sure. I'll pick it up, and bring it back next time."

"No," Carla said quickly, then, when she saw Jack knitting his brow, smiled. "I mean, the cat needs it now. Ears are really bothering her. Maybe you could bring it back tonight?"

"Sure," Jack said, sounding confused.

"And Delilah can go with you. Then you can show her what the right medicine is, in case I need more."

Jack looked at Delilah. "You up for a mall run?" he asked.

"Sure," she said. "I guess."

"Good," Carla said. "Then it's settled." She rubbed her hands on her dress, got up, and went over to a big black purse, which she opened and fished around inside until she came up with a smaller purse. Inside that was a little sort of coin purse, which she opened, and pulled out a twenty. "That'll do, won't it?"

"Carla," Jack said, "it's too much."

"Get something to eat. You don't expect me to cook for you, too, do you?"

Jack and Delilah emptied their pockets of cake on the road, hoping it didn't count as pollution. "The rain'll get rid of it," Jack assured her.

"Could run into the wells," Delilah said. "Toxic waste. We'll get arrested."

"We're born without asking to be, die without wanting to, and in between cause a good deal of pollution." He laughed his evil laugh, tossing crumbs out the window. "Anyway, I don't think they'll trace it to us."

"There's a lot left back there. What'll I do with it?" she asked.

"Pretend to take pieces up to your room to snack on, and flush 'em."

"Won't that hurt the septic?"

"Needs repair, anyway. Do you mind music? I like music when I drive."

She had no objections, and he popped a tape in his cassette player. It was something that sounded kind of New Age native, which she usually didn't like, but it had a nice beat and good voices, and the loud chanting suited her mood and the bright heat of the day. They rode in a comfortable balance of silence and talk, all of it general. He told her about the mall they were going to. It was a new one, just built the previous year.

"That's where I feel guilty," he said. "They carved up a section of pine bush to put it in, and—you know about the pine bush?"

"I went to school here," she said. "I know. A unique ecosystem that suits the needs of the Karner Blue butterfly and the spotted owl. The mall's after my time, though."

"Oh. Well, when you walk in, they've got a big picture of the butterfly on the wall, explaining all about it. Ha."

"Rude," Delilah said.

"Very. And they air-condition the hell out of it. It's frightening," Jack continued. "I think there may be a special place in hell for Americans. But I still go. Seems about impossible to do the right thing in the twenty-first century."

Delilah knew what he meant. She liked malls, enjoyed the marketplace atmosphere, the opportunity for people watching, and felt guilty about it. If anyone had asked her, she would have expressed a preference for the Karner Blue butterfly over the existence of yet another mall, but she couldn't unmake the imprint of humanity on the planet.

There was nothing she could do to push against the tide of change that suburbanized a nation, made it absolutely dependent on cars, and created malls. It was all too big, and the forces that pushed her into this or that behavior were beyond her capacity to shove back at. She could do only small things—not taking bags for purchases when she didn't have to, because she was sickened at seeing the ghosts of plastic bags hanging from trees. Things like recycling and composting and not using a blow-dryer, even though it was just a few drops of penitential water in an infinite ocean of greed. It was never enough, never would be enough, and she knew it.

"I leave the right thing to my mother," Delilah said. "I'd rather save the world."

"That your long-term goal?"

"Absolutely," she said. "Soon as I figure out how."

"Keep me posted," he said. "Meantime, maybe you could save the world by not going to the mall?"

"The only reason I'm going to *this* mall is because you're taking me," she noted dryly. "Usually, I frequent the old one. It has a better Macy's. And no butterflies were killed."

"Got me," he said, and laughed at himself, at her, at the craziness of a world that made shopping a moral dilemma. They pulled into a parking lot, found a space, and made their way into the mall. When they entered, Delilah felt the chill of the air-conditioning raise goose bumps on her arms.

"See," Jack said, watching her rub at them.

"Brr," she replied. Then, she spied a row of phone booths. "Listen," she said, "I have to make a phone call. Do you mind? It's important."

He looked a little perplexed, but didn't ask why she came all the way to the mall to make a phone call instead of calling from Carla's, which was good because she wasn't sure how she could explain. "Oh. Sure," he said. "Go ahead. I'm not in a rush."

She went to the bank of phones and used her phone card. Apparently her mother had been just sitting next to the phone waiting to hear from her, because she picked up before it finished the first ring.

"Delilah?" she said, before Delilah said hello.

"Was that a lucky guess? Or are those classes in psychic development working out?"

"Caller ID. The area code. I knew it had to be you. How is she? How are you? What's it like?"

"She's mean. I'm okay. It's weird, just like I said it would be."

"Does she know? I mean, you told her, didn't you, about who you are?"

"I told her. I'm not sure she noticed. She doesn't talk about it. Just puts me to work."

"Oh," my mother said. "Oh. Well, that's disconcerting."

"There's a good word for it."

"But does she seem okay? I mean, is she sick, and is her house a shack?"

"She drives her own car, and is well enough to order a small army of circus people around. Her house is a colonial. Very old. I've counted three fireplaces so far. There may be more."

"A colonial?"

"The real deal. With a pole barn. A pond. Turtles. Dwarves."

"Delilah, are you making this up?"

"Well, one dwarf. The rest is accurate." Delilah filled her in on the experience so far. When she was done, her mother was quiet.

"So what do you want me to do next?" Delilah asked. "I seriously don't know if she'll take money from me, but she'll sure take my labor."

"Then, probably you should stay and help for a bit. If all her other friends are away."

"How long is a bit?" she asked.

"I don't know, Delilah. Use your judgment. See what happens." Then, in a lower voice, "Is it really that bad?"

So far, it wasn't. Maybe her father was right, and she needed to get away, see some unfamiliar faces and places, be outside doing something physical instead of chasing tips inside smoky, noisy restaurants. After all, people paid lots of money to go work on dude ranches, and she was getting it for free. And it was nice to catch up with Monica.

"No," Delilah said. "It's not. I'll stay a while."

"Oh, good. What a relief. Now, don't rush her about meeting the rest of the family. Just see how it goes. In the meantime, you'll call?"

"Okay. I'll call. In a few days."

"I can always count on you, Lilah. Wait. Your father wants to talk to you."

She waited, and then heard his voice. "Delilah?" he asked.

The way he said her name expressed his concern. He could put a lot in one word. Years of lecturing, Delilah supposed. Or maybe he was just a man who used few words, so he had to make them all count.

"I'm okay, Dad," she said. "Really."

"You're sure?"

"Sure. There's a dwarf, Dad," she mentioned.

He chuckled softly. "Did you say the blessing?"

"Praised are you," she started in English, "Creator of the Universe." As she spoke, she glanced toward Jack, who was reading the mall directory. Behind him, entering the mall and staring at her as if he'd seen a ghost, was Michael.

"Who varies the forms of his creatures," she finished softly, as Michael's shock maneuvered itself into a broad smile. That smile she remembered. The one he put his eyes into. Those blue Irish eyes. She tried out a smile of her own, but wasn't sure if it was working.

"I better go, Dad," she said. "I'm in the middle of a mall and there's people waiting for the phone."

"Okay. You take care. Call if you need anything."

"I will." She hung up, and Michael advanced.

"Delilah," he said, as he reached her. As her name was said,

Jack picked up his head and turned to them just in time to see Michael put a hand on her shoulder and kiss her cheek. Over Michael's shoulder, she could see Jack, who looked confused.

"Delilah," Michael said. "This is so odd. I thought I was hallucinating. Aren't you in Florida or something?"

"Apparently not," she said, and he laughed. Michael's laugh was friendly and bright rather than wicked, but still very nice. "I'm here, visiting," she explained.

"Monica?" he asked. She nodded, not wanting to get into it. "How is she?"

"She's great. You know Monica. She's always great."

"One of the truly great women of the world," he agreed. He squeezed her shoulder. "Like you."

"Ha," she said. "Ha ha." Over Michael's shoulder, she saw Jack walking toward them, still looking bewildered.

"I think of you a lot," he said. "You know that?"

"I'm not sure how I would," she said. "Telepathy? Infomercials?"

He rolled his eyes. Those beautiful blue eyes. "Because I'm telling you," he said.

"Hey," Jack said a little sharply. "Old home week?" Michael turned around, and his hand slipped off Delilah's shoulder. His mouth opened, and he made an effort not to leave it that way.

"Jack," she said, "this is Michael. Michael, this is Jack."

Michael smiled, almost meaning it. "Any friend of Lilah's," he said.

"We're not friends," Jack said.

She bit her lip. "We just met. I mean, me and Jack. He's friends of a friend—grand—uh—relative of mine." She realized it wasn't going well. She turned to Jack. "Michael's an ex—old friend. Someone I've known. Knew. A while ago. For a while."

Michael's face was a study in questions while she blundered on. She wondered what he'd make of it. Good old Lilah, making everything as messy as possible. It was one of his complaints about her. That she just fumbled through things, without ever having a clear sense of direction or goals.

"Well," Michael said. "That's great. This is great. Um—listen, I have to run, but . . ." He pulled out his wallet and got out a business card—embossed, of course, with the state of New York seal on it. He got a pen from his pocket and wrote a number on it. "Here's my home number. Call me, okay?"

"Sure," she said, taking it and putting it in her bag.

"I mean it," he said. "I want to talk to you. Call me. Promise?"

She wanted to say something cutting about promises, but she couldn't come up with anything fast enough. "Sure," she said again.

He put a hand out to Jack, and they shook. "Nice meeting you," he said. "Maybe we'll meet again."

"Mm," Jack said noncommittally.

Michael nodded at Delilah, and disappeared into the mall. Delilah looked at Jack, who was frowning.

"Do you believe in ghosts?" she asked.

"Ghosts?"

"Ghosts. Dead people. Or people you wished dead a lot who just suddenly show up."

He pulled in a deep breath and let it out. "I have an ex-wife," he said. "Sometimes I run into her at the supermarket."

Delilah eyed him. "You have an ex-wife?"

"That's right," he said.

"What'd you do to her? To make her an ex."

"You assume it was my fault?"

"Sure," she admitted. "What'd you do to her?"

"I didn't do anything *to* her," he said. He fidgeted, shrugged. "She just figured out she didn't like men. When I see her at the supermarket, she's usually with her new wife."

"Ah," Delilah said. "Well. Let's get the kitty medicine."

They went on to their task.

water

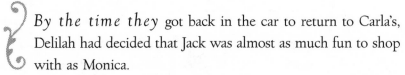 *By the time they* got back in the car to return to Carla's, Delilah had decided that Jack was almost as much fun to shop with as Monica.

He had stopped in the World of Science store to get a gift for the son of a friend, and of course then they had to play with a lot of windup dinosaurs and things that made noise before he made up his mind. Then they went to Brookstone to look at odd tools, and tried out the massagers and telescopes. Since Monica didn't really appreciate Brookstone, this was, in fact, better than shopping with her.

He squirmed a little in the pet shop, and told her he had an urge to take all the animals home. Delilah found it amusing to watch him manfully resist the kittens.

By the time they stopped for dinner in one of the mall restaurants it was as if they'd skipped all the usual protocols of friendship, and leapt ahead to just being comfortable with each other. He didn't ask questions about her background, didn't offer information about his. They just talked about what was in the moment. He wasn't flirtatious, so Delilah figured he wasn't attracted to her, which let her off the hook about how to behave to either encourage or discourage him. She tended to get those two mixed up, and often ended up encouraging when she meant to discourage and discouraging when she meant to encourage, so flirtation made her nervous. Then she would spill things. But she didn't have to worry about it at all.

There was only one uncomfortable moment when the waitress made a comment about his eye patch. "Dressing up early for Halloween, aren't we?" she said brightly.

He waited a moment, and the eyebrow over his patch went up a notch. Then he said without rancor but with a certain pointedness, "It's not a costume."

She turned red as the tablecloth, mumbled apologies, took their order, and left fast.

"Do you get that a lot?" Delilah asked him when she was gone. "About the eye patch."

He shrugged it off. "People seem made to notice differences," he said. "Probably some kind of instinctive thing. Too bad we aren't as good at seeing connections."

"Too bad," Delilah agreed. She was prepared to drop it, but he continued.

"It was a car accident," he said. "A long time ago. The eye is still there. It's just—scarred."

There were many things she could have said. Things like when did it happen, or how did it happen. But looking at his face, which seemed tense, as if he were braced for something unpleasant, she just felt bad for him. It couldn't be fun carrying a wound that waitresses mistook for a costume.

"Does it hurt?" she asked softly.

He opened his mouth, and shut it again. His eyebrows went up and down and he cleared his throat. Delilah was beginning to think she'd put her foot in the usual place and was getting ready to apologize, when he laughed lightly.

"Sorry," he said. "I guess—nobody's ever asked me that. But no, it doesn't. Not anymore."

The waitress brought their drinks, and Jack started talking about the process of brewing beer, and that was that. They ate some nachos, and he took her back to Carla's.

He dropped her off and she went inside and yoo-hooed to let Carla know she was back. There was no answer. All was quiet. In the kitchen, the black cat curled around her ankles and meowed. Delilah petted it, and it purred, then walked gracefully away. She reminded herself to ask Carla its name.

She went to the phone and called Monica, but she wasn't home. She'd said something about an important memo that needed to be written this week, so Delilah assumed she was hard at it. Monica was a dedicated worker. Delilah left a message, saying they had to talk. She needed counsel. When she hung up and turned around, Carla was standing in back of her.

"Christmas," Delilah gasped.

Carla smiled. "Scare you?"

"Yeah," Delilah said. "Thanks. A lot. I needed the adrenaline rush."

"You got the medicine?"

Delilah handed her the bag and she took out the bottle, held it up, and squinted at it.

"This is the right stuff?"

"I guess. Jack picked it out."

"Then it's right. He always gets things right. A good man." She paused for a moment, then added pointedly, "He's single."

"Oh, Jesus," Delilah blurted out. "Don't do that."

Carla pasted a look of fake shock on her face. "Do what?"

"Play matchmaker. It's so fu—funny. Not funny, I mean. I mean, don't do that."

Carla reverted to her more natural glare. "I don't like people cursing in my house," she said. "Especially the 'f' word."

"I didn't use the 'f' word," Delilah said.

"You were going to," she retorted.

"I'm sorry."

"No," Carla said. "You're not."

"Okay. I'm not. Only—please don't get any ideas about fixing me up with Jack or—or with anybody."

"What makes you think I was doing anything like that?"

"You're about as subtle as a sledgehammer," Delilah noted. "'He's a good man.' 'Single.' I mean, he's nice, but I'm not in the market."

Carla glared. "Not in the market? He's not a slice of meat."

"I have a boyfriend," she amended.

Carla eyed her suspiciously. "Hmmph," she said. "Can't be much of a boyfriend."

"How would you know?"

"He's not here, is he?"

"He's in Key West," Delilah said. "Where I live. He had to work."

"I only know what I see. And I see he's not here."

Before Delilah could reply to this, Carla waved a thin hand in the air. "Don't talk about it anymore," she said. "You'll just aggravate me. What's in Key West, anyway? Why do you live there?"

Delilah's surprise chased away her irritation. It was the first question Carla had asked about her. "My parents—your daughter and her husband—moved there when my sister got married and moved there. They wanted to be close in case any grandchildren occurred."

Carla stared up at the ceiling. "It's hot there," she commented after a while. "Lots of tourists. We used to go to Florida in the winter, with the circus. It was hot."

"That's right."

"You only have the one sister," she said, a statement rather than a question.

"Just Margo. I had a brother. A twin."

She nodded. "He died."

"How do you know that?"

"You said 'had.' 'Had a brother.'"

"Oh. Well, yes. He died. When we were ten. Childhood leukemia."

"That was bad, I'll bet," she said, and if there was any sympathy in her tone, Delilah couldn't discern it.

"Yeah," Delilah agreed. "It was bad."

"Why did you come, and not your sister?" she asked.

"Because she has a career and a husband and I only have a boyfriend and a job. As a waitress."

"How come? Are you stupid?"

"No. Of course not."

"Lazy?"

"No." Delilah flashed her a smile. "I'm an underachiever. Good at it, too."

"Most people aren't proud of that kind of thing," Carla noted.

"I'm contrary, too. I get it from my grandmother."

Carla cast her a quick scowl, then sniffed, and scratched at her hip. She looked around the kitchen and sighed deeply. "Well," she said, "it's late. I'm going to bed. Stan's coming tomorrow. Early."

"Stan?"

"Septic man. Work on the leach field. Might need your help, so you should get up." She moved toward the door that led to the narrow set of stairs.

Apparently, Delilah thought, the initial interview was complete. She wondered how she did, or if she'd ever know.

She thought about turning on the TV for a while, then decided against it. Instead she got herself a glass of juice from the refrigerator and went up to her room. She had some books she could read.

Once she was there, however, she didn't feel like reading. She just sat on the bed, staring at the Orange Moon Face, which leered back. After a while, she smelled smoke. Her grandmother, indulging in her secret vice. It made her crave one. To distract herself, she got off the bed, opened the closet door, and peered at the stuff inside it. She picked up one of the purses—a large black patent leather with a metal clasp—and opened it. Inside was a smaller purse, red patent leather. She pulled it out and opened it.

Inside was another purse—small brown leather. She pulled it out and opened it. Inside was an embroidered black change purse. She pulled it out and opened it. Inside was cloth. She tugged at it, until it was all out. It turned out to be a pair of men's pajama bottoms, white with red stripes.

She stuffed them back inside, and tried not to think about how they got there. This was Big Bertha's room, and though she hadn't met her, she already had pictures in her head about what she might look like. Again, the American prejudice reared its ugly head—only people who could be in a Calvin Klein ad have a right to a love life. But as she sat on the bed, she realized she was the one without a love life. Big Bertha had evidence of one. Even Carla might. Delilah was the one doing without. Go figure.

A scratching at the door interrupted her musings. She got up and opened it, and the black cat sat there, purring. She licked a paw, and casually picked her way into the room and leapt onto the bed, where she licked at her paws more.

"Chaos," Delilah said. "I think your name is Chaos."

She walked toward the bed to pet the cat, and on the way

noticed a picture lying flat on the bureau. She picked it up and looked at it.

It was an old-fashioned kind of photo—sepia toned, hand colored—showing an almost teenage girl, with a little boy. They were both smiling, big smiles. Real smiles, as if this were a good and important day. She had her arm around him, and he looked at her as if she were the best thing since sliced bread. She held a rose in one hand, and wore a white dress. And the little boy looked very much like her brother, Joshua.

She turned it over again, and saw that someone had written on the back, "Carla and Frank, 12/11/29.

It was Carla, and a boy Delilah presumed was her brother. She turned back to the picture and studied the faces. She could almost see the current Carla, mostly in the eyes, which were dark and large, not yet hooded by sagging flesh. Her hair was dark, too, and thick and long, much like Delilah's. And though the face was rounder, her smile wasn't unlike Delilah's, with half of the mouth a little higher than the other. Michael had often commented on it, saying it made her look sardonic.

So, Delilah thought. This was who Carla had been. The woman smoking in her room was who she had become. It didn't seem possible, or real. She didn't think there was any other animal on the planet that changed as much as humans did with age.

She looked again at the little boy. Of course, at a certain age little boys tend to look alike. Their faces are round and chubby, and they always seem surprised. So the resemblance could have been more one of age than of anything else. But it wasn't. Delilah could see Joshua's nose—turned up at the end, and the family always wondered where he got that from, given the noses he should have inherited from his parents.

And it was Joshua's smile, all of him into it. He tended toward the optimistic, a dreamer who spun stories, made up songs and riddles. Unlike Delilah, whose temperament was earthy and direct, Joshua had an otherworldly quality. He noticed pain quickly, and moved just as quickly to soothe it. If Delilah came home from school upset from a bad grade, he'd get solemn for a moment, then suddenly his face would break into that smile and he'd say something like, "I know. Let's play Teach the Teacher."

"What?" Delilah would ask.

"You know. Teach the Teacher. You be the teacher, and you teach the teacher how to give you better grades. You can use the water pistol."

Their mother said she couldn't take him to the grocery store, because he'd invariably find the saddest-looking person in the place and want to take him home.

That's how he was. Then, he got sick.

At first everyone thought it was the flu, but it didn't go away, and Delilah remembered the day he came home from the doctor with a white bandage on his arm from where they did the blood work. She didn't really understand what was going on. Only that something had happened that she could do nothing about.

He was sick for about a year. A year of hospitals and doctors, whispered conversations that she wasn't supposed to overhear. The smell of sickness pervaded the house, and Joshua was not available to play anymore. He had chemotherapy, and threw up a lot, slept even more.

Delilah's father explained what was wrong. He told her, in his calm, dry way, about leukemia and what it did to the blood cells, and how the doctors were working to fix it.

"Can I do anything?" she'd asked.

Her father looked pained, and she wondered if that was an impolite question, but then he hugged her and said, "Just be yourself, Lilah. Like you always are."

Later that week, she decided that if Joshua's blood was bad, and hers was good, perhaps she could share. Her mother found her in her room pricking her finger with a needle, trying to coax her blood into a cup for Joshua to drink, or put in his cereal or something.

Her mother had been upset, Delilah remembered. Margo told her she was behaving foolishly, and should try to be good since everything else was so horrible. Delilah didn't really understand, but then, she never understood Margo very well.

Then, there was the afternoon she went into Joshua's room to read to him—one of the Great Brain stories, she remembered. They used to read them together all the time, and try to figure out the mystery before they finished. Since he'd gotten sick, reading together was one of the few things they could still do. This time, when she went into the room, he looked at her with eyes made larger by the thinness of his face and the pallor of his skin. He smiled, but he didn't say anything. She tried to pretend everything was okay. She sat down and started to read.

When she looked at him again, he was asleep, and suddenly she was angry at him. Here she was, doing something nice for him because he was sick, and he was ignoring her. She threw the book across the room, and it slammed into the wall, knocking down a picture he had of the first moon walk. He woke up and startled hard, then gasped. Delilah went over to him to apologize, but he didn't seem to see her. He just kept gasping, as if he couldn't breathe. As if there wasn't enough air in the room.

She ran from the room sobbing. Her mother, coming down the hall at the noise, went right past her and into Joshua's room. Delilah pressed her back against the wall and slumped down to the floor, where she sat while her parents and Margo and then doctors came and went, going past her as if she were invisible.

At some point, her father came out of Joshua's room and found her still sitting there. It was probably very late by then. He squatted down next to her.

"Is he mad at me?" she asked, deciding to get the worst out of the way.

"Mad at you? Joshua? For what?"

"Hitting his picture."

A look crossed her father's face, which she couldn't name. It wasn't one she'd seen before. Not one she wanted to see again. In looking back, she recognized it as profound pain. A sort of world grief at the helplessness of all humans against death and illness and pain.

"No, pumpkin," he said. "He's not mad at you."

"Did I—did I make him sicker?"

"Of course not. Of course you didn't. He's just—sick. It's not your fault."

"Well," she said, truculent then, "when's he gonna get better?"

Her father sat down on the floor next to her. He lowered his head and rubbed at his temples with his fingers. "He's not getting better, pumpkin," he said. "He's dying."

And he started to cry.

His tears were silent. No sobbing. Just water running down his cheeks and his mouth twisted and his eyes scrunched up. It terrified her.

"Daddy?" she whispered. "Daddy? I'm sorry. I'm sorry."

He put his arms around her, hugged her. "You didn't do anything wrong," he kept saying. "It's not your fault."

To this day, she didn't know if she believed him. She didn't know that she wanted to. If it was her fault, at least she could do something about it. But if it wasn't, then there was no controlling it at all. Nothing she could do except feel horrible, and afraid.

Joshua died a few days later, and what she remembered from his death and funeral was a sort of generalized anxiety, coupled with guilty relief. She knew she was supposed to be sad, so she acted sad, but she'd been without him so long she didn't really miss him. And she was relieved to have the smell of sickness out of the house. Relieved to have no doctors or nurses, relieved that her mother was actually looking at her again instead of staring past her toward Joshua's room.

She was horrified at herself for feeling this relief. It took her years to understand what a normal response that was, and to forgive herself for it.

She wasn't sure if she'd ever gotten over the other lesson of Joshua's death—that the body betrayed you, without notice, and with no provocation. One day Joshua's body was fine. The next it wouldn't do anything it needed to stay alive. And if it happened to Joshua, it could just as easily happen to her. There was no reassurance in the world that would soothe that knowledge out of her.

She supposed she could have easily become a hypochondriac, but instead she fell in love with science, which seemed to her the only way to outsmart the body, trick it before it tricked you. At least it gave her the illusion of answers to the questions she couldn't even formulate yet. And science asked her only to keep trying to figure it out, with no emotional content necessary.

Margo didn't seem to feel any of that. She just was sad, and wept softly to the various boys she brought to the house when she told them the story. But then, Margo was the big sister. And the sense of betrayal was deeper for Delilah, because Joshua was a twin. They'd shared the womb, their cells tangling in that closed space, so the betrayal of his body felt like the betrayal of hers.

And now, she was looking at Joshua's face turned back in time. The face of her grandmother's brother. Joshua's face. And somewhere in there, in the smallest way—just one sparkling chromosome, perhaps—was her own face as well. If she had children of her own would they carry those same chromosomes? Come out with those same bright and oddly shaped smiles?

As she put the picture down, it occurred to her that it hadn't been in the room yesterday. Or had it, and she didn't notice? Or did Carla put it there because they had that little family talk? But no, she thought. She wasn't thinking clearly. She didn't have time to put it there tonight. And there was no reason for her to put it there earlier.

She decided she was getting as bad as Joshua, spinning stories out of nothing. She put the thought away, and climbed into bed.

When Jack got back to his apartment, he went to his room and started his usual routine of preparing for sleep. He often had to get up early, so he'd learned to take the advice one of his teachers gave him—sleep fast. Consequently, getting ready for sleep was little more than stripping and sliding under the sheets.

Tonight, he was halted in that routine. In his room he climbed out of his clothes, his eye patch coming off with his T-shirt. When he was naked he turned to throw his clothes into the hamper, and caught sight of himself in the mirror.

He walked to it, stood in front of it and looked. It was the same body it had been yesterday, a good body that worked well and looked okay. Keeping active made his muscles taut without being ostentatious. He was no body-builder. He didn't like the look. Neither did he want to get flabby, which was a danger, given his fleshy build.

He held a hand up to his scarred eye. The lines around it were tight, puckering the corners of his lid and making vision difficult. The eye itself was damaged, and scar tissue obstructed his vision anyway. Bright light refracted against it, causing him to see halos and rainbow rays of light nobody else saw. It disturbed the vision in his other eye, which was why he wore the patch.

He wasn't hiding his scars. No. Not at all. They weren't grotesque. Just different. His wife hadn't minded them, she said. But then again, she didn't really see him as a lover. She just hoped she would.

He hadn't actually thought about how they might detract from his looks in a long time. Not until Delilah asked him if it hurt. Something in the way she said it, the directness of her question and the heartfelt nature of it, got under his skin. Compassion was something he valued perhaps more than any other quality. The capacity to feel for the suffering of others was, he thought, what would keep the species alive long after survival of the fittest lost its value. Compassion *was* survival of the fittest. The only way. But he rarely saw it exhibited as easily or honestly as he had tonight.

She was a pretty girl, he thought, though not conscious of her attractiveness. He liked her eyes, which were large and dark. He liked her thick hair and the way her hips swayed from side to side when she walked, as if the motion of her body brought her pleasure.

She said she was a relative to Carla, but not what kind. Cousin? Great-niece? He didn't see a physical resemblance, but the age difference was so great, how could he? She seemed like Carla in being outspoken and, well, odd. In any case, she came from good stock. Probably would make good babies.

He stopped himself cold, and shook a finger at his reflection in the mirror.

"None of that, boy," he said. "You just met her."

He would take his time and get to know her before he began spinning stories in his head. Perhaps she was already involved, or planned to be a nun, or wouldn't be around long enough for it to matter.

In the meantime, she'd given him a pleasant evening, and he

was grateful. Pleasantness was a vastly underrated commodity, he thought.

He stretched his arms up over his head, and let them fall to his side. When he was tired, when the weather was shifting, and when he was feeling some great emotional change, the tiny muscles around his eye would twitch lightly. They did so now.

He touched them, wondering if there was to be a storm, if he was to sleep, or if he was about to fall in love.

There was no telling which it would be ahead of time.

NINE

earth

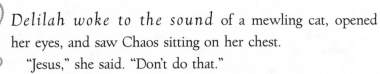 *Delilah woke to the sound* of a mewling cat, opened her eyes, and saw Chaos sitting on her chest.

"Jesus," she said. "Don't do that."

The cat mewled some more. Then, something loud happened. She sat up fast, and the cat ran away. At first she thought it was old man Bower, shooting at the early-morning bunnies, but the noise continued and it wasn't gunshots. It was an engine of some kind starting with a bang, and continuing with a lot of thumps.

She went to the window, pulled back the curtain, and looked out. A man was using a large device to open the earth on the side of the house. And he was smoking a cigar.

"Stan," she muttered, "the septic man. Who spends his whole life dealing with other people's shit." Stan, or one of his minions.

She got dressed, brushed her teeth without looking at herself, and went downstairs. As she entered the kitchen, she heard a sound that stopped her. Someone was singing.

"Blowout," a deep baritone rumbled, with feeling. "Sludge all over the place." His voice went up and down melodically, a little sorrowfully. "Need new lines, more sand. Not sure about the tank. Won't know until we dig."

Delilah made her way forward, and as she rounded the corner to the kitchen, she saw Carla standing at the kitchen table, one hand pressed to the surface as if she needed the support. "How much, Stan?" she asked.

"A lot," he sang softly. "Ten thousand, maybe."

She straightened her spine and pulled her hand off the table, held it at her side in a fist. "We'll have to work it out," she said stoically.

He patted her arm, and finished with a flourish, on a high note. "We will, Carla. Don't worry about it." He bowed to her, then made his exit through the sliding glass doors.

When he left, Carla sat down at the table and rested her face in her hands. For the first time since Delilah had seen her, she looked not only old, but also worn-out. Like a tree that stands by the side of the road and has taken in a little too much road salt. Delilah saw that her hand was trembling lightly.

"Carla?" she asked quietly. "Are you okay?"

Carla brought her head up, and her face assumed a more natural expression of irritation. "I'm fine," she snapped. "You always sleep this late?"

"I work nights," Delilah said. "Or I used to. Um—was that man singing to you?"

"He's got a stutter. Can't talk unless he sings."

Of course, Delilah thought. The logical explanation. "What're they doing out there?"

"Digging up the leach field. Gotta put in new lines."

"A shitty kind of day," Delilah muttered. Carla heard her.

"I told you I don't like bad language in the house," she barked.

Delilah sighed. "Can I do anything?"

"Yes," she said. "Make some food. The men'll be hungry."

"Food?" Delilah asked.

"Sandwiches. Salad. Come up with something. I'm going out-side."

Delilah did as she was told.

As she worked in the kitchen, coming up with potato salad, chicken that she found in the freezer and cooked for sandwich meat, and a platter of sausage with peppers and onions and tomatoes from the garden, she saw a variety of men in the yard. Some of them seemed to be with Stan, or maybe all of them were, but they also seemed to be friends of Carla's. They came in and out of the house as if they were used to doing so, and seemed to know things like where the water glasses were, and where she kept a six-pack of beer tucked away at the back of the pantry. One or two stopped to speak to Delilah, to ask what she was making, or to say it smelled good. Stan sang her a few lines about the sausage and peppers. They were all polite, and they all seemed to either smoke or chew on cigars. A party atmosphere prevailed.

While she worked, Delilah saw Carla outside, standing with her hands on her hips, shouting things to the men, laughing and smiling, waving at them coyly.

That was a surprise. Carla had a flirtatious streak. And Delilah noticed that the men flirted right back, not as if she were an old lady, but as if she were a friend. Someone had once told Delilah that women over fifty were basically invisible in America, but that couldn't be said of Carla. Not with these men.

Most of what they said was drowned out by the sound of machinery as the earth was opened up so that human waste could be dealt with, but Delilah caught bits and pieces.

"Hey," Carla shouted at one point. "You there. Mac. Don't be making comments about the help. She's smarter than she looks."

"She looks just fine to me," a man with a cigar shouted back. "I just wanna know, can she cook?"

"You tell me," Carla said wryly. "She's making your lunch."

Delilah realized that they were talking about her. She was a curiosity. Apparently not an unpleasant one. She found she didn't mind occupying that position. It seemed kind of nice, actually, all these people working together to clean up shit, and she was part of it all. Part of a movement, so to speak. She wondered what her mother would think of it. Or Margo. She smiled as she chopped another round of peppers for the frying pan.

"Delilah?" a voice asked.

She turned. It was Jack, not smoking a cigar, but dressed in old jeans and a torn T-shirt, with heavy work boots on. He had a package wrapped in white paper in one hand.

"Hey," he said. "How's it going?"

"Fine in here. How's it going out there?"

He shrugged. "It's getting fixed, but it'll cost a lot, even with all the free labor."

Delilah looked out the window. "Those men aren't getting paid?"

"Some of them. Most are neighbors, just stopped by to help out."

"People still do that?"

"They do up here. If you don't get mistaken for a bunny, it's not half bad. But it's still expensive work."

"I heard. Ten thousand. Carla seemed upset. Is she—can she afford this?"

"I doubt it. She doesn't have much except this house, and that needs work. Roof's gotta be reshingled before winter, and I'm worried about her furnace. I guess she's got some savings, and Stan'll let her take her time and pay. I don't know, though."

Delilah wiped her hands with a towel. "Jack," she said, "I can help her. I mean, my mother can."

"What?"

"My mother. My parents. They sent me here to find out if Carla needed anything."

He tapped the package thoughtfully against his leg. "What kind of relative are you?" he asked. "A . . . cousin?"

"I'm her granddaughter," Delilah admitted. "Don't tell her I said so. I think it pisses her off."

He looked her up and down, and whistled long and low. "Granddaughter?" he asked. "How the hell did that happen?"

"Well," she said, "there's this stork . . ."

"You know what I mean."

"My mom is her daughter. Carla gave her up for adoption."

"Huh," he said, then looked at her hard.

"I take after my grandfather," Delilah said. "I'm sure of it. At least, until she tells me he was the hairy man in the circus. Listen, if my family offers Carla money, do you think she'd take it?"

"Hard to say. I've tried a few times and she almost bit my left leg off. Maybe we can do an end run around her. I'll talk to Stan about the bill, see what we can work out. How much can your parents help?"

"Probably the whole thing."

Jack raised his eyebrows. "So you're not sailors or hippies?"

"Ex-hippies," Delilah said. "My father made good on the stock market, and he knows how to manage it, in spite of my mother's tendency to spend it on Vegetarian Suppers to Save the World."

"Um. Oh," Jack said.

"Yeah," she said. "Not an unusual reaction." She explained further about her father's unexpected arrival into money, and her mother being an activist, and how their house was usually filled with people she didn't know who had a lot of earrings or tattoos or both.

Jack grinned. "So this all seems like home to you, doesn't it?"

"Pretty much," she admitted. "No cigar smoking in my parents' house, though. And profanity is allowed."

Jack pulled out a chair and sat down, putting his package down in front of him. It hit the table with a thump. "What's it like being rich?"

"I'm not," she said, surprised. "I mean, it's not my money. I don't even own a set of dishes."

Or silverware, she thought, or furniture or much of anything. She'd given most of her stuff to the Salvation Army when she went back to Key West. It had all been college-grade goods, not worth burdening herself with.

"But it'll be your money someday," Jack said.

"They'll spend it before that," she noted. "Besides, I wasn't raised to think of myself that way. As—as privileged."

"You're young, white, American," Jack said. "You're privileged. Even without your parents' money."

"Uh-oh," she said. "I smell a political polemic coming on. Should I sit down? Get a beer? A cigar?"

He laughed. "No time for it now. Carla's got us all digging." He stood up. "I'll take a raincheck, though. Dinner, and a discussion of the arrogance of privileged Americans?"

She was about to say that'd be great, when she noticed that he looked nervous. That made her nervous, because the only reason for him to look nervous was if dinner and discussion also meant the other "d" word—date. Being nervous, she said the first stupid thing that popped into her mind.

"You been talking to Carla?" she asked. He blinked hard. She picked up a pepper and started chopping.

"What?" he asked.

"Nothing," she said. "Just—I hope Carla isn't making you feel obligated to entertain the relatives."

"I don't feel obligated," he said, shocked at the notion. He didn't act out of obligation except to his own sense of decency or pleasure, and so far that had been enough to keep him fairly responsible. "I just thought you might want to get away if you're not busy tonight."

"I am," she said quickly. "I mean, I'm busy tonight."

"Oh," he said, both perplexed and disappointed. "Well, then, some other time."

Seeing his confusion, Delilah decided to be proactive. "Look," she said, "you should know I don't date. I mean, I'm already involved. With someone. Anyway, I'm going out with Monica. Tonight, I mean."

There was a long silence. Jack cleared his throat. "With . . . Monica?" he asked.

"That's right. Monica. We were roommates in college. She lives in town."

"Well. Oh. Then, I guess . . . That's . . . nice. I mean, it's good to have . . . someone." Just his luck, he thought. Two out of two. He tapped the package against his leg again.

"What is that you're drumming with?" Delilah asked, hoping to shift the atmosphere.

He looked down. "That. Oh. It's for Carla. Goes in the freezer."

"What is it?"

"Stew. Venison stew. She likes it."

"Oh. I never had that. Where'd you get it?"

"In the woods," he said as he opened the freezer. "Where deer usually hang out."

"You—hunted it?"

"Had it butchered, then made a stew. Carla lets me hunt her land during the season."

He turned to the freezer and started moving things around, making room for it. Delilah hadn't ever known anyone who hunted the food he ate.

"Do you object to hunting?" he asked, as he closed the freezer door.

"Not on principle," she said. "We are predators. But I don't know what it's like. Is it—strange? I mean, watching an animal die. Knowing you killed it."

Jack did his trick of raising the eyebrow over his patch. "You never saw anything die?" he asked, then shook his head. "Of course not. Why would you? Well, did you ever see a baby born?"

She shook her head.

"Oh. Well, it's kind of like that. The same kind of—I don't know the right word. Energy, I think. It's a certain energy."

"The same as watching a baby born?"

"Yes," he said, more definitively. "It's like standing in a doorway where the wind is coming through. Doesn't matter if it's coming in or going out. It's just—a feeling on your skin."

"Is it like an adrenaline rush?"

Jack shook his head. "That's different. That's from the inside. This is from the outside. At least, that's as close as I can get to it. Nobody ever asked, so I never had to describe it before. You ask odd questions. Anybody ever tell you that?"

"Now and then."

"Well," he said. "You do. Listen, the dinner thing is still open. I mean, in a friendly way. And Monica could come along, of course. That kind of thing is okay, isn't it? You have friends, right? I mean, who are men?"

"Of course," Delilah said, confused. "I have all kinds of friends. I just don't want you to feel like you have to entertain me because of Carla."

"I know that," he said, frustrated. He wanted to spend time

with her, regardless. Couldn't she see that? "Jesus, you're an interesting woman. Person. Carla doesn't have anything to do with it. What the hell gave you that idea anyway?"

"You don't have to get truculent about it," she said.

"There," he said. "That's what I mean. You use words like 'truculent.' You make it fun to talk. So dinner and political discussion. With you and . . . um . . . Monica. Name the time."

It occurred to Delilah that there might be something in this for Monica. Not that she typically went for handymen in eye patches who hunted their own dinner, being an uptown kind of girl, but he was a nice man. A man the Foundation could approve of. She smiled at him. "I'll talk to her and let you know."

"Okay then," he said. "Do that. Good luck with the cooking."

"Good luck with the shit," she replied.

He laughed his evil laugh, and went outside.

The day passed in funky smells, noises, and a lot of food getting eaten. Delilah was allowed off the leash by dinnertime, but the men were still finishing the work so she couldn't shower. She went to Monica's and showered there, yelling at her from the bathroom about the meeting with Michael. She was clean and toweled off when she got to the part about his phone numbers burning holes in her pocket and her heart, and what should she do? Call? Not call? Devastation to all bad boys through their absence was the Foundation's policy in the new era, but maybe he was in a new era too, and no longer a bad boy, and how would she know unless she called?

Monica analyzed the situation rapidly, and came up with a suggestion.

"The Foundation," she said, "really needs to focus."

"On what?" Delilah asked.

"Accessories," she replied.

They went to the mall—not the one she'd been to with Jack, but the one she'd always gone to with Monica—and made their first stop at Ann Taylor.

"Didn't we used to shop at Macy's?" she asked Monica as she turned over a price tag on a silk summer sweater set. Delilah had seen Monica poor, and well off, but either way she had fine taste in clothes. And when poor, she had never once heard Monica complain about wanting something she couldn't afford. Somehow, knowing she deserved the best seemed to make her content with whatever she had at any given moment. Nor had Delilah ever seen her hesitate to spend a lot of money for something she wanted, if she had the money to spend.

"New era, remember?" Monica wandered over to the jewelry case, and peered into it. "That," she said, pointing into the glass case. "I think you should seriously consider it."

Delilah joined her and looked inside. "That" was a small silver necklace with a round zirconium or something else diamondlike at the center. Very subtle. Very sweet.

"Ninety-eight dollars," Delilah said. "Above budget for the Foundation."

Monica raised her eyebrows. "You have a card with you?"

"I don't want to run it up. This trip is already costing me."

"And whose trip is it?" Monica asked.

"What?"

"Whose trip? Who are you doing it for?"

"Well, my mother, of course."

"Then who will pay for it?"

"Oh," Delilah said. "Right."

Of course her mother would pay any expenses. She'd already said so, and sent her with a wad of cash as well. But though her mother's ideology didn't stop her from living in a mansion in Key West, it had taught Delilah that material ownership was not really a good thing. Having a Marxist economist for a father hadn't helped.

"The Foundation should not be confused about its relationship to material goods," Monica noted. "Yet I perceive it is."

"The Foundation is confused about a lot of things," Delilah replied. "It's a nice necklace, though."

"Try it on."

Monica got the saleslady to come over and open the case, and Delilah put it on, then gazed at herself in the mirror. Her first thought was that it was the kind of necklace you could have sex in. Some jewelry bounces around or jingles or cuts into the flesh when pressed. This would just sit there, sparkling like a small star at the base of the throat. She had a quick vision of Michael reaching up to touch it. She shivered.

"I shouldn't," she said, and took it off.

"You will," Monica replied, and said to the saleslady. "Could you take that to the counter, please. We'll be looking around some more."

She was glad to do so.

As they perused the racks of suits, sorting through possibilities—Monica always needed suits for her job—she said to Delilah, "The Foundation should begin discussion on the issue of its confusion. Material goods," she noted, "should be relinquished easily when necessary, and celebrated when possible. It's a Zen thing."

"Zen?"

"Zen is," she quoted, "Do what you want. Eat what there is."

"Who said that?"

"Jack Kerouac," she said.

"You don't read Kerouac."

"One of the men I dated did. He was fond of saying that. Of course, the way he lived it was a problem, but I think we can safely apply it to shopping."

"Okay," Delilah said. "I'll accept that. Are you trying that on?"

She had lifted a cream-colored suit from the rack and was eyeing it. "I don't know. It's not my color, is it?"

"It's definitely your color," Delilah said. Cream did something nice to the gold-brown of her skin.

She sighed. "I don't know why I resist cream."

"I don't either. Inner conflict?"

"My mother always told me it didn't wear well."

"Ah. More fashion issues emerge. Have you considered therapy?"

"Let's get back to the necklace," Monica said, always more eager to talk about someone else's issues. "Do you fear material goods, or growing up?"

Delilah opened her mouth and shut it again.

"Both?" Monica suggested.

"How can I grow up when I'm being dragged into my past?"

"Maybe," Monica said, "you're being dragged back so you can face it, and grow up."

"You say that," Delilah said a little defensively, "because you believe in plans. You always believed in a plan."

"You're nothing without them," she acknowledged.

"I don't think I believe in them," Delilah said. "I think—I think it's all kind of random. This and that happens. Lightning is a mystery. Nobody knows how the Rocky Mountains got there. Huge lumps of earth reaching up to the sky, and we don't know how they were made, much less why. If there is a plan, it's much too complex and obscure for us to participate in except by coincidence."

"Maybe," Monica said, *"how* is why."

"Oh, God," Delilah said. "That's too deep for me."

Monica handed her a suit. "Quick," she said. "Try something on."

Delilah eyed what Monica handed her. "It's a suit, Monica."

"Try it. New eras need new clothes. It's about how you see yourself. Choices you make for change."

"Michael would like it," she noted, holding it up and smoothing out the jacket. "He told me a really expensive suit or a short plaid wool skirt were the two biggest clothing turn-ons for him. I think it's a Catholic-school thing."

"So try it," Monica said.

"Still not my style," Delilah said. "You try on your suit, and I'll comment."

Monica gave up, and took her suit to the fitting room, Delilah trailing after with a few T-shirts and a pair of capri-length pants.

She tried each one dutifully but knew she wasn't willing to spend Ann Taylor money on T-shirts. She climbed back into her own clothes and emerged from her dressing room to see Monica at the mirrors in the cream suit.

"Nice," Delilah said.

"You think so? Doesn't make my hips look too big?"

Delilah laughed.

"At least," Monica said, "I try something on."

"I tried on the necklace," Delilah noted. "I'm even going to buy it. Isn't that enough? Or do you think it's a problem that I hate suits and Michael thinks they're sexy?"

"Not a problem," Monica said. "More of a statement. It says something about you, and about him, and about the two of you."

"Go ahead," Delilah invited. "Explain."

"That you would fall for someone who is inherently attracted to something you hate."

"My mother wears Liz Claiborne, and my father likes LL Bean," Delilah pointed out. "They're still married."

"Maybe your father likes to see Liz Claiborne, and your mother likes to see LL Bean. But it doesn't matter much, really. You and

Michael only connect at the edges anyway. Which is probably how you want it, since you prefer ideas to people."

Delilah thought about this. "Well, yeah. I do. They're more manageable."

"Exactly. Don't get me wrong. There are worse issues."

"Like issues with hips?" Delilah asked, as Monica continued to peer at her butt.

"You really don't think it makes me look fat?"

"I think it's a knockout. And it's on sale, isn't it?"

"Ye-es," she said hesitantly.

"Then you can overcome your hip issue by buying it. Now tell me what to buy to overcome mine."

She took a deep breath and let it out. "I'll have to think about it."

Monica went back into the dressing room and Delilah sat and stared at herself in the mirror. She was wearing her usual khakis and T-shirt, a sort of neutral outfit that she wore a lot, not because she thought it looked good on her, but because it was easiest. Picking out khakis and T-shirts didn't take a lot of thought, and she didn't have to worry about revealing too much when she wore them.

She heard her father telling her she didn't make choices, and wondered if that was why she wore what she did. Because it was easier than figuring out what suited her, and taking a chance on it. That was a depressing thought. She couldn't even connect to a fashion statement.

When Monica emerged again, she had the cream suit with her, ready to go. "Try on anything else?" she asked.

Delilah shook her head glumly. "I have issues with connection, even with myself."

"Lilah," Monica said, *"everybody* does. Don't let it stop you from trying something on, for God's sake. Go get a suit."

As Monica spoke, Delilah went ahead and made a choice. Not a very important one, but her own.

"No," she said. "No suits. You can't do field camp in a suit."

Monica nodded. "Now we're getting somewhere. Is that where you see yourself? This—what is it?"

"Field camp."

"It's not—an army thing, is it?"

"No, silly. It's what you do before you go and get a graduate degree in geology. Study rocks in the wild."

"Oh, well, then. Is that what you see yourself doing? The Foundation is turning inward, and needs to know."

Delilah closed her eyes. She'd considered it before she went to graduate school for business. And she rejected it. Because Michael had made noises about being a better team if she had a real job, as he defined it? No. She couldn't hand him that one. She chose not to go to field camp all on her own.

"I see myself outside," she said. "Not necessarily geology, though. Too specialized."

"Hmm," Monica noted. "Fear of committing to something you'd really connect with?"

She shook her head. "No. Something else. Something—Monica, remember when we got our apartment?"

Monica nodded. "I hadn't even met you. I walked in and there you stood with the landlord, talking about the place, and I thought you looked kind of wild and out of it."

"And I had no idea what your problem was. I mean, you were so polite and aloof. But it worked out fine, didn't it? It was a random thing. And we couldn't have made it happen if we tried, you know?"

As a Virgo, Monica didn't necessarily approve of the random. "I guess," she said reluctantly.

"I think I'm waiting for that. Something random. Something I can't predict. I keep thinking, I'll know it when it happens. It'll feel right. It'll settle in, somehow."

"But you can't wait forever. Sooner or later, you have to make choices."

"Maybe," she said. "But the only choice I have to make today is whether or not to call Michael."

"That," Monica said, waving it away. "You'll call him. We already know that. What we don't know is what you'll wear."

"The necklace," Delilah said.

"You may need something else with it. Just at first."

Delilah subdued a smile. "Do you think I'm being stupid?" she asked.

"It's necessary," Monica replied. "If you don't see him, you'd stay up nights wondering if you should have. If it turns out you're being stupid, you'll feel like shit, but you'll sleep better. Have you considered a cute little summer dress?"

"How about jeans and a T-shirt?" Delilah suggested.

Monica shook her head. "There are some lines I must draw."

They did find a Cute Little Summer Dress—denim blue, nice light cotton. When Delilah put it on and looked in the mirror, she saw someone who looked like the Delilah she imagined she might be, in a romantic moment. She bought it, and a few more like it. It was a choice made. Very satisfying.

They stopped for hamburgers and drinks at a pub near the mall, a place they used to frequent after shopping worked up their appetites. While they were eating, Delilah noticed how young the crowd that hung out here seemed to be—they weren't that young when she was in college, were they? And were they that much older now?

She thought of the picture she'd found in her room, of Carla as a girl. Carla had been young once and now was old, which led Delilah to believe that she might actually be old someday, too.

She looked at Monica and tried to imagine both of them old, going gray, getting fatter or thinner, blue veins popping up in their legs. She tried to see where the worst wrinkles would be—around the eyes, or the mouth? Sagging at the neck or jaw? And their hair—would that be patches of gray and brown, or a solid silver?

Delilah didn't think she would take aging well. She had recently found a gray hair, and she panicked. Her mother went gray at forty, all at once, and she'd been hitting the bottle ever since. She worried a lot about her roots, and was always asking Delilah if they were showing. Delilah didn't feel ready for that. She didn't want to be addicted to Loving Care. She'd read the ingredients. The first one was nonoxynol-9, and nobody could explain to her why a contraceptive was the main ingredient in hair dye.

But whether she took it well or not, it would happen.

She'd been blessed with a body that pretty much took care of itself. It did all its jobs with a minimum of maintenance, and most of the time she ignored it. When she got old, she might have to actually pay attention to things like diet and exercise. And things might happen to it that were out of her control. No. It wasn't that they might. They would. That's what aging was about—the body, out of control, doing stuff you didn't want it to do.

But she couldn't imagine what it would be like.

Would they be lively, healthy old ladies, or would arthritis bend their bodies into strange and painful shapes, osteoporosis hunch their backs, and glaucoma dim their vision? Or maybe by then, science would have taken care of all that. With the baby boomers aging rapidly, there certainly was a whole huge market for antiaging technology. Her father said it was a good investment bet.

"So you'll call Michael," Monica said, as they dove into their burgers and beer.

Delilah nodded. Then, she smiled. "Did you know," she said, "the first ingredient in Loving Care is nonoxynol-9?"

"Lilah," Monica said, "you know the oddest, most useless things."

Delilah clinked glasses with her.

"Yeah," she agreed. "I do."

TEN

air

She called Michael at work rather than home, thinking somehow that was more casual. He sounded busy, but glad to hear from her, and said he'd meet her at a bar they used to frequent, Pete's Place, that evening. When her heart stopped racing, and she got over her embarrassment that it was racing, she called home, and this time got Margo on the phone. She said Mom was getting antsy.

"Does she say anything about Mom at all?"

"Carla? Not a thing. Not yet."

"Well, have you asked? Did you bring it up?"

"I tried once or twice," Delilah said. "I still have my legs, but they got kind of cut off at the knees."

"What's that mean?" Margo asked. All the imagination in the family had passed her by.

"She didn't want to talk about it. Look, Margo, you have to

know her. She's—not very accessible. I'll talk to her. I just have to take my time. Tell Mom I'm working on it."

"I hope you know what you're doing," Margo said.

"If you think you can do better," Delilah said, and let that hang there.

Margo was quiet for a moment and then asked, in the same hushed tone her mother had used, "Is it bad there?"

Delilah was getting a little tired of that. They sent her, thinking she was heading toward a Third World ghetto. She had an urge to start making up stories about really big rats, but then how would she explain when they came to visit? "No," she said. "It's kind of interesting, actually. Not that different from home. Big house with lots of strange people in and out."

"Your room?" Margo asked.

"Old. You could roll a marble nicely down the floor. There's a fireplace in it."

"Really?" Margo perked up at that. "Working?"

"I think so. Most of them are. It's an old house."

"You should explore," Margo said. "Is there an attic?"

"There is. Maybe I will. She has a lot of stuff for me to do."

"Well, that's good, I guess. I mean, good that we sent you, if she needs help."

"The Foundation continues its legacy," Delilah commented.

"What?"

"Nothing. Listen, I better go."

"What's the rush? You got a date?"

"Of course not. I'm—I just don't want to run up the bill. I'll call again in a couple of days, okay? Or if anything changes in the meantime."

"Talk to her," Margo said.

"I will."

When she hung up, she realized she hadn't even asked about

Thomas, or tried to talk to him. But then again, he hadn't tried to contact her, or sent any messages of love through her family. That's the way it was with them. Which might explain why she was putting on a dress and going to meet Michael.

The day passed in a variety of tasks. There was always something that needed to be done there, but today Delilah was glad for that. It kept her from getting anxious about the evening, or scripting out elaborate plots of what might happen.

When she finished with the garden, vacuuming, laundry, and washing down the back deck to prepare it for restaining, which it needed desperately, she had just enough time to shower and put on her cute little dress. She decided against a ponytail. She'd just let her hair be free and wild.

She went downstairs to tell Carla she was going out and found her watching TV. *Homicide* reruns again.

"Um," she said, "I'm going out. You need anything anywhere?"

"Shh," Carla hissed. "I like this part."

Delilah waited for Lieutenant Giardello to finish his line about Italians being a cruel people, but they make good pasta so it balances out. Carla chuckled. The show went to commercial, and she twisted her head around to look at Delilah.

"I thought you said your boyfriend's in Key West," she commented.

"He is," Delilah said. "Why?"

"You're all dressed up," she said, wrinkling her nose. She looked tired around her eyes. A little puffy and faded. But her hair was sticking out at all its usual angles, so Delilah assumed she was okay.

"It's a dress," she said. "It's nice and cool."

"Yeah," Carla said. "Right. Who're you going out with?"

"An old friend," she said.

"What's his name?" Carla asked.

She was going to protest, then changed her mind. She'd be here all night if they got started. "Michael," she said. "Michael Swerton."

Carla's face darkened ominously, and she clucked her tongue. "Your other boyfriend know about Michael?"

"It's not like that, Carla," Delilah said weakly. "He's my—we were engaged. Then we split up."

"How come? He slept with someone else?"

"Maybe," she muttered.

"And you're going out with him? Again?"

"Just having a drink with him. Jesus, Carla. It's not like the old days."

"Modern times women are more stupid than we were?"

"I'm not—it's not like that," Delilah repeated, at a loss for any other defensive moves.

"Yeah. Right. Stop at the Pet Smart and pick up cat food."

"What kind?"

"The kind cats eat," Carla said. "A big bag."

"Okay. Hey. What's that black cat's name?" Delilah asked.

"What black cat?" Carla said, her attention back on the TV.

"The one that hangs out in my room at night."

"I don't have a black cat," Carla said. "If I'm asleep when you get back, don't make a lot of noise and wake me up."

"I wasn't planning on it," Delilah said.

Carla twisted around again, and pointed a finger at her. "I mean," she said meaningfully, "I don't want to hear noise coming from your room."

"Noise?"

"Noise," Carla repeated. "Creaking and grunting and groaning."

"What makes you think—" Delilah started, and then thought better of it. "No creaking."

"Or grunting or groaning."

"Or that," Delilah agreed.

Carla sniffed, and turned back to the TV.

Delilah left the house, and drove toward the city, stopping at the Pet Smart, which was in a shopping plaza that forced you to drive from one giant store to the next—Wal-Mart, Home Depot, Pet Smart, Office Max. She hated them, and thought they were actually worse than malls, which were at least female friendly in that they were one of the places women could go and not be harassed.

These kinds of plazas didn't even have that to offer. She had a theory that whoever designed them was in league with the car companies to make sure nobody ever got out of their car. There were no walkways and trying to get across parking lots from supermarket to massive discount center involved risking your life. So everyone drove, which meant nobody ever talked to anybody else, which meant nobody ever recognized anyone else as human. They just got pissed off because everyone was driving so badly, which was also forced on them by the poorly designed road entries and exits.

And of course, the more human contact was cut off, the more it became necessary to fill the gap by consuming goods you didn't really need, so it all worked out for capitalism. That was her theory. She thought she'd have to pass it by Jack, see what he thought.

By the time she left, with a big bag of cat food, she was ready for a drink. She made her way downtown, to Pete's Place.

She and Michael used to meet there regularly, joining up with groups of people from his job or her classes, hanging around for pizza, beer, and games of foozeball. When she entered it, the sights and smells of it reminded her of that time, and she felt a happy anticipation of a party. It wasn't crowded—midweek, early in the evening but after the happy hour—and since school wasn't in session it might not get crowded, but it still felt festive to her. She sat at the bar, and the bartender, a very good-looking man with dark, curly hair and an earring, greeted her with a smile.

"What's your pleasure?" he asked.

"Now there's a question," she replied.

"I know. That's why I ask it," he said, grinning at her.

Delilah laughed. "Tonight, I think just red wine."

"Tame," he noted.

"It's early," she said. "Wait until the moon comes up."

He got her wine. She was sipping it slowly, trying to keep her heart from leaping around inside her chest by focusing on the stupidity of CNN, when she felt a hand on her arm. She turned. It was Michael.

"Hi," he said.

"Hi," she said back. They stared at each other for a moment. He got on a stool. The bartender came over and he ordered scotch, no ice. His nervous drink, as she remembered.

"Stressed?" she asked.

He laughed. If Jack's laugh said that the world was full of weird and possibly dangerous but interesting things, Michael's laugh said the world was not something to be taken incredibly seriously. She thought both were probably true.

"I actually am a little nervous," he said.

"Afraid I'm gunning for you?" she asked.

He shook his head. "Your sharp tongue is not one of your prettier traits," he said.

"You mentioned that before," she said, and found something caustic rising at the back of her throat. "I think it was right after I walked in on you and what's-her-name fucking."

He stirred his drink. "Are we going to fight? Drag up the past and smash it around a little? I mean, that's okay. It's kind of what I expected, only let's get it over with. Here. I'll even help. I slept with Bonnie."

"And Kathy. And Cheryl. And some bimbo named Tiffany." Interesting, she thought, that she was still angry. She didn't know she could hold on to an emotion that long.

"I didn't sleep with Cheryl," he said. "I just—we just made out heavily."

"Sorry," she said. "My mistake. Anything else I got wrong?"

He took a long sip of his drink, and shook his head. "No. Mostly, it was me getting things wrong. Do you want me to grovel? Because I also came prepared to do that. My behavior was inexcusable. I know that."

She let that sink in for a moment. It wasn't part of any of the possible scripts she'd written for the evening. She wasn't sure what her lines were. She ad-libbed.

"You know that? Really?"

"Yes," he said. "Really. I think I knew it at the time."

She sipped her wine and looked at him hard. He was staring down into his scotch, his face quiet except for a small twitch at the muscle in his jaw. She knew that twitch as well as she knew his preference for scotch when he was anxious. It was what his face did when he felt pain. Seeing it dissipated her anger, not because she felt sorry for him, but because it seemed her anger had done what she wanted it to do. It had hurt him.

"If you knew it was wrong," she said quietly, "why'd you do it?"

He smiled grimly. "The usual bullshit. I was afraid. Not ready for a commitment."

Fear of connection, Delilah thought. They were made for each other. "I mentioned that at the time, I think."

"You did," he admitted.

"You said I was wrong. You said men weren't inherently monogamous and women were, and I said bullshit because the clitoris has eight thousand nerve endings and the penis has less than half that, and it doesn't work as well."

"I remember."

"So you're taking that back now?"

"I am," he said.

"How come?"

He twirled his drink around in his glass and stared at it, then lifted his eyes to meet hers. They were soft and serious, a little sad. That, she thought, was incredibly dangerous. Fortunately, she wasn't easily deterred by danger.

"I missed you," he said simply. "I mean, there were all these women, but I missed you anyway. Made me think I'd been kidding myself."

"Not," she said, "as much as you'd been kidding me."

"Look," he said, a little petulant now. "It isn't easy to admit this. You don't have to make fun."

"I'm not," she said. "It's just—unexpected. I have to rearrange my thinking."

"Here's to rearrangements," he said, and lifted his glass, touched it softly to hers.

Delilah sipped her wine slowly, to give herself time to think. She hoped he'd say something, but he didn't. He just sat brooding into his glass, something else she remembered about him. When he didn't have his public face on, he could brood deeply for a long time. When she was in love with him, she thought that indicated emotional depth. When they broke up, she thought it indicated an inability to communicate.

"So, is that why you wanted to talk to me?" she asked him at last. "Confession?"

"Mm," he said. "I was hoping for absolution, too."

"Pretty Catholic of you."

"I was raised Catholic," he said. "Any chance of it? Absolution, I mean."

"Doesn't penance come first?"

"Name it," he said.

Though she was not deterred by danger, neither was she a complete fool. And this was all happening a little too fast. There was too much for them to resolve, too much to talk about before he started looking at her that way.

She turned her face to her wine, and considered it in silence.

"Why'd you show up tonight?" he asked. "What was your agenda?"

She shrugged. "A sense of closure, before beginning the new era."

"What?" he asked.

"Closure," she said more seriously. "I wanted to see—a lot of things. Why I made the choices I made. What choices to make next."

"How's that going?" he asked.

"Moving along," she said. "This is helping. But why didn't you call me in Key West? Or write to me?"

"It's not the kind of thing I can do over the phone," he said.

"So if I hadn't shown up, what?"

"I guess I would've gone to my grave with regrets, like a good Irishman."

"I guess," she said carefully, "it wasn't important enough for you to make the effort."

"I was kidding." he said, "I've been thinking about it. I was considering calling Monica, getting her advice."

Delilah bit back a grin as she thought about what Monica might say.

"But I didn't have to," he concluded, leaning toward her. "You did show up. Just as if I called you. What do you think that's about?"

Monica, of course, would think there was a plan. Michael believed in fate. She thought it could be coincidence, and he was taking advantage of that. Opportunistic hunting. Her skepticism must have showed in her face, because he leaned away, and when he spoke again, the tone of his voice changed, became more matter-of-fact.

"I don't mean to push," he said. "I'm not—trying to talk you into anything. I thought maybe we could at least be friends. Any chance of that? I'm actually not a bad friend."

She wasn't sure how she felt about him backing down so quickly. Regret? Relief? Both? Either way, she wasn't going to be the one to push. The Foundation would be against that. "I think," she said, "we can take it out for a spin. See how it goes."

"Good," he said, sounding relieved. "Let's do that."

They were silent for a moment, both of them awkward as they tried to determine new ways with each other. It would be okay to be his friend, Delilah thought. He was a good friend, attentive and charming. And if he couldn't help flirting with her, well, he could hardly help flirting with anyone. As his friend, she'd have to accept him as he was.

"So," Delilah said, to get talk started, "are you still single? Dating anyone? I don't see a ring so I'm figuring you're not married."

"Nothing important going on in that area," he said. "My job's been keeping me too busy. You?"

"Single," she said. "Enjoying the hell out of it."

She felt immediate guilt, like Peter denying Christ, at not even mentioning Thomas, but she could rationalize it easily enough since she and Thomas didn't even have a verbal agreement about monogamy, and certainly hadn't ever talked about a future together. Still, it was a bad sign. It meant she hadn't actively decided to go further with him, but she wanted to leave it open as a possibility.

"I mean," she continued, "it's nice to be independent, isn't it? Make your own decisions. Answer to nobody but yourself."

"Do what you want and give what you can," he added.

"Do what you want and eat what there is," she responded.

"What?"

"Nothing."

He smiled, more relaxed now. "So this is okay, right?" he asked. "Being friends?"

"Peachy," she said. "As long as you keep acting like a friend."

"Okay," he said. "What's the rules?"

She got a napkin from the bar and asked him for a pen. Of course, he had one. She started writing it down under the heading RULES OF FRIENDSHIP.

"Number one is no lying."

"None? We tell each other the whole truth and nothing but, all the time?"

"Well, not all at once," she amended. "We're just getting to know each other, right? But important stuff, no lying."

"I'm good with that. What next?"

"The Aretha Franklin rule."

"Hmm?"

"You know." She sang, "R-E-S-P-E-C-T, find out what it means to me."

"Now that," he said, leaning over and reading as she wrote, "is a tricky one. I mean, what's respectful for one person is not the same for another."

"I get to tell you what feels respectful to me, and what doesn't."

"Okay," he said. "Here's number three, then. No laundry listing. Write it down." He tapped on the napkin. Reluctantly, she did so.

It was true that she had a tendency to save up offenses, then drag them all out at once. It was a form of tolerance. She'd tolerate and tolerate, then it would all come spilling out. She didn't like to bother with conflict unless it got big enough to make it worthwhile.

"Okay," she said, reluctantly. "I'll write it down. But I get the next one." In large letters, she wrote down the word TREATS.

"What's that?" he asked.

"Friends give each other treats now and then," she said.

"I gave you treats," he said. "Plenty of treats. Remember that time I brought you a hot fudge sundae for breakfast?" he asked.

"Because it was a Sunday. I remember. That was nice."

"What we did with it was even nicer," he said grinning. She giggled, then composed herself. She remembered it better than she would like to.

"Pay attention," she said. "We have more to do."

Then, his hand came down softly over hers. She stared at it, resting there.

"Let's just go back to number one a minute," he said.

"No lying," she said quietly, feeling a sudden dryness in her mouth and a drop in her stomach. He had that effect on her, but as Monica pointed out, so did roller coasters, and she hated roller coasters.

"That one. Delilah, if I'm being honest, I have to tell you I wanted to meet you to see if there was still a chance for us. If we could go back to what we had."

"No," she said. "I don't want to go back."

His hand pressed down a little more. "Then, forward. If we could go forward into something better. Didn't you think about that, when you agreed to meet me?"

"Yes," she admitted.

"I've been thinking about you so much lately, and the minute I saw you in the mall I felt—all kinds of things," he said, his fingers tracing small lines on the back of her hand. "We were so good together. Delilah, tell me honestly, is there any chance?"

His hand moved across her skin, like silk brushing silk. She had forgotten about his hands and how nicely they moved. She'd forgotten about how easy it was for them to laugh together, and simply enjoy each other's company. He might have been a bad boy, but he was also an easy boy—easy to be with, easy to go to bed with, easy to fall in love with. They'd gotten along so well. They hardly fought, and he was so attentive to her. That was what made his infidelity such a shock and so hard to bear. There was absolutely nothing else wrong between them that she could tell. And he'd had time, now. Time to remember that. Maybe time to see how hard it was to find anywhere else.

"There's a chance," she said. "There could be a chance."

"Do you want to go to my place and talk about it?" he asked.

Of course, she'd fantasized about this. But most of her fantasies ended with her rejecting him the way he'd rejected her. Now was her chance. She could do just that.

Then she thought how glad she was that she got that necklace and was wearing it. She thought about how the clitoris has 8,000 nerve endings in it, and how many orgasms the female body is capable of in any given session of sex.

"Honestly?" she asked.

"Quite honestly," he replied.

"I'd like that," she said. "A lot."

They paid their bill and left the bar.

In her room, Carla opened her dresser drawer too hard and got it jammed. She wiggled it, but it wouldn't move. She pulled at it, but it stayed stuck.

"Damn thing," she muttered. "Go one way or the other, would you?"

She tugged harder and felt it beginning to loosen, but it was heavy and she knew there'd be hell to pay if she pulled it out too fast and it fell on her foot.

She hated that. She used to be able to take risks like that, and the consequences were small, short-lived. Now, a cut could be a big deal, and she hated it. She couldn't even give herself the satisfaction of slamming her fist into the drawer. She gave one more tug, then gave up. She'd have to wait and have Jack or Delilah look at it.

She hated that, too.

She went to her nightstand, got out a pack of cigarettes, and lit one. It was her one remaining consolation. Of course, it would kill her, but not fast enough for whatever else came along first. So death allowed her a luxury. She supposed she should be grateful.

She felt the soothing nicotine enter her bloodstream and brain, and she began to calm down. Her irritation remained, but now it wasn't against her own body, or the bureau drawer. It was what really was eating at her—Delilah, and her foolishness.

Delilah, going out with her ex-fiancé, Michael. What was wrong with her brain? Had it stopped working altogether? Jack was there eyeing her all over, and if Carla knew Jack, he'd already made a move, but Delilah was out with Michael. She was a smart girl. She should know a good thing when she saw it, and not be out running around.

A small voice in Carla reminded her that intelligence had nothing to do with it. Hadn't she made her own mistakes, been drawn away from good men, right to men who would not be good to her under any circumstances?

Yes. Of course she had. More than once. As she mused on it, she thought there were one or two she wouldn't mind repeating, if she could. She drew smoke from her cigarette, and a slow smile moved across her face. She'd had her own Michael. In Cincinnati, where they stayed for two weeks with the circus.

She felt warmth spreading through her, just remembering it, and was grateful for the blessing of a good memory that allowed her these moments.

But that man was just a fling. A little nothing. Delilah might be taking her Michael seriously, and that was the problem. You couldn't take some men seriously, and there were some men that you couldn't treat badly enough. Surely Delilah knew that.

If she didn't, Carla thought, she'd have to learn. And she'd have to learn it fast. Carla didn't know how much longer she could wait to develop her own plans. Of course, when she thought about it, it was like her bureau drawer. She was helpless to push and shove it, short of hiring a hit on this Michael. And she wouldn't do that. She couldn't afford it.

So realistically, all she could do was wait for some circumstances to come to her assistance, watch for opportunities, and grab them. All very good, and she was good at it. She could do it. She just didn't like the waiting. She'd never been a patient woman.

She needed something to put her hands to, something not too strenuous, but not as dull as watching TV. She looked around her room to see what she might have. There were the boxes of photos she'd been sorting through. She could take care of them. It was a good night for it, and a fire would be soothing.

She was not too old to do that, and the boxes weren't too big for her to carry.

She tamped out her cigarette, lifted one box up, and started slowly down the stairs.

fire

Although Delilah didn't achieve the fifty to a hundred orgasms in an hour that women are supposed to be capable of, she had a very good time. She thought one of the good things about being raised by liberal ex-hippies is that she didn't have a lot of shame about sex. In fact, she could remember her mother explaining that a woman had a responsibility to her own pleasure, as well as to her own safety. This, when she was sixteen and was also given a stash of condoms to keep on hand, just in case the issue arose, so to speak.

Sex was taught as another function, an important but not all-consuming one. It was assumed she'd have it, and that she would like it. It wasn't necessarily assumed that all the sex she had would be about love, but it was also assumed she wouldn't be stupid about it. She was expected to bring a certain amount of self-respect and intelligence to the table—or the bed, depending on where she landed at the moment—and choose partners who would do the same. Her father told her she should find men who had an interest in her well-being, as well as their own. Her mother said she should find men who put the toilet seat back down. She thought they were probably the same thing.

So she was capable of enjoying sex, and she did, though she was also aware that with Michael, she was holding back. Not able to throw herself into it with the abandon they used to enjoy. If Michael noticed, he said nothing about it.

"Seems like old times," he said to her afterward, when they got out of bed to hunt for a snack, which was a custom they'd shared. But when they got to the kitchen, she wasn't really hungry, and shortly after that, she left.

"You don't want to stay?" he asked, not really inviting, but sounding surprised she wasn't going to.

She explained, then, about the family complications that brought her on this visit, and how she felt it was important to get back to the house. He made no protest, but he wouldn't. He wasn't the possessive type.

But she knew it wasn't really worry about Carla that made her leave. Perhaps she wanted to maintain some emotional distance to preserve her safety. Or perhaps she was enjoying not giving in totally, as a way of regaining a control she'd lost on the last go around. Monica might say that. Or she might say Delilah had issues with connection.

Michael said he'd call later in the week, and they'd give it another try, since this one worked out so nicely. She said okay, and tried not to think about Thomas. That wasn't difficult, since her more immediate concern was Carla. Delilah sincerely hoped she wasn't up, so she wouldn't have to face the glare or the comments she'd inevitably make. That was an odd thought, since it had been many years since her parents questioned her choice of partner. They didn't even say anything about Thomas, though her father sometimes got a worried look on his face when he saw them together.

Yet here she was, concerned about what an old lady she barely knew would think about her. And it was more than just not wanting to listen to her lecture, though that was a fairly large part of the equation. It seemed as if she valued Carla's approval, though she wasn't sure why. Because Carla was her grandmother? Because there was something intrinsically valuable about her approval? Maybe, Delilah thought, that was it. Carla had an instinct for bullshit, and if she smelled it here, it might tell Delilah something.

She was musing on this when she drove up the hill and rounded the corner that made Carla's house visible. The first thing she noticed was a bright orange something in the yard. Bright orange something took a moment to register, and resolve itself as fire.

"Fire," she said. "Shit."

She pulled into the driveway and got out of her car, ran into the yard, and saw fire. A big circle of it, and Carla standing at the edge, poking it with a stick. Her white hair, sticking out in tufts around her head, was backlit with orange. Her back was bent over her task, and she was muttering or humming to herself. Delilah saw that there were boxes next to her. She relaxed from her fight-or-flight mode, and walked over.

Carla turned and saw her, and surreptitiously tossed a cigarette into the flames.

"I know you smoke, Carla," Delilah said. "You don't have to hide it."

She shrugged, and went back to poking.

"What're you doing?" Delilah asked.

"Burning stuff," she said.

"Stuff?" she asked.

"Stuff," Carla replied.

Delilah sighed. And here she was, ready to value Carla's opinion.

"What kind of stuff?" she asked, peering into the box, then putting a hand in and pulling something out. "Hey," she said. "These are photos."

The one in her hand showed a woman standing in the middle of a ring, dressed in the sort of white tuxedo/bathing suit thing that circus or Las Vegas showgirls wear. She had white boots on, and a headdress with blue feathers. Her arms were raised high, and in front of her a great white stallion reared up on its hind legs. She was smiling.

"Who's this?" Delilah asked.

"Me," Carla replied curtly. "Put it back."

Delilah peered at it. It seemed so unlikely. "You?" she asked.

"Me," Carla grabbed for it, and Delilah pulled it back.

"What're you burning it for?" she asked. "It's a nice picture."

"It's over. Just clutter."

"No," Delilah said firmly, as Carla reached for it again. She reached down into the box, and Delilah grabbed for that, pulled it away as well. "No," she said more sharply. "No more burning."

"It's my stuff," Carla said.

"Yeah, well, it's bad for the environment to burn photos, first of all. Second of all, I want to look at it."

"What for?" she asked.

"Because it's—it's interesting," she said, taking refuge in her favorite neutrality. "And—and it's you," she added.

Carla was quiet a minute. "It's not all me," she pointed out.

"Other people you knew," she said. She pulled out another picture. In this one, a man in top hat and tuxedo stood in front of two tigers. Carla sat on the back of one of the tigers.

"God," Delilah said. "Wasn't that scary?"

She squinted down at it, and shrugged. "No," she said. "Not really. They're just big cats."

"Really big," Delilah noted. "And wild. You can't ever really tame them, can you? Wasn't there some circus guy who got his head bit off by one?"

"More than one," Carla said. "Using whips and so on, the cats got sick of it, I guess. You don't tame them. You work with them as they are. Most people think you have to boss 'em around. But they got moods, and preferences, just like any creature, and if you get to know them when they're little, you learn how to respect that. The best thing is to keep 'em fed, and be respectful. Work with them, not on them." She sighed. "'Course, they still could take your head off, but that didn't happen to me."

Delilah looked up at her and realized why she valued her opinion. She was a woman who had somehow managed to live her own life. She had whatever it took to ride a tiger and not get eaten. She understood things about the tiger that nothing on the Discovery Channel could ever teach. Unfortunately, she couldn't really teach it either. At least, not in words. Delilah thought maybe she'd learn it just by being around her, the way Carla learned about tigers by being around them.

"Was it fun? Working for the circus?"

She shrugged. "Circus is made to look like fun for other people, not be fun. And it wasn't Barnum and Bailey's or anything. Just a small circus. My uncle owned it. But I got to see a lot. I've been all over the country two or three times. And it beat working in a factory."

"How did you do it? I mean, did you have this house?"

"My brother took care of it then. Frank. When he died, I quit the circus. It was almost over by then, anyway. I was getting old. My uncle sold out a few years before, and the new owner wasn't good to the people or the animals. Wasn't any good anymore."

She said all this in a businesslike way, as if reporting on the activities of a concern not connected to her. Delilah decided the lack of emotion was about there being too much to feel, which she had to admit might have been pure projection on her part. Maybe it was just so long ago, there was nothing left to feel. But no. She wouldn't be burning it if it was nothing. She'd just dump it in the garbage in that case.

"Why are you burning all this?" Delilah asked. "Doesn't it make you happy to see it, and remember?"

"It's over. I like to stick to what's now. You're home late," she said.

"You're up late," Delilah replied, returning the photos to the box, but keeping it out of Carla's reach.

"Couldn't sleep," she said. "Old people don't sleep well. What's your excuse? Michael wouldn't let you go?"

"We had a lot to talk about. Y'know, I went to school around here. I've still got friends in the area. Not that you've been interested enough to ask or anything."

"I don't like to pry," she said, sniffing righteously. "Were you in bed with that man?"

"I thought you didn't like to pry."

"That's not prying. It's asking."

"Then what's prying?"

"Asking about your past. That's prying."

That, Delilah thought, was an interesting distinction. Maybe it was a circus thing. Maybe it was just a Carla thing.

"Well?" Carla asked, when Delilah didn't say anything. "Were you?"

"I don't think I have to answer that without a lawyer present," Delilah said.

"Hmmph. I hope he used a condom," Carla said. "There's all kinds of diseases these days."

"Look, I don't know what gives you these ideas—" Delilah started to say, but Carla cut her off.

"Your face," she said. "And eighty-one years of experience. I can tell when somebody's just been stupid."

"Were you always like this?" Delilah asked angrily.

"Like what?"

"Caustic and critical. I mean, does it come naturally to you, or did you have to practice in front of a mirror? No, I'm sorry. No mirrors here. God forbid you should look at yourself. Or maybe you're just bitter."

"I'm not bitter," Carla said, sounding genuinely surprised. "I've got nothing to be bitter about. I'm honest. You're bitter. Awful young for it, if you ask me."

"Bitter? I'm not bitter."

"Yeah. Something bit you and made you bitter," she said, chuckling at herself. "Bit you and made you bitter," she repeated.

"That's not true," Delilah said. "I'm just—I see the world, the way it is. I don't lie to myself about it."

"Only world you see is the one you're making for yourself. Maybe that's why you're bitter."

"Look, I'm not bitter. A little cynical, maybe."

"Cynical," Carla cut in. "Yeah. Cynical's the easiest thing in the world. Means you don't ever have to do a thing."

"Christmas," Delilah said. "I don't tell you what you're doing wrong."

"You just did," Carla said. "Unless 'caustic' and 'critical' were meant as compliments and I just didn't get it."

Delilah opened her mouth and shut it again.

"Well?" Carla asked, pushing at it like a sore tooth. "Was it a compliment?"

"We don't get along very well," Delilah noted, keeping her tone neutral.

"No. You know why?"

"Because you're caustic and critical?"

"Because we're alike. Every time you look at me, you see your-self. And you aren't sure you like it much."

"Does that work the other way around, too?" she asked.

Carla leaned back and dragged off her cigarette. "I suppose it does. I see all the things I did that were stupid. Some of them involved not using condoms."

Now there was a new and interesting idea. Carla was actually concerned about her? And this was her way of expressing it? But then again, there were certain implications in her comment that Delilah didn't like.

"What—you mean having my mother was stupid?"

"No," she said, making a face at me. "Babies aren't stupid. They're just—babies. The man. He was stupid. That was stupid."

"You're saying my grandfather was a stupid man?"

She looked away, her gaze focusing somewhere over the hills and far away. "Not stupid. Just not very responsible, I guess. The world was a place to play for him. Good-looking, though." Delilah saw her mouth soften into an almost-smile. It looked like she'd had some fun out of the deal, at least. That was good, somehow. Delilah was glad of that for her.

"Do you regret it?" she asked, then tensed, waiting for her to yell or say something critical. But she didn't. She continued con-templative.

"I don't regret anything," she said. "I've had a pretty good life. The circus, and all this." She waved a hand around, and Delilah had the sense that the land was waving back to her, acknowledg-ing her presence in a positive way. Just two old friends, saying hello of an evening. "Couple of things I want to see to, but that's not regrets," she added. "That's work."

"Things? Like what?"

She shrugged. "Just things. I'm working it out."

Delilah didn't pursue it. She'd had almost a whole paragraph of being nice. That might be her limit.

"Can I have one of those?" she asked, pointing to Carla's cigarettes.

"No. They're bad for you."

Delilah laughed. Carla grinned back. "I'm old," she said. "You're not. When you're old, you can smoke."

"I used to smoke," she said. "I quit. But I miss it."

"I used to have sex and eat chocolate fudge. I miss that, too," she sighed. "So you can have sex and eat chocolate fudge, and I can smoke." She made a sound that was a rusty laugh, with the same touch of wickedness in it that Jack's had.

"Okay," Delilah said. "That's a deal." She stuck her hand out, and Carla surprised her by taking it. They hadn't actually touched before. Her hand was dry and her skin felt thin and papery, like a lizard's, but her shake was firm and positive. Delilah was prepared to let go, but she pulled on it, jerking it. Delilah looked at her, questions on her face.

"What about that boyfriend in Key West?" Carla asked.

"What about him?" she replied, staying neutral.

"I was right about him, wasn't I?"

Delilah shrugged.

"Hmmph," she said. Then, "Are you hungry?"

She checked in with herself. "No. Not really."

Carla stared at her hard a minute, still hanging onto her hand. She seemed to have a conversation with herself, her lips moving a little. "You should find someone else to have sex with. He can't be very good."

"Well, jeez, Carla," Delilah said. "How the hell would you know?"

"Watch your mouth. If the sex is good, you oughta be hungry. That's how it works. Find someone else."

Delilah was opening her mouth for rebuttal, but Carla dropped her hand and waved at the fire.

"Get the hose," she said, "and put this fire out. I want to go to bed."

She threw her stick in the fire and walked away, leaving Delilah with the task of putting out the fire, and carrying the boxes back inside.

TWELVE

combined elements: water and earth

Delilah's visit extended itself beyond her wardrobe, and she had to seriously shop with Monica for more shorts, more T-shirts, more summer dresses. Summer became deeper all around her, and hotter and muggier. She wondered if it was worse in Key West, but when she called home to check on the temperature there, it didn't seem like it.

Over time, Carla was a little less caustic with her, though no more forthcoming. When Delilah suggested that her mother wouldn't mind coming to visit, Carla pointed a thin finger at her and said, "I don't want to talk about it yet. When I'm ready, I will."

Delilah wondered if that kind of directness was a result of age. Maybe when you got old you were sort of honed down to an essential self. And that could be a great thing, or an awful thing. It certainly supported the need to make sure you were doing okay as you went along, or someday you might wake up old and horrible.

Which, given Carla's statement that they were alike, made Delilah wonder if she'd wake up someday old and Carla. And would that be a bad thing? She couldn't tell. But she wanted to find out.

She started by sorting through the box she'd saved from the fire, and picking out some of the best pictures. She asked Carla questions about who the people were, and sometimes Carla actually told her, either smiling or snarling at the names as she said them, talking about their job in the circus, how long they stayed, what happened to them when they left. Many were dead. Some were friends. Some she called jerks, and waved them away.

Other times, she told Delilah to leave her alone. She was tired. Or her eyes hurt. Delilah noticed that she blinked a lot, and wondered if she had cataracts. Carla said no. No cataracts. Her eyes just bothered her sometimes. Probably just haying-season irritation.

Delilah began to notice other infirmities, and how she worked to hide them. She found Carla with her shoes off, rubbing at her feet one evening during *Homicide* reruns, which she began watching with her.

"Hurt your foot?" Delilah asked.

"It's nothing," she said, and put her socks back on. "Aren't you going out tonight? With Michael?"

She said his name with disdain. But Delilah went out anyway, or more accurately stayed in with Michael. It seemed to be going well between them, which was one reason she was willing to extend her visit. They were laughing, talking, enjoying each other. But then again, they always had. He even said something to her about a job he knew about in the area, working for Consolidated Energy Products, one of the bigger petrochemical companies that made stuff like components for nuclear power plants and plastics.

"Plastics," Delilah wrinkled her nose. "You know I'm always fighting the plastic wars."

He'd seen her in the grocery store, refusing bags, reusing bags until they fell apart. Of course Delilah knew that landfills were primarily filled with paper products, but something about the permanence of plastic and Styrofoam bothered her more. Humans had made something they couldn't get rid of. Thin, white plastic supermarket bags hung from the trees like little ghosts, haunting us with our own ingenuity and lack of wisdom. It seemed dangerous.

"What would I do in a plastics company?" she asked.

"They've got this problem with the river. In quite a few rivers, actually. Stuff they put in it. PCBs and whatnot. Now they have to figure out whether to dredge or not. They need people with geology backgrounds to help out."

"Oh, great. So I'll sign on to be one of the people who tells them they don't need to. I'm not a company girl, Michael."

"No, Delilah," Michael said. "I know that about you. But you could be one of the people who tells them they do need to. Work from the inside for change."

"That'll keep me moving up the company ladder," she noted.

"It will, if you do it right. Get some political connections. I can help you with that."

Michael, offering to be her political connection. That was more romance than she'd counted on.

"The only thing is," he said, "they're an international corporation."

"What's that mean?"

"They might put you somewhere else at first. I know most of their geo-interests are local, as far as the rivers go, but they could ask you to work in some of their offshore locations, just to start."

"Offshore?"

"Alabama. Georgia."

Delilah eyed him. "Trying to get rid of me?"

"I like visiting Georgia," he said. "And they might keep you local. Anyway, it's something to think about. I'll get you the name of one of their people and you can call, talk to him about it. Time for you to get yourself a career, don't you think?" He slapped her on the behind, then, and the games began.

So they went on. During the day when nobody was around and she wasn't helping Carla with some chore or other, Delilah spent time wandering around the land, watching the turtles raise their little butts in the pond or exploring the woods at the top of the ridge. She got to meet Big Bertha, who really was big, one night when she came back from Michael's and found her sitting at the kitchen table with Carla and a six-pack. They were giggling. It reminded her so much of herself and Monica, she wanted to offer them a napkin to take notes on.

"Hey," Bertha boomed out at her, in a friendly way. "Sit down with us. You might learn a few things."

"Don't start," Carla said. "She already knows too much."

"Come on, Carla. Don't be such a bitch. She's such a bitch, isn't she?"

Delilah laughed, and sat down with them, noting that apparently it was okay for Bertha to swear in the house. It wasn't until she sat down that she noticed Bertha had only one arm. The other stopped at the elbow. Bertha saw her staring, and cleared her throat.

Delilah looked up at her. "Tiger?" she asked.

Bertha shook her head. "Bear," she said, and drank more beer.

After her third she seemed to forget about her bad arm, and tried to pick things up with it, then laughed at herself.

"You'll never learn, Bertha," Carla said, pointing the beer toward her real hand. Bertha laughed, and drank some more.

They had other visitors, too. Old man Bower stopped by for coffee now and then, and complained about the bunny problem, which seemed to be his personal crusade in life. Stan the septic man came around to admire his handiwork and sing to Carla. Jack had made arrangements with him for his checks to come from Delilah's parents, and to keep his mouth shut about it. When Carla asked why the bill was so small, he only sang at her that her friends' labor had gotten her a lot more savings than he thought it would.

Somebody Delilah didn't know came by to hay the back fields, leaving giant rolls of brown hay standing around the perimeter of the land like still lifes of strange, headless hippos. And of course Jack came around and fixed things, often asking her to help.

Now that they were over the whole question of dating, she could enjoy his company. He had a funny way of seeing the world that suited her, and he often laughed at her jokes, and even more often listened to her talk about things she'd seen on the Discovery Channel, or in the pond, or in the woods, as if he were really interested in them.

She told him she was working on that dinner, but Monica was busy with some funding crisis, and probably wouldn't get her head out of work for another week, which was true. She helped him dig up and reset some of the paving stones in front, and his evil little laugh made her feel good.

But she was feeling good in general. The nights were warm. The days were long and sunny and even warmer. The heron was visiting the pond every day. The smell of the earth filled the air, and she liked just walking around the ridge and seeing what she could see. She got to know the trees and what lived in them, the places where deer had clearly been grazing around them. Jack showed her how to tell where they bedded down at night, so if she wanted she could go out and watch them under the moon. When she did so, she sometimes heard coyotes howl in the distance.

Jack taught her how to recognize tracks—raccoon and fox, and what he thought might be bobcat once.

"How'd you learn all this?" she asked.

"My grandfather taught me," he said.

"How'd he know?"

Jack had shrugged. "His father taught him, I guess. They were raised on the Res, and everyone hunted up there."

"The Res?" she asked.

"I'm part Mohawk. On my mother's side."

"Oh," she said. "Well, that's cool."

He looked at her wryly. "I'm half Polish, too. Is that cool?"

"I guess," she said. Then she frowned. "Brown? Polish?"

"Bronoski. Shortened at Ellis Island."

"But—you don't live on the Reservation?" she asked, not sure how that worked.

"My mother left when she married my father. They died when I was a teenager, in a car accident. Drunk driver hit them. That's how I got the eye patch. After that, I went back and forth between my father's people and the Res. I go back sometimes. Visit people, do a little work. And there's some Mohawks around here, too. Have a powwow coming up. Wanna go?"

"Sure," she said. "I'll invite Monica, too."

"That's great," he said. "Just great."

At night, sometimes she'd sit out on the deck, staring at the summer stars. Sagittarius in the south. The Great and Little Bears in the north. The Corona Borealis near the west. Sometimes Jack stayed into the evening and sat and had a beer, and once or twice

Carla joined them. She'd sit in a lounge chair with her feet up and not say much, but nobody else would either. They'd just sit there and listen to the night.

"Figure out how to save the world yet?" Jack asked her once in a while.

"Not yet," she said. "I'll let you know."

Delilah began to think she might have found something like a new era after all, and it was filled with peace.

Of course, there were problems. She couldn't get Carla to appear at the same time as Chaos, or even acknowledge the cat's existence, which troubled her in a fundamental way. Michael was certainly being nice, but they just as certainly weren't talking directly about anything beyond the moment. Besides his suggestion that she get a job, she didn't have any sense that they were actually going anywhere they hadn't already been.

That was only natural. It was early days in the new era. After all, she'd only just discovered that she liked cute little summer dresses. She was willing to go slowly with anything more demanding in terms of decision making.

Her mother was another problem. She and her father were more than willing to send any money Carla needed, but Delilah had to placate them about Carla's not wanting a visit yet, and Mom was getting impatient. Delilah didn't know if someday she'd just show up. Thomas was a bit of a problem, too. She'd talked to him once or twice, but didn't mention Michael. Doing that sort of thing over the phone just didn't seem right, but letting it go unsaid seemed just as bad.

Then, of course, there was the continuing problem of the house, which seemed to break in a new place every day. There was a staircase that was threatening to come apart, and Jack found a part of the roof that not only had a lot of shingles missing, but also had way too much bounce.

"We can take care of that, though," he said.

"We?" she asked.

"You're pretty good with a hammer," he noted. "Heights scare you?"

She looked up. It wasn't that high, and the pitch wasn't that steep. "I'm okay," she said.

"Then, we. Carla doing okay?"

"Seems to be," she said. "Why?"

"I was in the kitchen, working on the sink, and saw that she left the stove on. God knows how long. It was on low, and had a pot of beans burning pretty good. You were out," he added.

"I was," she admitted, but didn't elaborate.

"Monica?" he asked.

She didn't lie. "I went to school here. I had some friends to catch up with."

He tilted his head and regarded her with his one good eye. She was beginning to appreciate how much expression he could put into one eye. "Michael?" he asked.

"He's one of them," she noted, trying not to show her surprise that he remembered. "He might have a job for me. Working for CEP."

Jack frowned. "CEP. The plastics company? Don't tell Carla."

"Why not?"

"She'll kill you."

Delilah stared at him blankly.

"A few years ago they wanted to build a complex up here. Just offices and something they called light industrial, whatever that means. The town was for it. Carla wasn't."

"What'd they want with land way up here?"

"It's accessible to the highway, but relatively unpopulated and far enough away from the urban places that they wouldn't run into zoning problems. And they preferred Carla's because it's right at the top of the hill, surrounded by about two hundred unbuildable acres."

"She has that much land? Jesus. How does she pay the taxes?"

"She only owns about twenty. The rest is a lifetime rent agreement with the town, signed years ago. They tried like hell to break the lease, believe me."

"How'd she manage to stay?"

"She made a fuss, started a sort of grassroots movement. Mostly made of neighbors and friends. You can imagine."

Delilah certainly could. Kootch and Big Bertha as environmental activists. It was a formidable prospect. "And that worked?"

"For the time being. Local papers got behind it, made a lot of noise about taking land away from old ladies. Carla had her picture on the cover of the Sunday papers. Pissed her off because she didn't like the way her hair looked. Then, people in the area who don't want their property values going down got in on it. So it's stalled, but the town and CEP are still trying to see if they can do an end run around it, and it may come up again."

"So," Delilah said, "you don't like them much."

"Well," Jack said, rubbing at his chin. "You know they messed up the river. Won't take responsibility for it. Let's see, what else? Ruined some land up at the Reservation. Got kids sick because the school's on a toxic-waste site, and there's no cleanup planned because they deny it. Then, there's what they make intentionally, besides the toxic waste. What's your friend Michael got to do with them?"

Delilah realized she didn't really know. She assumed his politics were in line with hers because otherwise, why would she sleep with him? But then again, he didn't talk much about his work, beyond saying things like he'd had a hard day, or he was working with so-and-so on an important bill. So-and-so was always a name important enough for her to recognize, and he always said it in a sort of fake bored way that irritated her. "I think he's trying to get me to help them change their evil ways," she said.

"That save-the-world thing?"

"Something like that."

"Will you?" Jack asked. "Work for them, I mean."

"I haven't even looked into it yet," she said, and changed the subject. "Is Carla always forgetting pots, or is that a new trick?"

"Relatively new. Can you let me know if she comes up with any other new tricks?"

"Actually, she's been rubbing her eyes a lot lately. Says it's allergies. And her feet seem to bother her. If I say anything, she yells at me, but I'm getting used to that."

"Y'know," he said, "you could have a little more patience with her. Getting old takes tremendous courage."

"Courage?"

"Think about it," he said. "You have to watch every resource you ever relied on fail, and keep improvising new ones to support you. You have to work with less and less, watch your friends die, your body fail. It takes some guts to do it and stay human. Carla's doing a pretty good job, I think."

"I read somewhere that survival past menopause allowed humans to develop civilizations, because it created a whole group of people who could think ahead, prepare for the future."

"Old women rule," Jack said. "Never forget it."

"When do we start on the roof?" Delilah asked.

And so it went. She was settling into a routine. Almost.

Then, on a Wednesday morning on a day that the weather forecast said hazy, hot, and humid, high in the high eighties, she was woken to the sound of someone calling her name.

It seemed soft at first, and flowed in with a dream she was having about standing somewhere under the earth, with a little old lady gnome trying to get her to wash dishes. Then, it got louder, harsher, and she was awake.

She shot out of bed, and the voice was still calling her. It was Carla. Delilah put on a bathrobe and went down the hall to her room, and opened the door. Carla was standing there, absolutely naked.

"Don't just stand there with the door open," she said. "Come in and sit down."

"I can wait until you're dressed," Delilah said.

"Sit down," Carla said. "You might as well see what you'll look like."

Delilah sat on the edge of the bed. She didn't stare, but she had to meet Carla's challenge directly, or be called on it, so she did look. There was Carla's body, which had eighty-one years on it. Surprisingly, it didn't look that bad.

Her breasts weren't perky, but they didn't hang down to her knees. And the parts of her skin that hadn't been exposed to the sun were pretty smooth and elastic. There was a clear line of demarcation between the wrinkles of her face, and where they stopped at the skin of her chest. The skin of her arms, too, had the leathery quality of the sun written into it, and it stopped where the sleeve line must have been, reminding Delilah that she should keep using that sunblock and maybe, as Monica suggested, buy a nice hat. Carla's legs had blue veins showing under them, but they weren't too flabby. She walked a lot, and Delilah thought that was another plug for regular exercise.

As Delilah watched, Carla rummaged through drawers until she pulled out something that looked like a one-piece bathing suit, and a pair of shorts.

"What's that?" Delilah asked.

"Swimsuit," she said. "I'm going to Lake George."

"Um—Lake George?"

"Waterslide World," she said. "Haven't been in years. I wanted to let you know."

Delilah let that sink in. It took a moment, because of all the things she'd anticipated Carla saying, this wasn't on the list.

"Oh," Delilah said. "Waterslide World. Great. A great day for it. I'll just—get my bathing suit."

"I said *I'm* going," she said.

"I heard you. I want to go, too."

She didn't, really. She was supposed to meet Michael after work for dinner, but she certainly wasn't going to let Carla go alone.

"I had things for you to do."

"And I wouldn't mind a day off. I want to go," Delilah insisted.

Carla eyed her. "Why?" she asked.

"Because I've never been. I mean, not here. I've been to things like that in Florida, and I liked them. A lot."

Delilah sat there, while Carla pulled herself into her suit, hefting her breasts into the bra portion of it. When this was done, Carla turned and stared at her.

"Well," she said, "Hurry up. I'm not waiting around for you."

Delilah went to her room and threw stuff into a bag—a plastic grocery bag that she found in the cupboard since she didn't bring a beach bag and didn't want to start digging through old purses in the closet—and was ready to go. Then, downstairs to the phone to make a quick call to Michael, to let him know she'd gotten tied up with Carla. Almost out the door she remembered that Jack was supposed to come by later in the afternoon to start on the roof, and she was supposed to help. She wrote him a note and left it on the kitchen table, while Carla stood at the door tapping her foot impatiently. Then they left the house, and Delilah headed toward her car. Carla headed toward hers.

They both stopped and looked at each other.

"What're you doing?" Delilah asked.

"I'm not walking to Lake George," Carla said.

"I know that," Delilah said. "I'm driving."

"I can drive."

"I want to drive."

"Why?" she asked suspiciously. "You don't like the way I drive?"

"No," Delilah said. "I don't. You're too slow. And I'm neurotic. I don't trust anyone else driving. If you drive, I'll be clutching the door the whole time and by the time we get there I'll have a stomachache."

She chuckled. "Okay. You drive. But I pick the radio station."

"Oh, God," Delilah said.

Carla surprised her and picked a station that had a lot of oldies. Oldies for Delilah, not for her.

"This one," she said, when Santana played "Black Magic Woman." "I like this one."

"You do?"

"They used to use it for circus routines," she said. "I'd come out all dressed in black, and ride the tigers. I was pretty damn hot, even if I was already too old."

"Carla," she said, shocked. "You swore."

"We're not in the house," Carla replied, and she sang along, way out of tune and loud. Delilah joined in, mostly to drown her out. Even so, it was better than having her drive.

They got there, and there wasn't much of a line. Wednesday was always the best day to go to these places, because the weekenders were mostly in transition and the crowds were down. It was already hot, though, and Delilah worried about that.

"Let's find a spot in the shade," she said.

"No," Carla said. "I want the sun."

"It's too hot," Delilah said.

"I want to feel it on me," Carla said. "You can't feel it in the shade."

She marched over to a lounge chair that faced the wave pool, and sat down. "There," she said. "That's good."

Delilah peered up at the sky. Not a cloud. "I'll go get some drinks," she said.

Carla opened her bag. "Got drinks," she said. She began unbuttoning the housedress she had over her suit and shorts, then leaned back on the lounge, and sighed in deep contentment.

Okay, Delilah thought. She knows what she's doing. At least, it seemed that way. But somehow, sitting in a lounge chair with not too much on, she looked more fragile than she did around her own home. There, Delilah never quite separated her from the land around her, which had a solidity and permanence to it. Here, where the sun glared off white cement and blue chlorinated water, Carla became almost transparent, only partially fleshed out. It made Delilah aware of her age, and nervous about it.

She pulled off her tank top and shorts, and leaned back on her lounge chair, prepared to relax if it killed her. She even closed her eyes.

The sun felt good, as if it got into her skin and worked its way right to the heart, doing nice things there. Delilah knew it was bad for her, but it was also necessary.

That's what she told herself, as she began to let that drowsy feeling overtake her. It didn't last long.

"Huh," Carla said.

Delilah opened her eyes. "What?"

"You're dark-skinned."

"Yeah," Delilah said. "My father suspects there's some Romanian gypsy in him. He's kind of dark. My mom is fair, though. Like you, I guess."

"Her father was dark," Carla said. "She was pretty light, though. Given to rashes."

Delilah paused. How would Carla know that? "She was?"

"Yeah. A little squiggly thing, all white with no hair. Her head was pointy from getting stuck in me. She got stuck for a while. That was the tough part," Carla leaned over and spoke confidentially. "I hear women talk these days, thinking they can beat the pain, like it's a sin to talk about having any. But don't ever let anybody tell you it doesn't hurt. It's a lie. It hurts like hell."

"Huh," Delilah said, again remaining neutral.

Carla went back to reclining. "Disgusting, to lie to women that way. Anyway, she came out in the end and we were both fine, and when I took her home, she broke out in these red bumps. Scared me to death."

"You . . . took her home?" Delilah asked cautiously.

"I did," Carla said. "For two weeks. Kurt helped some, not much, but some. He even talked about maybe marrying me, and I'd stop working, take care of the baby."

"Kurt?"

"The man. The stupid man. Your grandfather."

There was a long silence. Delilah let it play out, and then took the biggest chance of all. "If you took her home, why didn't you keep her?" she asked.

There was another long silence, during which Delilah waited for Carla to tell her to mind her own business, but she didn't.

"Kurt died," she said, her voice quiet and without noticeable emotion. "Got himself killed riding his motorcycle too fast after he drank too much. Killed a couple while he was at it. After that, I had to go back to work. Couldn't take care of her properly. So, I let her go where someone could."

Delilah thought about her at thirty, realizing she was just a year older than Carla had been when she gave birth to her mother, which seemed somehow remarkable. She tried to imagine herself, getting pregnant, hopeful that the father was going to marry her and make a family with her. Then having the rug pulled out. Finding out he was dead, and had killed other people along the way. Too many dreams shattered at once.

She could imagine the shock of it, and the sense of rage Carla must have felt. At least, Delilah would have felt it. How dare he get drunk and die? How dare he leave me with a baby and no support, just because he wanted to get drunk one night? All that, she could imagine. What she couldn't imagine was what it must be like to let go of the baby. Surely nine months in the womb and pushing the damn thing out and caring for its bumps and rashes, knowing it was your genetic material, your connection to the future, your connection to love, must make that as painful a decision as you could possibly make.

"It must've been so hard to do," she said softly.

There was a long silence. Delilah risked opening an eye to look at Carla, who reclined on her lounge, her eyes closed, her face giving nothing away.

"She had a life," she said, a little defensively. "And I had a life. We just couldn't live them together."

Delilah wanted her to understand that she wasn't making judgments, but she didn't know if anything she said would tell her that. She had no answers. Only more questions.

"How did you know it was the right thing to do?" she asked.

"I didn't," she said. "I only knew I had to do it, if I wanted her to have a good chance in the world."

"Maybe," Delilah suggested, "she would've liked the circus."

"Maybe," Carla replied, caustic now, "I couldn't do it. Take care of her and work. Maybe I'm just someone who couldn't do that, and I knew it. I know there's kids raised to it, raised in it. I was around them. But I didn't think I could do that. Anyway, it turned out okay, didn't it?"

"Pretty much," Delilah agreed. "She's had a good life, too."

"There you go. That's how you know, then. It turned out okay. I want to go in the water."

Delilah heard her rise, and looked over at her. She didn't look upset. Or sunstroked. Carla-like, she started to walk away.

Delilah rose quickly and followed her toward the wave pool. Carla put her feet in, splashing them around and sighing deeply in contentment. Delilah noticed there were small sores on them, sort of scattered around. Before she could ask about them, Carla was walking out to her waist, then diving in and swimming. Delilah caught up.

"I don't want you following me around," Carla said when they were in the deep part. "Get back to the other side."

Delilah turned around and did as she was told, but kept an eye on Carla. After a while, she emerged on the shore, as unlike the Venus on the Half Shell as you can get, but kind of beautiful in another way. Like the turtles. Old and full of the world as dirt and grass. Fragile and permanent. She stood on one leg and hopped, poked at her ear and shook her head. Then she pointed at the tubes.

"I want to go on them," she said, and started walking. Once again, Delilah followed until they were at the entrances, where you got the tubes or mats you needed, and they surveyed the various options for slide rides.

"That one," she said, pointing at the Devil's Plunge, which went straight down. She walked toward it. Delilah scampered after.

"Wait," she said. "Wait up." Carla stopped and turned.

"You can't," Delilah said.

"Why not?" she asked.

"You're too short," Delilah improvised.

Carla rolled her eyes. "You're a lousy liar," she noted. She turned back and watched the kids come down. One of them screeched all the way down, hit the water hard, and came out shaking, his eyes real big.

"Maybe not," she said.

"How about that one?" Delilah suggested, pointing to a large blue tube that seemed to have a gentler curve. Someone popped out the bottom smiling.

"Okay," Carla said. "That looks good."

"Maybe I should just go down first and check it out?"

Carla gave her an evil look and walked ahead. They got their tubes, and ascended the stairs with them. Delilah was totally uncertain about it, especially when they got to the top, and the attendant who helped them into their tubes looked at her as if she were committing a crime.

"You sure you want to go?" she asked Carla.

"If I wasn't, would I be sitting here?" Carla asked sharply.

"Okay," she said, pushing her down.

Delilah heard a short whoop, but it didn't sound unhappy. And there was nothing she could do except go down after her, which she did.

It felt great. Delilah thought it felt like what breath must feel like, leaving the body. Sitting in a big soft inner tube, she went down and around sloping curves smooth and easy. It was absolutely effortless, just fast enough to feel good, but not fast enough to scare her. And very Zen. No action necessary, except setting her internal receptors for maximum enjoyment of the moment. In fact, what was important was to do nothing and let water and gravity carry you down and out. Let the laws of nature do their work while you took the ride.

She whooped, too, and popped out of the blue and back into the sunlight a happy woman.

Carla was standing at the entrance, still holding her tube.

"Again?" she asked.

"Again," Delilah agreed.

Carla smiled, her grin as wicked as Jack's could ever be.

They went up and down quite a few more times, letting the water lead the way, before Carla said she wanted to go back in the pool for a while.

"Okay," Delilah said, prepared to follow. Carla stopped and turned to her.

"After that, I have to go to the bathroom," she said. "You gonna follow me into the stalls?"

"I just thought . . ."

"I know what you thought. Will you go sit down and let me be for a minute or two? I'm used to being alone now and then."

Delilah supposed she was, and let her go. She went back to the lounge and sat there, trying to keep an eye on Carla, but there were too many people, and she was soon lost among them. She let it go, and contented herself with people watching.

What she noticed primarily was how many different kinds of bodies there were. A bleached-blond woman in lime green tank top with lime green shorts, five feet tall and five feet around—a true sphere—sat at the edge of the wave pool reading a romance novel. Delilah wondered what her thoughts were. Was she longing to be beautiful and loved? Did she wish she looked like the woman illustrated on the cover, with breasts pouring out of a slightly torn bodice and her waist nipped in to almost nothing?

A round man came up and sat beside her, put an arm around her, and looked at her adoringly. She returned his gaze. Got that one wrong, Delilah thought. Apparently you don't have to be thin to be loved.

A robust woman sitting on one side of her, wearing a paisley muumuu, was smoking a cigarette and talking to a friend whose skin shone with oil. Her voice, which was as robust as her body, called Delilah's attention away from the lovers.

"So I smoke," she declaimed loudly. "I told my niece. We all have something. My niece, she's fat. She goes to the beach and wears a T-shirt. I tell her, you're fat with the T-shirt on, and you're fat with the T-shirt off. Take it off and enjoy the sun."

It seemed like good advice.

A group of children ran by squealing, and Delilah watched them. They didn't care what their bodies looked like yet. As Carla might have counseled, they only enjoyed the feeling of having them and using them freely to explore motion, the pleasure of sensation, the power of control, and the freedom of the lack of it.

Delilah watched them run and romp around and in the pool, skittering like insects among the many kinds of bodies gathered there. Women with beautiful faces and a little roll at the belly. Women with truly fabulous breasts and bony knees. Men with protruding bellies and marvelous biceps. Men with hairy backs and six-pack abs, or balding heads and strong jawbones. Everyone had something that worked, and something that didn't. Praised are you, she thought, who varies the forms of your creatures, who freckles, scars, bulges, and builds them. Praised are you.

She was enjoying the abundance of all this, when the worst happened.

She heard a murmur pass through the crowd. She looked up to see what caused it, and saw the Perfect Body with the Perfect Face walking straight toward her. It went almost beyond perfect, into airbrushed.

Full perky breasts that weren't overwhelming. A Barbie-sized waist, and hips that curved just right down into long, lean legs with just enough fat content to smooth out any bones. Heart-shaped face with high cheekbones and large blue eyes, complimented perfectly by her sun-streaked blond hair. And her skin was smooth and golden brown, with not a wrinkle, pouch, dimple, freckle, or scar.

The worst got even worse a second later, as Perfection sighed, and tossed her bag on the lounge chair to the left of Delilah's, which was empty. She sat down and added insult to injury by oiling her perfect skin until it shone. Then, she laid back, closed her beautiful eyes, and rested, just as if she weren't a goddess. As Delilah sat there, trying not to feel inadequate, men walked by and paused just long enough to catch their breaths.

"Shit," she muttered, wishing Carla was there to make some kind of rude comment. Thinking that, she was suddenly aware that Carla had been gone a while. She left the goddess to her other worshippers, got up and went to the wave pool and looked around, but Carla wasn't there. Next, she tried the bathrooms, but the only occupants were three teenage girls who stood in front of the mirrors examining their bodies. Delilah startled as she looked over at them, and suddenly saw her own face staring back at her from a mirror. She'd already grown unused to seeing it. It looked okay, she thought. Sun-kissed. Not too tense. She could use a haircut, but that's why God made rubber bands. She fluffed her hair up a little. In front of her, the teenage girls turned this way and that, examining themselves.

"Does this bathing suit make my hips look big?" one of them, a blond, asked.

"Oh, God, no," a teenager whose hair was blue and fuchsia said. "It looks great on you. I wish I had more boob for this one, though." She tried to lift her small breasts, and failed. The other girls giggled.

"I think it's nicer to have small ones," the third girl, a rather voluptuous brunet said. "These are so heavy, and I can't go with-out a bra or anything. I know they'll sag bad when I get old."

"I wish my thighs weren't so big," another one said.

They all sighed, concerned with the capacity of their bodies to appeal to others. Delilah felt like taking the mirrors down, and telling them to get outside and have some fun. Go look at the round people in the pool, who get to enjoy love, sex, and food. The only thing they don't have is public approval, but you can't get that unless you're airbrushed anyway. Or a goddess, like the one waiting to make her feel inadequate back at the lounge chairs.

But she knew they wouldn't listen. They would just look at her as if she were crazy. They'd look at her the way she looked at Carla sometimes.

Which reminded her. Carla. She started looking under stalls for feet. They were all empty.

She was a little panicked now, and made her way through the concession stand, thinking Carla might be there getting something, but she wasn't. "Shit, Carla," she muttered. "Where'd you run away to?"

She went back to the lounge chairs to get her bag and maybe go check the car, see if Carla was sitting inside it, frying. The god-dess was still there, and at rest, but to Delilah's relief, so was Carla. She was leaning back in her lounge chair, eyes closed.

"Hey," Delilah said. "How's the water?"

She didn't answer. Delilah was used to that, but she didn't like Carla's coloring. She was mottled, red splotches on skin that looked too pale.

"Carla?" she asked.

"Fine," she muttered. "Fine."

"Carla?" Delilah said again. "Do you want some food? Something to drink?"

"I'm *fine*," Carla said, her voice was rising in pitch, getting strident. "Didn't you hear me goddammit."

"Okay," Delilah said softly. "I heard you."

Then, Carla opened her eyes and looked around, frightened, as if she didn't know where she was. She sat up and reached over to clutch Delilah's arm.

"Where's Frank?" she asked. "He knows how to handle Daddy. Get Frank."

"I'll get him, Carla," Delilah said. Was she having a stroke? Heatstroke? What the hell should she do?

She didn't have much time to think about it. Carla made a strangled noise, and pointed at the goddess. "Who's that girl? Is that mine?" she asked, getting loud now.

The goddess opened her eyes, and Carla leaned over Delilah to look at her hard. "Is it you?" she asked. The goddess blinked and looked to Delilah, her mouth caught in the shape of the letter "O." She gasped, and sat up.

Carla leaned over more. "It'll all go away in the end. You know that, don't you?"

The goddess blinked hard, and Delilah watched as her eyes filled up with water, which ran over the rims.

"No point crying about it," Carla said. "It's what happens."

The goddess pulled back, and put a hand to her mouth. Delilah put herself between them, blocking Carla. She had to get her out of here. She had to get her in the car and headed toward home.

"Let's go find Frank," she suggested. "You come with me, and we'll find him."

Carla looked at her hard, as if she were a stranger. Her eyes were younger. Innocent of experience. They looked into Delilah, piercing through here and now to a place she wasn't sure she was ready to visit.

"It's the wind," Carla whispered. "The way it whistles through you. You know?"

"I know," Delilah whispered back, and she did, because it felt like it was whistling through her now. As if they were both just wind, whistling through each other, disembodied, acknowledging a different kind of existence. Then she leaned back, and closed her eyes. Delilah leaned toward her, uncertain if she was passed out, afraid of what she'd find if she put a hand to the pulse at her neck. She was reaching toward it in spite of her fear, when she felt a hand on her shoulder. She turned quickly, and saw Jack standing there.

"What're you doing?" he asked sharply. "What's going on?"

"She's— Something's—she's," Delilah stuttered.

Carla's eyes opened to slits, and she muttered something unintelligible, waved a hand at Jack, who sat down on the lounge next to her. "I'm here, Carla. It's okay." He reached toward a bag he'd put down on the ground next to him. A little black bag. What looked to Delilah like a doctor's bag. He opened it, and took something out. A syringe. "Here you go, Carla," he said, and pinched some skin on her arm, jabbing it in.

He put one hand on her wrist and held it, looking at his watch.

"Jack?" Delilah asked softly.

He held up one finger, indicating she should wait a minute, and continued looking at his watch. Then, he put her hand down, and pressed her eyes open with his fingers, looking into them.

"Jack?" Delilah asked again.

"What were you thinking of, bringing her here?" he muttered.

"She brought me here," Delilah shot back. "I didn't have a choice. Didn't you get my note?"

He didn't say anything for a moment. Carla opened her eyes and looked at him as if she knew who he was. "Hullo, Jack," she said. "Didn't expect you here today."

"Yeah," he said. "Me neither." He turned to Delilah. "We should get her home. I'll drive her. You can follow. If I pull over, you pull over, too, okay?"

"Jack?" Delilah asked again.

He looked at her. "She's diabetic," he said. "I just gave her glucagon. I'm her doctor."

THIRTEEN

combined elements: fire and air

"*I don't need to be* walked to my room," Carla snapped. "I can walk by myself. I know where it is."

"We're aware of that, Carla," Jack said, keeping a tight grip on her arm while Delilah stood the rear guard in case she stumbled. "I want to check you before you go to sleep."

Once they were in her room she jerked her arm away and sat on the bed. "Go away," she said.

"Not yet," Jack said. He knelt down on the floor at her feet. She swatted at him as if he were a fly.

"Go away," she said, more emphatically.

"Not yet," he repeated, and took off her shoes, examining her feet. "Did I tell you not to go barefoot?" he asked.

"Can't wear shoes down the blue tube," she said, and grinned at Delilah, who bit her lip, trying to look stern.

Jack looked over at her. "There's a bottle of saline solution in the bathroom cabinet, and an ointment. In a tube. Could you get it? Bring some gauze bandages, too, and a washcloth."

Delilah did so, and when she returned he was massaging her foot. He took the saline solution and rinsed a space between her toes, applied ointment, then the bandage. Delilah knelt beside him and began rubbing Carla's other foot.

"Cut it out," Carla said, trying to pull away. "I feel stupid."

"You are stupid, Carla," Jack said. "If you can't listen to your doctor's good advice."

She pulled harder and Delilah had to hang on hard enough that she was afraid of breaking something. "Jeez, Carla," she said. "Women pay a lot of money for this sort of thing, and here you're getting it free."

"I don't want it," she insisted, but she stopped pulling. They massaged for a while longer, then Jack looked over her feet thoroughly, and put a pair of socks on her. When he was done, he sighed, ran a hand through his hair, and pushed himself to his feet.

"Okay. Time for sleep. I'll come by to check that foot tomorrow, and you're to make an appointment for blood work. And no smoking," he added.

"What makes you think—"

He pointed to the bureau. "The ashtray. Dead giveaway."

She lifted half her mouth in a grin and snickered as he gathered up the saline and lotion. He laughed his evil laugh, touched Delilah's arm, and they went out.

"Hey," she called. They turned.

"Say good night," she said to Delilah.

Delilah looked at her for a good long moment. She seemed not the worse for wear. Just tired, maybe a little faded and pale, but she was suddenly filled with delayed fear at what she'd almost done to her.

"I'm sorry," she said.

Carla squinted at her. "For what?"

"I—Carla, I could've killed you."

She felt Jack touch her shoulder. "It's my fault," he said. "I didn't tell you. If you'd known what to do—I should've told you."

"Oh, for God's sake," Carla cut in. "Will you cut it out? It's my life, isn't it? I wanted to go, and I went. And if it kills me, well, at least I did what I wanted. Don't I get a say in how I go out?"

"Carla," Jack said sternly, "if you're trying to—"

She waved a hand at him as if he were a fly in her face. "If I do that, nobody'll know what I'm up to. And nobody's to feel bad about it. You got that?"

"Carla," Jack said, but she cut him off again.

"You got it?" She looked at him, then at Delilah. They said nothing.

"Look," she repeated. "You two—you're young. Go have your own life, and let me have mine. Don't try to be so responsible for me. I don't need you. You got *that?*"

"I got it," Delilah said at last. She looked at Jack, then turned back to Carla.

"G'night, Carla," she said. "It's been a fun day."

Carla lay back on the bed. "Fun," she murmured. "I had a good time, dolly. Love that blue tube."

They were quiet going down the stairs, and then Jack said, "I want to check her insulin supplies. Okay?"

"Okay," Delilah said, not sure why he asked. Polite, she thought. He was polite. He was a doctor. Who knew?

She went downstairs to the kitchen, intending to get something to drink, but instead heading toward the sliding glass doors and then out onto the deck. Once there, she looked up. The sky was so full of stars it couldn't hold another one. A good clear night. She walked off the deck and soon found she was walking around the pond and up the ridge behind it. Halfway there she realized she was tired, and sat down. Then she lay on her back and stared at the sky. It was clear enough to spot the Milky Way, and see Sagittarius, aiming true at Antares in the heart of Scorpio.

The sky reminded her that it was a big universe after all. Tonight, she felt small and wrongly made within it. She closed her eyes. After a little while, she heard the crunching of footsteps. They stopped, and for some time there was no sound except the crickets. Then, as if he'd been standing there all along, there was Jack's voice, saying, "Hey."

She opened her eyes.

He looked funny from that perspective. Hugely tall. "Hey," she said in return. He sat down. She stayed where she was.

"You okay?" he asked.

"Fine, Dr. Brown. Except for the patches of guilt and horror beginning to raise on my arms and back."

Jack leaned back on his elbows. "It's not your fault. I should've told you."

"Why didn't you?" she asked.

He sighed. "Carla swore me to secrecy. She said you didn't have to know yet, and if you did, she'd be the one to tell you."

"Christ Almighty."

"Yeah. But she's been good about taking care of herself. I didn't think it'd be a problem."

"You could've mentioned that you're a doctor."

"Then you would've treated me differently."

"I would?"

"People do. They elevate you. And women—sometimes they look at you like you're a good catch. Or a savior. Not quite human anymore, with faults and so on."

"Your ex-wife do that?"

"She said she married me because she thought I could cure her of being a lesbian. Then, of course, she figured out it wasn't a disease. I was enjoying just being Jack Brown. It was pretty selfish."

"There's worse things you could do," Delilah pointed out. "Kick dogs. Club baby harp seals. Rob convenience stores."

"Yell at young women at Waterslide World. I'm sorry about that, by the way. I guess I was scared." He twisted his head and looked down at her. "Do you think about me differently now?"

She put her hands behind her head and continued looking up. "It adds another layer. Maybe it even elevates you a little. I mean, as a handyman, you hold the life and death of a washing machine in your hands. As a doctor, you potentially hold my life and death in your hands. That's—different."

Jack sighed. "I know. It's just—uncomfortable."

"Your cross to bear. Why don't you tell me about it now? The diabetes, I mean."

He leaned back on his elbow, picked a blade of grass, and chewed on it. "Carla started taking meds when she was in her late sixties. Now she gets shots every day. Her dose has been getting higher in the last year or so, which isn't uncommon in someone her age. She's been good about policing it—mostly because she hates the thought of being really sick—but lately I've seen some behavioral changes. She's forgetting things. Being impulsive. Wandering off now and then. I'm worried about that. If she forgets her meds, or takes too much because she forgot she took them, she could kill herself. And her protein's been high, too."

"What's that mean?"

"Kidneys aren't doing what they ought. Diabetes puts a burden on them, and after a while, they just go. If it keeps progressing, she might be looking at dialysis. I'm thinking I need to sign her up for regular health aide visits to check her feet and double-check her sugar levels and so on, but I don't know if that's covered."

"Bank of Mom'll cover it," Delilah said. "Her guilty conscience is boundless. Or—could you teach me how?"

"You'd be willing?" he asked.

The thought made her a little queasy, not about the needles, but about the responsibility. But the thought of not taking care of Carla made her even more queasy. "If you think I wouldn't mess it up," she said.

"It's not hard," he said. "You could do it. But when you leave, we'll have to get someone else anyway. I'm on a limited-practice schedule, so I can be here a lot, but I'd rather she had someone else, too. She won't admit it, but she needs some looking after."

"Don't we all," Delilah said.

He made a noise at the back of his throat, then cleared it. Then he shook himself, and spoke. "What you could do," he said, "is just make sure you check in with her. Ask her if she took her shot, sort of look her over to see if she's seeming balanced. And keep an eye on her feet. She's got neuropathy from poor circulation, which means wounds can get ugly fast, and then you have to start cutting things off. Do you think you'll stay? At least until Eleanor gets back."

"I'll stay," Delilah said. "Though I get the feeling she doesn't like Eleanor much. Not that I think she likes me much, either."

"Oh, she likes you."

"How can you tell?"

"I know her."

"How do you know her, Jack? I mean, all this time I thought you were just a handyman, and now there's these huge gaps of information. How did it start?"

He took in breath and let it out. "I met her at the clinic

when I first started working there. About six years ago now, I guess. I work three days a week in a group practice, two nights at the clinic. I didn't want to do the career push thing. Just wanted to be a doctor, you know? Anyway, she came in for a checkup, and I rubbed her feet. Like I did tonight. She was funny. Kind of flirtatious and ornery at the same time. While I was doing that, the PA came in to ask me about some volunteer work we were doing with an alcohol rehab place. Carla, of course, butted in and asked why I did that, and I told her about my parents being killed by a drunk driver. She got real quiet, then she invited me to come have dinner with her. I didn't, of course. Not professional, you know? Then she called me at the clinic and asked if I could come and look at a funny wart on Kootch's face. She said he was too stubborn to go see a doctor, so if I could come up as if I was just visiting, and maybe check it out, that'd be a help. I went."

"And the wart?"

"Just a mole. Perfectly benign. But then I saw a front step was coming loose, so I fixed it. And then something else needed fixing, so I came back again. And so on."

Delilah chewed on his story for a moment, then said, "Carla told me that my grandfather died in a car crash. He was drunk. I guess he killed another couple, too."

"She told me about it," Jack said. "She thinks getting me here to work for her somehow makes amends for that. Funny thing is, I think she's right. Being here, fixing things—it's been good for me. Not something I necessarily would've chosen on my own, but good."

"You know," Delilah said, "if you told me all this before, I wouldn't have elevated you. Thought you were neurotic, maybe, but not elevated you."

He smiled. "I don't usually tell people I'm part Mohawk, either, for the same reason. People look at me like I have some in with the spirit world. Makes me feel like a living anachronism."

"Then if you tell them you're Mohawk *and* a doctor, they must think you're a minor deity."

He raised his eyebrows. "Why minor?" he asked.

She laughed. "Only because they don't know you well enough. Listen," she suggested, "maybe you know the wrong people."

"Probably. I guess that's one reason why this place is good for me. Everyone else I know is so regular. Got an eye on the career. Looking for the wife and the house in the suburbs. Here, it's different."

"That's a good word for it."

"But you know what I mean, don't you? You feel it, too. It's not just the people. It's in the land, and in the sky."

Delilah stared up at the sky full of stars. She did feel it. It wasn't big or startling, like seeing the Grand Canyon for the first time, with the skin of the earth pulled back and all the working parts revealed. It was softer, slower, like hands moving over you gently as you slept, and the whispered voice of lullabies that seeped into your dreams. You didn't necessarily remember it when you woke up, but you were aware of how rested you felt, and how right.

She didn't know how or why a certain portion of the earth became a friend, what unseen energies moved up from it and into her to make that so, but she was aware of it happening.

"I'm beginning to know," she said. "Look at that," she pointed toward the southern horizon. "There's Sagittarius. My constellation, by the way. And the Milky Way. Did you know we go around its center every two hundred million years, and we're smack in the middle of our fortieth trip?"

"I didn't know that," he admitted.

"The Mayans call it the World Tree. Right near the elliptical, where Sagittarius hangs out, they think is a special place. And see that," she said, pointing more to the upward dome of the sky. "It's the Corona Borealis. The Greeks said it was Ariadne's crown that Dionysus threw into the sky when she died, and the Shawnees say it's a circle of dancing star maidens. Busy sky, huh?"

He squinted, then looked back at her. "I don't think I actually see any of that. It just looks like a bunch of stars all clumped together to me."

"Sure," she said. "It's right there. No, wait." She pointed back to Sagittarius. "You can see Sadge. Look for Antares—that bright red-orange star—and follow it back."

He shook his head. "I'm not seeing it." He tapped on his eye patch. "Monovision. Screws with your depth perception. You see Sagittarius. I just see stars."

"Just?" Delilah said. "Just? *We're* just stars. Made of all the stuff you need to make a star. You know. 'We are stardust, we are golden. We are billion-year-old carbon.' Though I'm not always sure about that golden part. Look. Try this." She sat up and grabbed his hand, and pointed with that, trailing it along the tip of the archer's arrow toward Antares. "See?" she asked.

He stared first at her hand on his, and then resisted the urge to close his eyes and enjoy that feeling and disciplined himself to follow where she had him pointing. As if her motions created the image she saw, it suddenly became visible to him, too. "Huh," he said. "That?"

"That," she said, feeling satisfied. She released his hand. He turned and looked at her.

"How'd you learn to see the stars?" he asked.

"Actually, it was my brother who was in love with them," she said. "And since he was—well, we were twins, so we did just about everything together."

"You have a brother?"

"Had," she said. "He died when we were kids."

Delilah waited for him to ask questions, but he didn't, which somehow encouraged her to continue because it was more like talking to herself. She told him the story of the leukemia, and then just kept talking, telling him how Joshua was someone she thought of as being as permanent as her own body, just a fact of life like the sun in the morning, and how the world changed when she discovered that wasn't true. How they had been each other's shadows and how, to this day, somehow he was still hers, lingering, getting more or less visible at any given time, but always there, attached to her in a way she didn't understand.

Then, she stopped talking. There didn't seem to be anything else to say. For a while, there was silence. She wondered if Jack was thinking this was what women did when you were a doctor— they told you death stories. She wondered if she should be embarrassed. She became aware that Jack had lain down on his back and was staring up, his hands behind his head.

"I'm sorry that happened to you," he said quietly.

"Me, too," she agreed.

"When my parents died, I felt all of that. Everything seemed pretty ephemeral. Pretty fragile."

Above them, a meteor streamed its way across the sky and faded into darkness somewhere behind Ursa Minor. A thrill ran through her, the way it always did when she saw that. She knew it was just chunks of rocks flying around, but that didn't matter. Something happened in the great wide sky, however brief, and she was there to witness it.

"Beautiful," Jack murmured.

"Mm," Delilah agreed. "Right into the little bear. See it?" She pointed up and traced it with her fingers.

"I'll take it on faith. You can see the patterns. I can't." Jack said.

"Staring up like this makes me feel like I'm falling. Not falling down. Falling up, into the stars."

Delilah knew what he meant. When she lay on her back and stared up at the sky, she often felt as if they were sucking her up into them, as if she'd fall up and up until she was one of them. "It's nice, isn't it?" she commented.

"A little weird. Like a trust fall."

"A what?"

"Trust fall. You know. When you fall back and hope that someone catches you? We had to do them in one of my classes, for psych rotation. It was supposed to help us understand what it was like to be a patient."

"And did it?"

"Actually, it's pretty informative. You want to try it?"

"Try it?"

"A trust fall."

"But—where'll I fall?"

He pushed himself to stand up. "You'll just fall straight back."

She sat up and looked at him. "Have I mentioned that this land is Taconic orogeny. A combination of shale and clay?"

"I'll catch you," he said, and put his arms out. "Come on. Try it. Or are you chicken?"

At that, she stood up. "You sure know how to sweet-talk a girl. So what do I do?"

"Stand there," he said, and positioned her, then went somewhere behind her. "Okay."

"Okay? Okay what?"

"Just—fall."

She twisted around to look at him. He stood behind her, with his arms held out. "Turn around," he said. "You can't be looking when you fall."

"Are you nuts?" she asked.

He laughed. "You'll know that as soon as you fall back, won't you? Turn around."

She turned away from him. She thought of every Charlie Brown comic she'd ever read where Lucy pulls the football away at the last minute. "Just fall? Just like that?"

"That's right," he said. "Go ahead. Count of three."

He counted. When he got to two, Delilah stopped him. "Wait," she said. "Wait."

"I'm not going anywhere," he said. "What's the problem?"

"What if I'm too heavy?"

He laughed again.

"No, really. What if you drop me?"

"I don't drop women," he said. "Throw them, maybe. But I never drop them. Count of three," he said again.

This time, when he got to three, she dropped straight back. There was a swift moment that seemed suspended in forever where she didn't know if he'd catch her. Somewhere between the decision to drop and the being caught, eternity seemed to reside, quiet, and full of peace. It seemed to last a long time, and it felt good.

And then, she felt his hands on her arms and back, and saw his face, inverted.

"How's that?" he asked softly.

"Way cool," she said, staring up at the stars from this position. "Wow way cool."

"Thought you'd like it," he said.

She closed her eyes and smiled, trying to recapture the feeling of that moment of suspension. The between time of trust and fall. She became aware that he shifted position, and was squatting, holding her sort of halfway on his lap. She became aware that his breathing had changed slightly.

These were warning signals, and she recognized them, but she

wasn't afraid, nor did she feel the need to respond. She was content to just lie there, half in his lap, half on the ground, his hands
holding her sides, her arms folded mummylike on her chest.

Part of her thought she should worry about herself at this
point. She had a boyfriend in Key West, sort of, and she was sleeping with her ex-fiancé, but her body was saying this felt good. Just
her body talking, she told herself, and decided she really did need
to introduce him to Monica. Someone should be enjoying this on
a regular basis.

"Delilah," he said softly. "I have to tell you something."

"Mm?" she asked.

Then, she heard a screech. Carla's screech.

She rolled over to her side on the ground and scrambled to her
feet. Jack was on his feet, too.

"Delilah," she screeched. "Phone for you."

"Jesus Christ," she muttered.

"Mary and all the saints," Jack amended.

"Who is it?" Delilah called back to her.

"Some jerk named Thomas," she shouted.

"Thomas," she said. "Hell. It's Thomas."

"Who's Thomas?" Jack asked.

"My boyfriend. Sort of," she said, moving toward the house.
He grabbed her arm at the elbow.

"Boyfriend?" he asked. "You have a boyfriend?"

"Sort of," she said. He looked shocked. "I told you. Didn't I tell
you?"

"You told me . . . Monica?"

"Monica? She's not my boyfriend. She's my friend." She
frowned at him. "Did you think . . . you did, didn't you?"

"I guess . . ." he drew himself up a little. "I didn't know. I guess
I hoped . . ."

"Hoped what? For the opportunity to see a little girlie action?"

"No. Of course not. Jesus. What do you think I am?"

"A man," she said.

"Look, you said you were going out with her."

"Out shopping."

Carla screamed from the deck, "You taking this call? Some of us want to get to sleep."

"On my way," Delilah said, and went toward the house.

FOURTEEN

air

$\mathcal{C}$ *The conversation with Thomas* was hampered in a variety of ways. First, there was the guilt she felt about Michael. Then, there was the fact that both Carla and Jack hovered over her shoulder the whole time. Jack seemed like he was still adjusting to her heterosexuality, not sure if he was happy about it. Carla just seemed pissed off.

"Why are you staying so long?" Thomas said, a little whiny about it. He wasn't possessive, so Delilah figured he must have another project for her to take part in. What this time, she wondered. Banana cream pies?

"You know why," she said, and quickly changed the subject. "How are you?"

"I'm good," he said. "The show went well. I sold some pieces. The blue in the Jell-O came out really sharp."

"I'll bet. So what're you doing now?"

"Well." He brightened some. "Your mom thought maybe you'd like me to come visit, so I am."

"You are?" she said, trying to sound bright and happy. "How nice. When?"

"Day after tomorrow," he said. "My flight comes in around noon."

"Wow," she said. "You must've sold quite a bit at that show."

"Your mom's treating. It was her idea."

She thought, not for the first time, that Thomas actually took more money from them than she did. And he took it with less reluctance. "Well," she said. "Well, well, well."

"Can you pick me up at the airport?"

"Sure," she said. "That'll be great. You'll like it here." She looked around at Carla and Jack. "Everybody's so friendly, and concerned."

Jack scowled. Carla made a face. Delilah didn't want to talk to Thomas more, but kept him on the line for another ten minutes because she knew that when she got off, she'd just have to explain it all to both of them.

When Delilah picked Thomas up at the airport, he was his usual self, full of talk about his art, kissing her quickly, and then getting on with the motion of life. Though he was no different, Delilah was aware of him in a different way. His need to stay in motion and therefore detached from anything he actually moved around disturbed her. The way he didn't really ask about her too much beyond the perfunctory "how are you, how's it going?" made her feel almost invisible. And the way he took it for granted that he'd be staying at Carla's made her uncomfortable. She couldn't see him joining in the work crew, and she couldn't see Carla appreciating his inability to do so. Some life-forms, she thought, do not adapt well to new environments.

Of course, she wasn't sure how much of her irritation at him was simply guilt because she was sleeping with someone else and not telling him, which she had to justify by seeing him as absolutely the wrong person in every way. He'd been satisfactory enough in Key West, and he hadn't really changed.

But she had. Being here had changed her in ways she couldn't yet define.

She was glad when Carla made it clear that Thomas didn't have permission to share her room. Of course, Thomas being Thomas, that wouldn't be a problem. And she'd temporarily dealt with Michael by telling him she'd be unavailable while she straightened out some family matters. Michael being Michael, that wasn't a problem either.

"Do what you have to. You know me," he said. "I can amuse myself."

None of her men were possessive, she thought. What a grand thing. The response of mature individuals, able to let people be who they are. She couldn't help but wonder why it made her feel like whining.

"Hey—listen, I got the name of the man to call at CEP," he told her. "You want it? They'll be posting the job in the next couple of weeks, but you can get to him ahead and talk a little, right?"

"Right," she said, and took the name and number. Though having Thomas at Carla's made Alabama look better by the minute.

"Well," she said to Thomas as they dragged his suitcase and camera case into the house and set them down in the living room. "Here we are."

He looked around, pushing his glasses up his nose. "Cool," he said.

"We like it," she replied.

A banging in the kitchen drew her attention, and she yelled out a hello. After a while, Jack appeared, a wrench in his hand, looking like he was in a bad mood.

"What?" she asked. "The sink again?"

"Toilet," he said. "Backed-up pipes."

"Oh. That's not too bad. Need a new one?"

"It's the pipes," he said impatiently. "Not the toilet."

"Right. Jack, this is Thomas. Thomas, this is Jack. He's a friend of mine."

When she said that, Jack opened his mouth and closed it again, subdued the scowl on his face, and came forward to shake Thomas's hand. "Pleased to meet you," he said.

"Sure," Thomas said, looking at and then around him vaguely. "This is quite a place."

"Yeah," Jack said sullenly. Delilah resisted the urge to kick him.

"Where's Carla?" she asked.

"She went out to do errands," he said. "I don't know when she'll be back."

"Okay. Well, I better show Thomas to his room. Good luck with the pipes."

"Thanks," Jack said. "Oh—and don't put him near Kootch's room. Kootch gets upset."

"He's not here," Delilah said.

"Coming back early. He's upset about the melting ice caps, and plans to do some lobbying for a global warming accord."

"Joy. Thomas is next to me, anyway," she said, and left before he could respond.

When she got Thomas up in his room, the first thing he did was take out a camera and snap a few shots of the peeling wallpaper, close-up. The pattern was roosters and little orange flowers, faded.

"You sure you don't want a hotel room?" Delilah asked him.

"And miss this? No way." He snapped a few more. "God, this is great. What's it like outside?"

"Big," she said. "And dark. At night, that is."

"Lot of grass," he noted.

"Turtle butts, too."

"Huh. That could be cool, I guess." He put his camera down, and grinned at her. "I'm being rude, aren't I? Why don't you come here and make me feel welcome?"

He held his arms out.

A wave of repulsion passed through her. Nothing, and she meant nothing short of Richard Nixon, seemed less appealing. She felt guilty as hell about it, but there it was. She wanted none of it, and when she thought of times past with him, it was like viewing a picture of herself from the distant past.

"We can't," she said quickly. "Carla's got rules."

Thomas's mouth opened in surprise, and then he shut it. "What?"

"No creaking or groaning. We can't have sex here, Thomas. I tried to tell you."

"Oh," he said, sounding more surprised than disappointed. "Really?"

"Really," she said firmly. "You have no idea what she's like when she's upset."

"Okay. Anyway, it's good to see you."

"It's good to see you, too, Thomas."

Behind her, she heard someone clearing a throat. She turned, and saw Jack standing in the hall, still scowling. "I'm sorry to bother you, but there's a call for you."

"For me?"

"It's Monica."

"Oh. Right. I told her to call." She turned to Thomas. "Why don't you get settled while I go take this, and then we can walk around. Get something to eat."

She trailed Jack down the stairs to the phone in the living room, wondering if his front looked as miffed as his back. She didn't like it. Not at all. He had no right to be angry with her. She hadn't done anything to make him angry. And if he was actually angry at something else, he had no right to take it out on her. They were supposed to be friends.

"Hey," she hissed at him. "Since when am I the enemy?"

He stopped walking, but he didn't turn around or say anything.

"I didn't kill anybody you love, or start working for CEP yet. I didn't even break the damn pipes. So what's your problem?"

He turned around, his face looking less like a scowl. "I don't have a problem," he said.

"Good," she said. "Then you can deal with mine."

"What's that?"

"Did I do something wrong that I don't know about? Sometimes I do that, but if you don't tell me there's no way I can fix it, is there?"

The muscles on his face moved around some, and ultimately came to rest in a rather sheepish smile. "You didn't do anything wrong," he said. "I'm just in a bad mood. It's not pretty, I know. I'm sorry."

"Is it something to do with Thomas?" she asked hesitantly.

"I guess—I guess I'm surprised about that," he said. He struggled with his feelings for a moment, trying to get them to take shape in words. This wasn't easy. Especially since what he felt was something he didn't think he had a right to feel. It grew out of the meanderings of his own wishes and fantasies, which, apparently, she didn't share.

"I still feel stupid for thinking you and Monica—thinking what I thought," he said. "And—well, I got used to having you at my beck and call. For roof fixing and star watching and so on."

"Oh," she said, thinking that at least one of the men in her life was possessive. "Well, that's—kind of nice. But you don't have to worry about Thomas. He won't be a burden. Not that kind, anyway."

"Okay, I guess," Jack said reluctantly.

"Trust me," she said. "Honest to God and all the turtle butts."

Jack continued to stand there, looking at her.

"I better get the phone before Monica thinks I've been abducted by aliens," she said.

"Right," he said. Then he stopped again. "Oh. Hey. The powwow's next weekend. You still interested in going?"

"Oh. Sure. That'd be great. When?"

"Saturday. Around noon."

"Great. I'll tell Monica to come along. And Thomas'll like it."

"Sure," Jack said. "Great."

They moved forward, though she noticed his back was looking miffed again. When they got to the living room, he disappeared into the laundry room and Delilah picked up the receiver lying on the small end table only to hear Monica saying, "And you better have a good reason for keeping me on this line talking to myself."

"Oh, God," Delilah said with heartfelt relief. "Thank God you called."

"Lilah?" she said. "Are you okay?"

"Not," she said. "And I can't talk too much. Thomas is here."

"Oh my. Oh—that's not—were you expecting him?"

"Not until two nights ago when he called to tell me he was coming."

"Well," she said gleefully. "Doesn't this put a little cramp on love's developing story?"

"Bitch," Delilah said.

"Yes, well I owe you a few, don't I? So what are you going to do?"

"Tell him, I guess. I—guess."

"Honey, if you see any other options, you go ahead and show them to me, okay?"

She was right. Clearly, she had to tell him. But she didn't really know how. "Monica, I've never been the dumpee. Always the dumped. How do you do that?"

"How did Michael do it?"

She thought about that. "Tacky," she said.

"Anti-Foundation," she agreed. "Maybe you should try . . . let's see . . . being honest?"

"Honest?"

"Mm-hmm. As in, 'Thomas, I've fallen back in love with my ex-fiancé. It's not that there's anything wrong with you, and I hope we can still be friends.'"

"Oh, God," she said. "That's what they always say to us, isn't it?"

"Afraid so. And here you are, in the seat of the enemy. How's it feel?"

"Shitty," she said. "And—and is it honest? I mean, am I in love with him, Monica? Or am I just sleeping with him?"

There was a pause. "That's a question for you?" she asked.

"Maybe?" she suggested.

"If it is, I can't answer it."

"Damn," she muttered.

"Really, Lilah. Is it a question?"

"I guess it must be, sort of, since I asked it. Only, I don't know if it's just a question because I'm nervous about Thomas, or because it really is a question."

"Maybe," Monica said, "you should take it one man at a time. The Foundation likes to keep things simple."

"Okay," she said. "Okay. First, Thomas."

"When?"

"I don't know. He plans to stay a week. Today's Thursday, right? Maybe tomorrow, then. Or—Saturday—no. Sunday. There's a powwow on Saturday."

"Priorities, girl," Monica coached.

"No. I mean, yes. Priorities. The powwow. I want you to come. So you can meet Jack. Remember I told you about him?"

"I remember," she said. "And you notice I haven't been jumping up and down with enthusiasm. I remember what happened the last time you fixed me up with someone."

"There was nothing wrong with Charles."

"Oh, yeah. Nothing except that little Witness Protection Program thing he was in."

"He said he was an international surfer. How was I to know?"

"And this one's a handyman with an eye patch."

"Actually, he's a doctor, as it turns out," Delilah said. "Works in a clinic, and a group practice. And he's nice-looking. The patch is romantic. And he's patient and kind. Smart—not just brainy, but human smart, you know? And honest."

There was a long pause, while Monica digested this. "Tell me something," she said. "He's all that, why don't you snatch him up?"

"Monica," Delilah said, "I'm trying to break up with one guy so I can keep sleeping with another one. What makes you think I've got room in my schedule?"

Another long pause. "Okay," she said. "I'll meet him. That's all, though."

"Saturday," Delilah said. "At the powwow."

"Oh. A cultural event. That can be lovely. Where is it?"

"I'm not sure. I'll find out and call you back. Listen, I better go."

"Okay. One question," she said.

"Shoot," Delilah said.

"What do you wear to a powwow?" she asked.

Delilah told her jeans, sneakers, and a left-wing political T-shirt would probably suit just fine.

fire

The rest of the week proceeded without major crisis. Carla met Thomas, snarled a few words, and retired to her room. Delilah took Thomas out a lot, to keep him out of her way, and they drove around, looking at places like the University, and the apartment she used to live in. She wasn't sure why people liked to do that kind of thing—see places from other people's past, as if just viewing a building would tell some secret about who she was—but they did. Thomas snapped a lot of pictures while Delilah had jitters about the possibility of running into Michael.

Then, every night before she went to sleep Delilah checked to make sure Carla had taken her insulin, in the right measure, and to take care of her feet.

"You don't have to check on me," Carla growled at her as she carefully applied ointment with a Q-tip, as Jack had instructed her, to the small wound that still hadn't healed.

"I don't care," Delilah said. "I am checking on you. No swelling in your ankles? Urine strips coming out okay?"

"Yes. And it's a fine day," Carla commented, "when a little girl who dates boys like Thomas gets to check up on me."

"Someone has to take care of you," Delilah noted.

"Me," Carla snarled. "I take care of me. You think I *want* to have my feet chopped off? Go on dialysis?"

"Good night, Carla," Delilah said, and left the room.

In this way, they somehow got to Saturday, which started out overcast and uncertain. Carla was taciturn at breakfast, while Thomas, always chatty in the morning, asked her questions about the house, which she answered in monosyllables, using glares for punctuation. Delilah had managed to avoid breakfast before this, saying she preferred to have time alone with Thomas, which was a lie, but at least no blood had been shed.

Halfway through the English muffins, Thomas picked up his camera and aimed it at Carla, and Delilah thought all her efforts were about to go down the tube, but Carla did the right thing. She got up and left the room.

Delilah watched the sky, fearing for rain the way you do when you're a child looking forward to the beach. This was a big day, after all. Delilah would start it by matchmaking Monica and Jack, and end it by breaking up with Thomas, since she had a date with Michael on Monday night and didn't want to miss it.

She knew it might have been jumping the gun to arrange that, but she did, calling him while Thomas was investigating the pole barn, telling him she'd have her family stuff cleared by Monday, and was he free for pizza? He said he was, but he was at work and sounded distracted, so he didn't talk long. He also said he missed her, and looked forward to it, which was nice to hear.

The overcast turned to sun instead of rain, with a lot of feeling in it. A nice warm day in late summer. Delilah had gotten directions from Jack and passed them on to Monica, and they'd decided it was best, given the delicacy of the various situations, that they all arrive under their own steam. She and Thomas got there first.

The powwow site was an open field, with vendors' tents set up in a circle around the perimeter, and a roped-off section in the middle where drumming and dancing was already going on. People in tribal regalia, people in jeans and T-shirts, people wheeling babies or walking with canes shopped at the vendor booths, or sat and watched the dancing, eating buffalo burgers and fry bread.

"Wow," Thomas said, spotting a man in full-feathered headdress and carrying a tomahawk. "This is pretty cool." He had his camera out, and started pointing it at things.

"Thomas," Delilah said, "some places have rules about photos. Maybe you should ask first."

"Oh. Right. Who do I ask?"

"At the entrance, I think. They'll tell you."

He wandered off in that direction, and she saw him stopping to talk to a woman in a deerskin dress and moccasins. She found a seat on the ground outside the dance circle and sat to watch the dancers. Knowing Thomas, it would take him a while to remember where she was, and that maybe he should hang around with her a little bit.

A group of dancers were just finishing up something they called a deer dance. She admired what they wore, then closed her eyes and listened to the drumming and the chanting. The open-throated singing that's always best outside where it can reverberate against the hills and wind its way up to the sky, along with the drumming that was deep enough to feel inside her chest, seemed to clean her out somehow, and calm her at the same time.

When they were done, the emcee got to the mike and said,

"We're bringing out some people from Mexico City, here to share some Aztec dancing with us."

Three people entered the circle—a man, a woman, and a little girl. They wore short deerskin skirts trimmed in gold and red and blue, and headdresses with feathers streaming out behind for at least three feet. On the front of each headdress was a grinning skull.

"Looks like fun," a voice said behind her.

She twisted her head around and looked up. It was Jack.

"Hey," she said. "You got here."

"I did," he admitted, and took a seat next to her. "Aren't you here with . . ."

"Thomas," she said. She waved a hand in the direction of the crowd. "He's taking pictures, I think. Shh. They're starting."

The man stepped to the center of the circle and spoke. "Hi. I'm Felix Ruiz, and this is my wife, Luisa, my daughter, Celinda. We say this is a dance in English, but really we're doing sort of cosmic movements. And we start with asking permission for the four directions to open up."

He began beating a drum. The little girl made a circle, stopping at each direction to blow into a conch shell, the sound rising like another kind of singing, while the woman—her mother—walked behind with burning sage. Delilah, stealing a glance at Jack, noticed that he was paying close attention, occasionally nodding and humming to himself.

"You know this?" she asked.

"It's the four directions," he said, as if everyone knew what that meant. "You always start there."

She turned back to the dance and as the dance progressed, and she saw how the dancers placed themselves in each direction, she thought she understood. There was something important about talking to the unseen forces of a place, and knowing where you stood in relationship to them. It was not prayer in the traditional sense of asking for something, but it was prayerful. It was, she thought, about being who you were, where you were, and staying in touch with what was around you.

When they were done, they went back to the center of the circle, and Felix spoke about the next dance, which he called Dance of the Smoking Mirror, which was to honor some of what they called the darker forces in the world.

"It's to honor some of what you might call the forces of darkness. We know they exist," he said, "and they can't be ignored. If you try, well, it's a mistake."

The sun beat down and heat encased the area. Delilah and Jack were silent, watching. Something the dancers were doing—their song, the smoke from the sage, or perhaps the drum—seemed to change the air around them. Made it more liquid, as if they danced under water, or as if beings made of liquid energy that reached up from the earth swirled around the legs of the dancers, touching them lightly, enfolding and releasing them. Delilah had no way of naming it, or explaining it. She only knew she perceived it. Like lightning, it was a mystery. Delilah squinted over at Jack, who was staring hard.

"You see it?" he murmured.

"Mmm," she said.

"Good. Then it's not my eye."

Was it possible that they'd called up darker forces, and danced with them? Was it possible that such forces actually did exist? Delilah, raised by Marxists, had no religion to speak of. Her father was a secular Jew, and never insisted on any kind of education in that area for his children. And she had no interest in it after Joshua died. She couldn't imagine a God who would let that kind of thing happen.

But maybe there were gods who didn't have good intents toward humans. Maybe there were gods like lightning, who had no intent at all, and just did what they did, regardless. Maybe dancing was the only way to deal with them, after all.

Delilah watched the way the three dancers used their feet and hands. The way they bowed to the earth and turned their faces up to the sun from that position. Keeping it all in balance with their bodies, she thought. That's what this is about. And as far as she could tell, it worked.

When it was done, she let out a long sigh of satisfaction.

"That's for sure," Jack agreed.

The dancers acknowledged the applause with thanks, and then said they were going to do a social dance. "So Felix will come around and invite you in," Luisa said. "It's really polite to say yes when he does, by the way."

Jack shifted, as if to go, and Delilah turned a look at him. "Oh, no," she said. "You're not going anywhere. I can't leave, and I'm not going in alone."

"Ha," he said. "Ha ha."

"That's right."

Felix reached them, and extended his hand. Delilah rose, and nodded at Jack, who also rose, and they went into the circle with a lot of other people.

"This is fine," Felix said. "Now, I'm going to show you some steps, and you just have to do what I do. Okay?"

They all nodded. The men looked nervous.

"But let's just try it out with a few people first. I want some beautiful women. Could some beautiful women raise their hands, please?"

Delilah laughed, but then Jack grabbed her arm and raised it. "There's one now," Felix said. "I want about three more, and then I need some ugly men. Any ugly men here today?"

Delilah recognized an opportunity when it slapped her in the face. She pointed at Jack. "There's one," she said.

Felix grinned at him. "Come on over here," he said.

When four beautiful women were facing four ugly men, Felix said he'd teach the steps to the dance.

"Like this," he said, and did something rather complicated that to Delilah looked like a cossack's dance. It involved squatting and kicking at the same time, and twisting his heel around, too.

"Now you do it," he said to the men.

With a lot of reluctance and not much panache, they tried, though Delilah noticed Jack had that evil grin on his face, and he really was able to do that kicking thing. He stared right at her, daring her all the while.

"Now it's the ladies' turn," Felix said, and repeated the steps.

The women, of course, acquitted themselves marvelously, making up for a lack of training with a maximum of attitude.

"Now that was nice," Felix said, as the audience applauded. "Which one do you think did better—the men or the women?"

The women won based on the volume of cheering, but Felix said he couldn't quite tell which it was, so they had to do it again. Everybody laughed.

"Maybe just a couple of people this time, though," he said. He looked at Delilah. "You," he said. He pointed at Jack. "And you."

Delilah wasn't laughing anymore.

Jack mouthed words at her. She thought they were, "I'm going to kill you for this," but she couldn't be sure. Everyone else sat down, and she and Jack were left in the middle of the circle with Felix, who showed them another complicated series of steps, this time enlisting his wife to dance with him. They involved not only squatting and kicking, but also dancing around each other back-to-back, and then Felix linking his arms in Luisa's, and flipping her over his back, whereupon she landed on her feet and leapt up at him, chasing him around.

Delilah looked at Jack. Now he was grinning. It didn't look good.

The drumbeat started, and like good sports, they began the squatting and kicking. The audience started to clap in time, and Delilah noticed in her peripheral vision that Monica had arrived, and was standing outside the dance circle, wide-eyed. In back of her, she could see Thomas nearby, snapping pictures in the other direction. So far, he didn't seem to notice what she was doing. That, at least, was a mercy.

They got to the dancing back-to-back part, when someone in the crowd shouted, "Flip her. Flip her over." Monica's eyes got bigger.

Delilah thought she heard Jack swear, but by then everyone was chanting, "Flip her. Flip her. Flip her."

Delilah felt his arms link hers, and she was up off the ground. She rolled with it, thinking of the trust fall, thinking he won't let me fall too hard, he doesn't drop people, thinking I hope he doesn't have a bad back or anything. She thought she saw Thomas, looking somehow closer than he could possibly have been, taking pictures of it all.

She was briefly airborne, then her feet were solidly on the ground. Her relief was immense. Then, as Luisa had done with Felix, she leapt up and chased Jack around, kicking her heels as she went. The crowd clapped and whooped, and she felt triumphant. She'd been lifted off the earth, and returned to it in one piece, and she was sure she was a goddess, albeit a minor one.

The drumming gave out just before she did, and while everyone applauded, she and Jack were called into the center of the circle. Felix handed them each some long, dark feathers like the ones in his headdress.

"You guys did okay," he said, "but there's something you should know." He looked to his wife.

"That's right," she said. "Felix here performs the marriages in our village, and what you two just did was a wedding dance. So, you're married. You can kiss the bride."

More laughter from the crowd. Delilah wished she could see Monica's face, but she couldn't because Jack's face, looking a little stunned, was blocking her view.

"Kiss the bride," someone shouted.

"Yeah, kiss her," someone else added unnecessarily. Before they started chanting, he pulled Delilah to him, shrugged a little apologetically, and put his mouth against hers.

It didn't last long. Not long enough to call it a real kiss. If Thomas saw it, he wouldn't think anything of it at all. Jack broke away and was preparing to leave the circle, but somebody in the crowd booed.

"That's no kiss. Kiss her, man. Can't you kiss her?" somebody called out.

"Yeah, kiss her. Kiss her," other voices joined in.

Mob mentality is vicious, Delilah decided, but didn't get farther than that in a polemic on the topic because this time Jack made a sound like he was growling, put a hand on her arm, and pulled her close. Then his hand was on her face and his mouth was on hers, this time really kissing her, with his lips soft and tender and his hand at the back of her neck, making her skin tingle.

She grabbed at his arms so she wouldn't fall down because there was something roaring in her ears. Her knees felt weak and the kiss seemed to go on and on, though she really couldn't tell if it was a minute or a month because it was like the time in the trust fall that came between falling and being caught. An eternal now, impervious to any normal measure of time. Just his mouth on hers, and her body feeling the electricity that seemed to buzz all around his skin.

Then, she felt a tap on her shoulder, and heard someone clearing a throat. She pulled away, and Jack released her and they stood facing each other, slightly out of breath. His jaw was tight, and the muscles around it were moving. She was sure she was gaping, but didn't know what to do to change that.

"That was—um—fine," Felix said, and she turned to see he was standing behind her, looking a little nervous.

Someone shouted, "Kiss her again." For a minute, Delilah thought Jack was going to, but Felix took her arm and started leading her out of the circle.

"Okay, you two," he said. "Save something for the honeymoon."

More laughter. They left the circle, clutching their feathers.

Jack waved to the people gathered outside, who applauded him. From behind his smile he said, "Bet that's the last time you make me dance."

"Maybe," she said back, "and maybe not."

He stopped his steps and twisted around to look at her with his good eye.

"Oh, look," Delilah said brightly. "It's Thomas, and Monica. Everybody's here. How nice."

"Hey," Thomas said, coming up to her, smiling. "I got it all on film. Some great shots. Especially that flipping stuff. You two were great."

No, she thought. Her men weren't the possessive type. Not most of them, anyway.

"We were, weren't we?" Jack agreed, looking a little triumphant.

"Jack," Delilah said, "this is my friend Monica. Monica, this is Jack."

"So nice to meet you," she said, putting out a hand. "And you didn't drop Delilah. How good of you."

"I don't drop people," he said. "Throw them, yes. Drop them, no. Delilah knows that about me."

"You know what?" Delilah said. "I'm hungry. Anybody want anything? A buffalo burger or something?"

"I'd like that," Monica said. "Why don't we go together?"

This was not her plan. Not at all. She thought fast. She reached down and grabbed at her ankle. "I think that flip maybe did something to my ankle. Would you mind if I sat down a minute? You can go with Jack. He knows what's good to eat. I'll wait here with Thomas. Do you mind?"

"Not at all," Jack said with feeling.

Monica gave her the look that translated to the word "bitch," then put her social grace on. That's what the state pays her big bucks for, Delilah thought. And off they went. She sat down, and Thomas joined her, shooting a few random pictures.

Her thoughts were confused. Her feelings were confused. Had she just been kissed for real? More important, did any of this count, for instance, in the afterlife? When she died, would she wake up married to Jack Brown for all of an Aztec eternity? She stopped a moment and asked herself how she felt about that prospect, then decided she didn't want to think about it. She had too much else to deal with. She turned to Thomas.

He was staring up at the sky, his mouth open.

"What're you doing?" she asked.

"The bag," he said, pointing up.

She looked where he pointed. A plastic grocery bag had been caught up by the wind and was rising into the sky like a balloon released from a hand.

"I didn't know they went that high," he said, snapping a few shots, then lowering his camera. "Look at that."

She did. It rose almost straight up, caught in some current that was invisible, couldn't even be felt by those on the ground. But it was lifting it up, and up, and up some more. They stared, waiting to see if it would fall back down. Things that go up are supposed to come back down. So all the laws said.

"You think it'll get caught in an airplane or something?" he asked.

"Mess up a bird is more like it," Delilah said.

But it continued to rise until it was nothing more than a speck, and then it disappeared into a cloud. Gone. Defying gravity. Defying all visible means of support. Just gone. Delilah wondered if it would ever come down to hang like a ghost of sin in a tree, or if it would just keep going up, in a moment of flight and absolution. She had the distinct sensation of something ending, in a very complete way.

"Cool," Thomas said. "But out of range."

Thomas smiled and touched her hand. She couldn't help herself. She jerked away.

"Thomas," she said. "We have to talk."

He blinked at her and adjusted his glasses. "Okay. Go ahead."

"Maybe not right here. Maybe we should leave. Go back to the house and talk there."

"This sounds serious," he said. "Is something wrong?"

"No. Not wrong. Just—we have to talk. We should go."

"But we have food coming." He waved at Monica and Jack, who were approaching. Monica was smiling, but Jack was not. He was scowling. At her.

"Buffalo burgers," she said with feeling.

They arrived, and food was handed out. Delilah noticed Jack didn't have any.

"Not hungry?" she asked.

"I have to leave," he said. "I've got the clinic tonight."

"On a Saturday? I thought you worked there Tuesday and Thursday."

"They asked me to take an extra shift. Somebody sick." He put a hand out to Monica. "It's really nice to meet you. I'll see you again, I hope?"

"I'm sure you will," she said, smiling brightly. "All my pleasure."

He tipped a nod at Delilah, then one at Thomas, and then he left.

"Well," Monica said. "After all that excitement, I'm just starved. You?"

"Ravenous," Thomas said.

"How about you, Delilah? Didn't all that make you just starved?"

"Right," she agreed, giving Monica an evil look. "Famished."

But she actually was pretty hungry, so she ate, and then they went around to the booths and bought stuff. But all she could think about was that she wanted to get back to the house and talk to Thomas. Get it over with, before Monday made a dishonest woman of her one more time.

combined elements: water and fire

Delilah didn't break up with Thomas that night. After the powwow they went to see a movie he wanted to catch, at the same theater they'd been to the night before. An independent film about people who are confused about love. How appropriate, Delilah thought. When they got home, he was so tired he just plopped on the bed. When Delilah went into his room to talk to him after she brushed her teeth, he was already fast asleep.

In the morning, the first thing that happened was a knock on her bedroom door. Delilah sat up hard.

"What?" she said. "Who?"

"Get up," Carla's voice said. "Come to the kitchen."

She got out of bed, dressed quickly in shorts and tank top, and made her way downstairs. She stood in the kitchen. "Carla?" she asked. No answer.

However, there was a clatter from the room that housed the

heating units, so she went toward that. Another catastrophe? She hoped not. She didn't know how even her parents' budget would hold up.

She opened the door and looked inside. It wasn't a door she'd opened yet, and she wasn't sure what she'd find there, but all she saw were pipes and machinery. "Carla?" she asked again.

"Nope," Jack's voice answered. "Just me."

Delilah scratched her head. "She told me to come downstairs. Is something wrong?"

He leaned back from some pipes he was doing something to and looked at her. "Just plugging another leak," he said.

"Better than taking one," she said. "Ha ha. Get it?"

"Hmmph," he said.

"You aren't laughing at my stupid jokes anymore? I count on you for that."

"Right," he said, and banged a pipe with his wrench. He muttered something.

"What?" she asked.

"Nothing," he said sullenly.

"Are you vexed?"

"Vexed?" he asked. "Vexed?"

"Vexed. Upset. Peevish. In a mood."

He mumbled something else. A mood, Delilah thought. Or hoped. "Hey," she said cheerfully, "isn't Monica great? I'm glad you got to meet her. I mean, she's really something. Smart, and has this great job. She's not driven or anything, but she's conscientious about her work, you know? A woman of character. She's great, right?"

He looked at her fiercely. He took in a big breath and let it out. He put down the wrench.

"I told you my parents were killed in a car accident."

"Yes," she said tentatively. "Yes. You did."

"You know what that taught me?"

"Um—what?" she asked.

"To hate waste. I hate waste. In any form. Human or other-wise. That's why I'm vexed. Hell, not vexed. Mad at you."

"At me?"

"You," he said.

"I'm sorry, but I don't know what the hell you're talking about."

"You don't? Not a clue? That's convenient."

"What?" she asked. "What is it? Tell me what it is I'm doing wrong. Don't do this background-noise crap with me."

"Background-noise crap?"

"Yes. You're too chickenshit to come out and say what's eating you, so you bring up background noise. You hate waste and so on. Human Waste 102. I recognize crap when I smell it."

He sounded for all the world like a jealous lover, or wannabe lover, but if he didn't come out and say what he wanted, she couldn't tell if that was her ego, or the truth. She did know that he was not saying something, and it pissed her off. She was no good at guessing games.

They glared at each other.

"Your turn," Delilah said at last. "Come up with something good."

"It's—it's watching you throw your life away," he spit out. "No job. No direction. Sleeping with that loser."

Delilah was shocked. How did he know who she was sleeping with? Had Carla said something, damn her busybody tongue?

"Michael?" she spit out. "He's—he's not a loser. He works for the legislature. He has a nice apartment. He's involved."

When she saw his jaw begin to gape open, and a look of com-bined shock and pain form on his face, she realized her mistake.

He wasn't talking about Michael. He didn't know about

Michael until she told him. He was talking about Thomas. Delilah, who wasn't sleeping with Thomas, didn't think of him. Her sister always said she took things too literally. She opened her mouth to try to reclaim her losses, but it was clearly too late.

"Michael? You're sleeping with Michael? That old friend of yours who wants to get you a job with CEP?"

"Actually, ex-fiancé. We were engaged. We broke up. Then . . . I just ran into him, and, well, things happened."

"That's the way you see it? Like you don't have a choice? Things just happen?"

"They do," she said. "At least a lot of them do. And I'm not saying I didn't have a choice. I just—I chose that."

"But—what about Thomas?"

"I'm going to break up with him," she said. "I've just been waiting for the right time."

"And the right job, and the right man and the right life? Jesus, and I thought you had integrity. You sure talk like you do. My mistake."

He picked up his wrench and started doing things to pipes.

"I haven't been sleeping with Thomas," Delilah said. "He sleeps in the other room. Carla has a no-creaking-bed rule. And I knew it wasn't going anywhere."

"And now you'll use love to justify any number of lies."

"I didn't say love," she said vehemently. "You don't have to be in love to sleep with someone."

He stopped doing things to pipes and looked at her, saying nothing. Apparently sleeping with Michael without being in love was even worse.

"It's complicated," she continued. "There's history, and—and trying to figure things out and—Jesus, you don't have any claim on me. I can sleep with whoever I want. I don't have to explain myself to you."

"No," he said, calm now. "You don't. You have to explain it to him."

He pointed behind her.

She turned slowly, with a bad feeling in her stomach. Thomas was standing there, looking shocked.

"Oh," Delilah said. "Hi."

She turned back to Jack. "I'll just be going now. See you around."

"Yeah," he said. "Good luck with that integrity thing."

Having ruined her life, he went back to doing things to pipes.

Delilah closed the door to the furnace room, and stood looking at Thomas, who stood looking at her.

"Well," he said, drawing on his dignity, "I guess that's pretty clear. I wish you'd told me, though."

"Thomas," she said, "I'm sorry. I tried. I told you we had to talk."

"Yeah. Wish you'd done it before I took pictures of you kissing him."

"I'm really—what?"

"I mean, that's kind of tacky, isn't it? To kiss him right there in front of me?"

"Who?"

"Him. Jack. Who you're sleeping with."

"I'm not sleeping with Jack," she said trying not to laugh. "What makes you think that?"

"Jeez, Delilah. I'm not stupid. He's yelling at you for telling lies. You're telling him you can do what you want. I mean, duh, right?"

"I think," she said, "you missed the pertinent parts. For the record, I'm not sleeping with Jack. I'm kissing with Jack. No. I mean, what you saw yesterday wasn't that."

"What was it?"

She struggled for words. She couldn't honestly say it was nothing, but she didn't have a clue what it was, except that it felt wonderful, which troubled her.

"I'm *not* sleeping with him," she said at last. "Truly I'm not. He's been—a *very* good friend." And that, she thought, at least that much, was certainly true. A good man. A good friend. She had a moment of sorrow, thinking that might end.

Thomas looked slightly mollified. "I thought it was just for show, but the way he was talking to you I get the idea it's not."

"How was he talking to me?"

"Well, like it mattered to him."

Delilah thought about that. Thomas was right. Jack argued with her like it mattered to him. And she was arguing back the same way. The one man she wasn't sleeping with was the one who seemed to care the most what she did with her days. She began to feel like she should have a headache. She rubbed at her forehead, but none came.

"It's not Jack," she said. "I'm sleeping with Michael. My ex, remember?" she added when he looked momentarily blank. "Jack is pissed at me about it. I don't know why, so don't ask. I guess—it does matter to him. My life matters to him. And the thing is, it never seemed to matter to you."

Thomas adjusted his glasses. "I care about you, Lilah," he said.

"I know. I'm not criticizing you. Maybe it just doesn't matter enough. Or in the right way, for either of us."

Thomas grimaced, and held up a hand as if to point a finger at her and yell, then he dropped his arm and shrugged. "Maybe you're right," he admitted.

He sighed. She sighed. There it was.

"What do we do now?" he asked.

"I think you go back to Key West."

"Where in Key West?" he asked a little plaintively.

"Well, to my parents' house."

"That doesn't seem right."

"They like you for who you are. Besides, everybody stays there. You know that."

"I guess. Couldn't I stay here a while? It's nice here."

She shook her head. "If you stay, she'll make you work. You don't like to work."

"Maybe that's why we got along so well," he said.

"No," she said, realizing a new truth. "I like to work. I really do. I just haven't found the work I like."

"I guess. Look," he said. "No hard feelings, okay?"

No, she thought. It takes some kind of feeling to have hard feelings, and that was the problem. They didn't have enough feeling at all.

"No hard feelings," she agreed. "None at all."

Jack worked for another hour, though he knew he could have finished the job in fifteen minutes if he'd hurried. Instead, he took his time, going slowly and double-checking everything he did.

When he heard the sound of a car starting outside, he peeked his head out of the room. All clear, he thought. He went to the living room, looked out the window, and saw that Delilah's car was gone.

He didn't know where she'd gone, or if Thomas went with her, but he didn't care if Thomas was around. He just didn't want to see Delilah.

He went back into the furnace room and cleaned up, put his tools away. He picked up his tool case and brought it to his car, threw it in the backseat. Then, he went around the back of the house and sat by the pond.

Once there, he asked himself a serious question: Why did he always fall for crazy women?

No, he thought. Not crazy. Just—well, a little wild. Off the beaten track. Outliers. His first girlfriend used to paint blue under her eyes to ward off evil spirits. The woman he dated for two years when he was in med school was a practicing witch. The only woman he'd slept with since his divorce liked to take all her clothes off and dance in the rain. Which he didn't mind, except that she liked to do it in the city park.

He'd married his now ex-wife because she seemed unlike that. She was so calm, so gentle. When they made love, she stroked him endlessly, didn't scream during orgasm, and never cried afterward the way some women did, for reasons he couldn't figure out. But it turned out she was an outlier anyway. Somewhat outside the bell curve. A statistical anomaly.

He'd been stunned when she told him. It just wasn't what he expected to happen between them. And he couldn't figure out how she could have hidden it for so long.

"Did you ever like sex with me?" he remembered shouting at her.

"I *liked* it," she said, still calm, still gentle. "But with women—well, I *love* that."

It figured, he thought.

And then, there was Delilah.

She at least, didn't give any illusion of calm, or normalcy. He couldn't rest in denial, telling himself she was an easier kind of person to be with. With her, he had to admit to himself that he simply preferred crazy women. He just wished he knew why, so that he could at least have a possibility of changing that behavior.

Was he playing doctor? Savior? He didn't think so. He could get that urge satisfied on the job, ten times over. He didn't seem to want to fix them, anyway. He just wanted to be with them.

The piercing cry of a hawk slid over the sky and down to him. He looked up, shielding his face from the glare of the sun, but he couldn't see it. He could only hear it. It was a sound that went through him, and he liked the feeling of that. Maybe, he thought, he just liked wildness in general, and that liking extended itself to women. He liked the way it went right to the heart, and stayed there.

He did seem to prefer all things that were unique, oddly made, slightly irregular. He wondered if it had anything to do with his own life, the fact that he was an outlier, and like was drawn to like. Son of a Polish immigrant and a fairly traditional Mohawk, he didn't truly fit in any one place, though he was comfortable in many different places. He could sit through mass and sing all the hymns, or sit in a longhouse and listen to the Thanksgiving Address roll out for hours, as one of the elders went on and on, thanking all things, each in their own peculiarity.

He often said the Thanksgiving Address by himself, in fact, turning to the earth, the sun, all living creatures, one by one, and saying the ritual words. To say it alone felt odd at first, because each thanking ended with the line "and now, our minds are as one." But after doing it a few times, he realized that his mind was becoming one with each thing he thanked, and so it was appropriate. Each time he did so, he grew closer to the earth, the rivers, the trees and plants and animals and fish. And that couldn't be anything but good.

"And now," he said to himself, "we turn our thoughts to the crazy women of the world. Creator put them here to . . ."

To what? he asked himself. Because that was the thing about the Thanksgiving Address. It named the tasks of all things on the earth, and gave them thanks for doing it. The moon, which was responsible for all things relating to women. The birds, which were painted brightly and sang beautifully so that when humans felt they couldn't go on, their hearts would be renewed by seeing their colors and hearing them sing. The waters, which cleansed everything, and the stars, which lighted the night.

Everything had a task—even humans, who were here to live in harmony and give thanks. That was all. Nothing more. At least, that was what the chiefs said, though he had an uncle who told him the job of humans was to tell stories. It amused the animals, so that they could keep up with their job, which was basically to run the world.

Story makers, Jack thought. That was what humans were. Nothing more or less.

Personally, he thought the job of humans, who were highest on the food chain, was to simply take care. Take care of each other. Take care of things like turtles, and ants, the land itself. Take care of rivers and trees and so on. Having evolved an inordinate amount of power and intelligence, their job was to think about ways to love all that, and care for it, in every way they could.

It was simple, but like most simple things, it wasn't necessarily easy. It had to be worked out in the details, and to really love had something complex and fierce and burning at the center of it, like the earth itself, hot and molten at the core. It involved stretching the self in ways that aren't always comfortable, and an acceptance of unpredictability, lack of control, potential loss. Because love was always unpredictable. And slightly out of control.

And maybe, he thought, the job of crazy women was to remind men of that, thus doing their part for love.

He felt a shiver, signaling for him the arrival of a truth.

There it was, he thought. He was falling in love with Delilah because she reminded him that love was not neat, or subject to his needs. It was something you gave, wild and free, regardless. And he would have to own up to it, regardless. Stop hiding behind the background noise, and get real, with himself, and even with her.

"We turn our thoughts to crazy women everywhere," he said. "They teach us how to love, without restraint or reason. If we didn't have them, men would forget that they were alive. If we didn't have them, much of the beauty of the world would go unseen, and so we send to them our thanks, our greetings, and our love."

As he spoke, some motion in the house, or just a sense of energy shifting, drew his attention. He looked toward it, and saw Carla's face at the sliding glass doors. She was watching him, intently, and when he turned her way, she nodded.

"And now," he finished, "our minds are as one."

SEVENTEEN

earth

Thomas left that night, booking a red-eye. After Delilah dropped him off at the airport, she stopped in at Monica's.

"You decent?" she asked when Monica answered her intercom. "And alone?"

"Both, I'm sorry to say. Why didn't you use your key?"

"In case you weren't. I thought Jack might find solace in your arms."

"Come up," she said, and buzzed her in.

As soon as she entered the apartment, Delilah saw that Monica was seated at the dining room table with a napkin and a pen.

"Uh-oh," she said. "What's that?"

"The minutes of a Foundation meeting. You weren't available, so I had it in your absence."

Delilah sat down and watched her write.

"What's it say?" she asked, peering at it. Monica had an awful scrawl.

"It notes improvement in the Foundation's choice of men. Jack is a lovely man."

"You think?"

"A lovely person. You know that about him right away."

"You do?"

"Of course you do."

"How?"

"Well, by the way he treats other people, of course. He's very kind. A kind man."

"Then why didn't you stay with him?"

"There was something else you know about him right away." She wrote some more. Delilah tried to see what it was, but couldn't.

"What?" she asked.

Monica sighed. "It's obvious to the most casual observer."

"I'm not. The most casual observer. You know that about me."

"Tell me this, first. Are you seeing Michael tonight?"

"Tomorrow night."

"Then we'll table this for future discussion, and move to the next item on the agenda." She put the pen down and folded up the napkin. "Is Thomas gone?"

"Dumped and gone," Delilah said.

"How did it go?"

"Quietly. But there wasn't ever much heat between us, so it ended the way it started."

"It always does. That's what my mother told me. Only she said it in Spanish, which sounded much better. So you and Michael? Moving forward?"

Delilah shrugged. "I think so. He said something about helping me find a job. I'm figuring that means he'd like me to stay."

"Oh my. Will I have my wedding after all? With dresses and cakes and guest lists? Coordinating linens?"

"Can't," Delilah said. "I'm already married. Aztec style."

Monica waved it away. "The Foundation isn't yet prepared to discuss the implications of that. Unless you are?"

Delilah shook her head. "There's no implications. Just good clean fun. Though . . ."

"What?" Monica asked.

Delilah shrugged it off. "Nothing. Men are all nuts, I think. It's the testosterone. But I still can't promise you a wedding to Michael."

"Because of him, or because of you?"

She opened her mouth to say because of him, of course. She didn't know if she could trust him again. She didn't know if he meant it. And so on. Then, she realized that she was the one who didn't know. If she could trust herself. If she meant it. And only some of that had to do with not trusting him.

"You know," she said, surprised at herself. "For two years, since we split, I've wondered on and off what it would be like to get back together with him. Now that it's here, I'm not sure. Maybe both."

"The gods have given you a great gift," Monica said. "Tell me this—if he asked you tomorrow, would you say yes?"

She frowned. "I wouldn't leap to it," she said.

"Then you wouldn't say yes," Monica noted. "Marriage is a leap of faith, based on gut instinct. If you're not leaping, you better stay home."

"More like a trust fall, I think," Delilah said.

"A what?"

"Nothing. I'm just babbling. I'm tired, I guess. I should go home now."

Monica looked confused. "You're going back to Key West? Tonight?"

"No," Delilah said. "Of course not. Whatever gave you that idea?"

"Well, you said home."

"Oh," she said. "You're right. I did. Huh. I meant Carla's. Now that's scary, isn't it?"

"Maybe. Or maybe not. There's worse homes." Monica eyed her. "You must have a lot to think about. Or not think about, as the case may be."

"Yeah," Delilah said. "As the case. I'll call you."

"Say hello to Jack for me," she said. "Such a lovely person."

The house was quiet after Delilah left, taking that stupid boy with her. Carla had shuddered, meeting him, but resisted saying anything because after all, who did she have to blame but herself?

She had been the one to give up her daughter. And giving up her daughter, she'd also relinquished all the lessons she might have taught the granddaughter that would have kept her from stupid boys like Thomas.

But Delilah was doing the right thing there, at least. She was sending him away. Not that Carla was surprised. She didn't even have to do anything about it anymore. Delilah had started listening to the land, and that was a voice she could never walk away from again. It might even take care of that other stupid boy. It should.

Carla was satisfied. And the house was quiet.

She wandered its silence like a cat, padding from room to room, touching things, burying her face in the curtains and smelling their particular odor. As much as she was glad to have Delilah here, she was glad to be alone. Years in the circus, living in trains and trailers, had robbed her of alone time and now she coveted it the way some people coveted money after they'd been poor.

For all the time since then it had been a tenuous balance for her, that between being with people and being alone. Fortunately, her house was big enough that she could have both at once if she wanted to. And still she craved more.

Soon, she thought. Soon she'd have enough and then some.

She had the sense of things coming to a head. She had the sense of something about to break—this time, not anything in her house.

She went into the front parlor and turned on the TV. She could watch *Homicide* in peace tonight. She would enjoy it while she could.

fire

 Delilah slept well that night, and got up the next morning thinking, "It's Monday. Pizza and Michael day. How nice."

She felt like an honest woman, too. Like she could really focus now. Monica was right. The Foundation needed to focus on one thing at a time.

When she got up and looked out the window, she saw that Jack's car was not in evidence, which was a relief. She didn't want a scene with him, or even his dark mood raining all over her parade. Just because he'd been her friend and kissed her at a powwow didn't mean he had the right to judge her life. She hadn't asked for the kiss. He hadn't even asked for it. It was just something that happened. But she could make a choice now to dismiss it, and him, and focus on what was real. Michael, and pizza.

She went downstairs and made herself breakfast, and then she and Carla sort of moseyed around the house, not talking much, though Carla kept casting glances at her. They weren't angry, or even irritated. Just glances, like she was trying to figure something out.

"Carla," Delilah said to her when she stood staring at her while she washed lunch dishes, "what is it?"

"What's what?" she asked.

"You keep looking at me like you expect me to turn into a lemur or something."

"No I don't," she said.

"Yes you do," Delilah countered.

"I don't even know what a lemur is. What is it?"

"A small furry animal. Our forebothers. Don't change the subject. Carla," she said, deciding it was time to make a frontal assault on a pressing problem, "my family wants to come see you. Can I tell them it's okay?"

"Your family?" Carla asked, just as if this were a new topic. Sometimes Delilah worried about her mind.

"Your other granddaughter. Your son-in-law. Your daughter."

Carla scowled, then smoothed her face. "I'll think about it," she said, and walked away. Delilah had to think of it as an evolutionary step forward, and let it be.

The rest of the day was quiet, and she had mostly the wind coming down off the ridge and the sound of birdsong as a companion. She found she was nervous about the evening, anxious for the hours to pass until nine, when she told him she'd get there, and to calm herself she worked in the garden, turned the compost, washed dishes, and then made sure that Carla had enough of the right food for dinner—Jack had mentioned that her albumin levels weren't getting any lower, and he had her on a strict diet. The hours passed, but she was acutely conscious of every one, until she showered and got dressed, then went downstairs, where she found Carla watching TV.

"I'm going out," she said.

"What for?" Carla shot back, not looking at her.

"To get a life," Delilah replied. She waited a moment, but Carla didn't say anything else, so she left.

When she got on the road, Delilah realized that what she said to Carla was the truth. She felt like it was time to get a life, whatever that meant. To Gen-Xers like her, according to all the surveys, that wasn't easy. They were known as the noncommittal generation. The ones with no defining moment like Vietnam or Pearl Harbor or walking on the moon or the Civil War. Because of that, they didn't really know where to put their energy, or how to direct it. Nothing defined that for them, and in fact, they were unwilling to have their lives defined. They didn't want to be pinned down.

Of course, it affected everyone in different ways. Michael was very committed to his work, and willing to put in the long days and nights. So was Monica. But neither was married. As far as Delilah could tell, Monica wasn't even close. And for herself—well, that was sort of the question. Sort of.

Maybe she wasn't ready to leap if Michael proposed, but she was ready to explore the possibilities, and she thought that was actually a very mature choice. Monica might think marriage was a leap, but Delilah thought it should be considered in a serious, sober way, thinking it through carefully before reaching a decision. She'd acted impulsively with him before, but now she knew better. She'd sort through the options and see what worked best for her. Besides, she wanted to settle the question of a job, which was also sensible. She should have her own life in order first.

She was still considering making a call to the man Michael

knew at CEP. It could be her opportunity to save the world. And even if it wasn't, at least she could earn her own living. After all, there were the environmentalists, and there were the people who created an economy so everyone could have houses and SUVs and so on. Maybe she was meant to be the latter, which could be a relief. To just work, and not worry about the world so much she couldn't actually do anything in it.

She could get an apartment, be near enough to Carla to help out, see what would develop with Michael. She didn't have to tell Carla who she was working for. Then again, if CEP hired her, they might send her to Alabama, which would be a whole other set of issues, and would certainly delay the question of marriage. That, she thought, might also be a relief.

And of course, they might not hire her, but there were other jobs, and if she didn't restrict herself to getting one that was politically correct, it might be easier to actually find one.

That was all longterm, though. In the short term, she was just where she wanted to be, doing just what she wanted to do, with the person she wanted to do it with. And how many people could say that out loud? By the time she got to Michael's apartment she was feeling very warmly toward him because she could.

She parked her car, and noted how fast the night was coming on these days. Though it was still summer, the days were getting shorter, which always gave her the same sinking feeling she'd had as a child, when back-to-school specials started their advertisements.

She ascended the front steps and glanced at the first-floor windows, which were his apartment. He not only had the whole first floor, he also had his own entrance. Inside was only dimly lit. He couldn't possibly be asleep, though. It was way too early for that, and Michael didn't take naps. She wondered if he'd gone out for beer or a movie, but she saw his car parked in front. Maybe, she thought, he was walking.

She pushed at the front door, which was open. It was a funny door, and if you forgot to push it just right, it wouldn't lock. He'd told her about it, to make sure she got it right when she left. It was unlike him to leave it open, she thought. He must have been anxiously awaiting her arrival. Or maybe he had some nice little surprise for her—champagne and candlelight, with him sitting at the table naked and a pizza in his lap.

She smiled. That would be like him.

She went inside, to his apartment door, and knocked. No answer. She put her hand on the knob to see if that was open, too. It wasn't.

"Michael?" she called in, knocking again. "It's Delilah. Monday night, remember? Pizza and me?"

She was about to give up and sit on the stoop to wait and see if he came home, when she heard footsteps, then his voice on the other side of the door.

"Delilah?" he asked.

"That's right," she admitted.

She thought she heard him say "oh shit," which should have tipped her off, but then again, maybe he stubbed his toe in the dark. The door opened, and he stood there, in his bathrobe. It was a nice bathrobe. Blue with a hood. She had bought it for him on the Christmas they got engaged.

"Delilah," he said, not moving from the door. "I had you penciled in for Tuesday."

"Oh," she said. "I see."

He continued to stand there, and she continued to see. Finally, she pushed him back and went inside, walking around him and toward the bedroom.

"Delilah," he called after her, with a different emphasis this time, simultaneously pleading and scolding.

She pushed the bedroom door open. The woman who sat in his bed clutching the sheets to herself was blond, and pretty. Michael always picked pretty women.

"Tiffany?" she asked.

"Amber," she said. She had a sultry voice. Michael liked a sultry voice. She turned around and walked back to the living room.

Michael was there, looking chagrined. She stopped and considered him, looking more angry than chagrined.

"Haven't we done this before?" she asked. "Only her name was Tiffany."

"Bonnie, actually."

"Right," Delilah said.

"Delilah," he said. "I'm sorry. I guess I thought it was Tuesday you were coming over. I mean, you said pizza, and most good places are closed Mondays."

"Right again. What happened—you lose the napkin?"

"What?"

"You forgot about number one on the list? That not-lying thing."

"I didn't lie," he said. "I didn't lie to you."

"You said . . ." she started, but then didn't know where to go with it.

"I said I wanted to sleep with you," Michael said. "I didn't say anything about wanting to sleep with *only* you."

She was quiet. He was right. His logic and his integrity remained intact. Even more intact than hers, since she'd actually had a boyfriend she hadn't told him about. It seemed they were doomed to never get close enough to be real with each other.

"Lilah, I didn't make you any promises. If you heard them, you were making them up for yourself."

"Yeah," she said. "I'm good at that."

"Don't be mad. Please don't be mad."

"I'm not," she said, and realized that she wasn't. Not at him, anyway. Because how could she be when she was no better? "I'm just—disappointed at myself, I guess."

"Why?" he asked. "You didn't do anything."

Yes, she thought. Even in this moment he knew how to placate, how to create sympathy and warmth. She laughed.

"Michael," she said, "you think you're the one who fools around, and I'm the one who claws at you for monogamy, but it's not true. I'm just like you," she said. "Terrified to make it real. Terrified to—to live it. And all this time, I've been blaming you."

"I don't think I understand," he said slowly, carefully.

"No," she said. "Neither do I, exactly. I just know the smell of crap when it wafts my way. Human Waste 102. I'll see you around."

She left his apartment, got in her car, and started to drive.

At first, as she drove, she felt nothing much. She was just thoughtful, trying to absorb the implications of the revelation she'd just had. Then, she felt more and more heat rise in her, and while she still didn't feel angry at him, she was, in short time, burning mad at herself. She was really, really mad. Mad with the kind of fury that wants to break things and scream obscenities and probably get arrested for doing stupid things. She'd allowed herself to be led into this game, do it all over again. Hell, she'd chosen it, when she had every reason to turn it away.

"Fuck this," she said, and pulled into the nearest liquor store.

She needed to do some damage.

She bought a bottle of tequila. A cheap tequila. Nothing good would do the kind of damage she was thinking about. There was a phone booth outside, and she called Monica to see if she wanted to help do damage, but she wasn't home. Another late night at work for her. Delilah took her bottle, and went back to Carla's. She was good enough not to open it until she got there.

The house was quiet, but that suited her. She sat down in the kitchen with all the lights off, opened her bottle, and started to drink. She had gotten one good slug down when the sliding glass doors opened, startling her and making her dribble tequila down her shirt.

"Jesus," she said. "What is it?"

In the shadowed doorway, she saw the outline of a small person. She squinted at it. Then she remembered something Jack had said about the melting ice caps and Kootch.

"Kootch?" she asked.

He took a step toward her. "Glasses are in the cupboard," he noted, and glided past her, out of the room.

"Thanks," she said to his receding back, "but I don't think I'll bother." He didn't respond. She raised the bottle again, and drank.

As she drank, she thought. She thought about what mistakes she made this time, why she made them, and most important, how she could avoid making them again. She considered the question, but found no answer, so she had another sip of tequila to oil the works. It didn't help, but it made her feel better.

"Fuck the question," she said, not too softly, after another sip or two. She clapped a hand over her mouth, waiting for Carla to leap out of a cupboard and yell at her. When she didn't, Delilah was emboldened to try it again. "Fuck the question," she said a little louder. She stood up to say it again, and knocked over her chair. When she picked it up, she set it back upright as hard as she could. "Ha," she said, really loud. "Ha ha ha. Stupid men. Stupid fucking questions."

She sat down, and wondered if she was actually getting

drunk, and decided she wasn't. She was just still really pissed off. She sat and nurtured the feeling for some time, feeling how it grew when she watered it with the tequila. Periodically, she stood up and named something else that needed fucking. Fuck thinking. Fuck maturity. Fuck fucking. She didn't think she was being very imaginative in her litany, but it felt good. Once or twice, she knocked over the chair again, and got to slam it around some more.

She didn't know how long that part of it lasted, because Carla believed in clocks only slightly more than she believed in mirrors, so Delilah had nothing to judge the passage of time except her internal signals and the motion of moonlight across the kitchen floor.

Though her internal signals weren't all they could have been, she did notice a shift in the plane of moonlight that lay across the floor, and that she was fairly far down in the bottle when she heard the front door opening and closing. Soft footsteps walked down the hall and up the stairs. She had no idea who it was, and didn't much care. Maybe Kootch came back down to show her where the straws were, since she didn't want a glass. Maybe a burglar was coming in to steal things and kill her. Maybe Carla had snuck out to meet Stan the septic man and was just returning from her rendezvous of love. The thought didn't shock her. After all, why should being old make you immune to folly? Or make you want sex less, which came down to the same thing.

She went back to her ruminations. She'd picked a partner to suit her. One she could count on not to stay. To pick something different was to wander into a realm of the unknown, and that was risky, unpredictable. Humans, she decided, not only noticed differences more, they feared them, and ran to sameness at the expense of all wisdom.

The question was, how did you change that, if what you feared most was the change itself? Or was it best to just accept your limits, and get what you could?

She raised her bottle. "Do what you know and be damned," she said, and chugged some more tequila.

Then, the lights went on. She closed her eyes against the shock.

"Turn those off," she snapped. "If you're gonna rob me, you don't want me to see you, do you?"

"Delilah?" a voice asked. Jack's voice.

Great, she thought. Just what she needed. Another critical voice.

"You come here to tell me what a shit I am?" she asked. "Because if you did, you can skip it. I heard you the first time."

She heard him walk toward her, and opened her eyes. The lights were off again, and she could see him, her eyes more adjusted to dark than light at that moment. He ran a hand through his hair. "I came over to check on Carla. She called and asked me to come out and look at her foot."

"That's so nice. How's her foot?"

"Nothing wrong with it at all," he said, adding, "Kootch is back."

"I know."

He frowned at her, then at the bottle. "What are you doing?" he asked.

"Getting drunk," she said. "Or trying to. I'm not very good at it, y'know. I have an inordinate tolerance for liquor. Must be in my blood. Circus blood."

"What're you drinking?" he asked.

"Tequila. It's a cure for bad love. Drink two bottles. If you wake up the next day and you're not dead, you'll be cured."

She wasn't slurring her words yet, but the world was beginning to feel like a warmer, fuzzier place than it had been. She tilted the bottle, keeping at it.

Jack sat down at the table. "What happened?" he asked.

"Me," she said. "I happened."

"You happened?"

"I happened to walk in on Michael with another woman. For the second time in our history together."

"Oh," Jack said. "I'm sorry. I really am."

She looked at him, and saw that he didn't look upset. In fact, he was chewing on his lip like he was trying to control its motions.

"Are you laughing at me?" she asked. "That would be very rude."

"Of course not," he said. "I said I'm sorry it happened."

"That's what your words say. Your face is saying something else," she pointed out.

He raised a hand palm up, then let it drop. "I didn't like him," he said bluntly.

"You only met him once."

"He seemed—fake. Phony."

Delilah was going to say something like fuck you, but then changed her mind. "He is," she said. "So why didn't I notice that before? Huh?"

"I—I don't know," he said. "Why didn't you?"

"It's not a riddle. I'm looking for answers. You want some?" she asked, offering him the bottle.

"I don't like tequila."

"More for me," she said, and took another swig. "Maybe I didn't notice he was a fake because I'm a fake, too. Maybe he's just a reflection of my tortured, inadequate soul."

"Maybe you just had to figure it out and now you have," Jack said calmly. "It's not that bad."

Delilah wondered what would happen if she tried to stand up, and then realized she didn't have to, which made her feel more cheerful. "You're right," she agreed. "It's not that bad. You know what bad is?"

"What?" he asked.

"Dead is bad."

"You're right. Dead is bad."

"Yes. I know that because my brother died. Did I tell you that?"

"Yes," he said. "You did."

"I did, didn't I? I don't know why I told you. I never tell any-body. I never told Michael and I was engaged to him."

"Delilah," Jack started to say, but she waved his words away.

"I'm trying to explain something. The way you explained about your parents. You know what my brother dying taught me?" she said, no longer sure she wasn't slurring.

"What?" he asked.

"Not to trust anything. Not any goddamm thing at all. Least of all this body." She tapped for her chest, hoping she'd actually hit it. She did. "Because this body lies to me. It tells me lies."

"No," he said. "No it doesn't."

"Yes, it does. It told me to sleep with Michael. Again. The clit-oris," she said with some authority, "has eight thousand nerve end-ings, all of which have betrayed me. Every single damn one of them. Did you know that?"

"They didn't betray you," he said. "Your fear betrayed you."

Dammit, she thought. He was saying what she thought. How dare he do that, without knowing anything about it? He had no right. "You think you're so smart, Dr. Brown," she said. "Minor deity and all that. So what the hell do I do about it, huh? Where's the answer to that?"

He tapped a finger against the table. "Are you really drunk?" he asked.

"After all the alcohol I consumed, I sincerely hope so. Don't change the subject. I say my clitoris betrayed me."

"Jesus, you're stubborn. That wasn't your clitoris. Not any part of your body. That was your mind. You just tend to get your signals mixed up, then you trust your mind too much, and your body not enough."

She raised the bottle. "Here's to my mind," she said, and took a big gulp, then coughed some of it back up.

Jack laughed his evil laugh, which suited her mood. "Your body's probably telling you to put that bottle down now," he said.

"However, as you note, my mind disagrees." She raised the bottle again, but he put a hand on it.

"Wait a minute," he said. "Just—give it a minute, okay?"

She gave him what she hoped was a disdainful look. "Is this the part where you lecture me about my integrity? Or lack of integrity? Or lack of direction? Or general lack?"

"No. Look, I'm sorry about that. What I said—well, the reason I said it wasn't what I said it was."

"Try again," she suggested. "Use more nouns."

"Come with me," he said. He grabbed her hand, and she was raised to her feet, which, surprisingly, held her up just fine. It's a bitch when you can't even do some damage with tequila, she thought.

"Where're we going?" she asked.

"Outside."

And they were. He led her through the sliding glass doors and out into the yard, his one arm around her.

"I can walk on my own," she said, realizing she sounded like Carla.

"I know," he said. "That's not why my arm's around you."

"Then why is it?"

"Figure it out," he said, and walked her to the pond, where

they stopped and he waved a hand around. "Look at that," he said.

She blinked. "Can't see the turtle butts. Too bad."

"See," he said. "That's what I want to tell you."

"That I can't see the turtle butts? I already knew that."

"No. That you want to see them. That it matters to you. The thing about you, Delilah, is that you're wild."

"Oh no," she said. "I always play it safe. Stick to what you know. Losers."

"No. That's the fear. That's not you. You're wild. And it scares the hell out of you because you can't control it, so you just stop doing anything except looking for losers, to try to keep that wild part down."

"That," she noted, "doesn't make sense."

"Yes it does," he said adamantly. "You know what kind of love you're capable of. You knew it when your brother died, didn't you? And you've been running from it ever since."

She frowned. Something in his words was sinking into her belly, getting under the tequila and making her feel a heavy sort of sorrow she didn't want anything to do with.

"No," she said. "Just—no."

"C'mon, Delilah. You know I'm right." Jack put a hand on her neck and tilted her head up toward the sky. "Look at that," he said. He pointed toward the sky. The night was clear and the sky was filled with stars, all of which seemed to be spinning just a little more than she should have been able to discern.

"Ooh," she said. "It's Cassiopeia. Where's that bottle? I want to drink to it."

"There," he said. "You *see* the pattern in what's wild and full of chaos and—and life. You can see it. You can name it. You ought to let yourself live it, too."

His words went a little bit deeper, and began to ache.

"I don't know how," she whispered. She brought her head down, overcorrecting a little, then swung it back up. "I'm just a little bit of stardust floating around a strange and wicked world."

"You're a beautiful, wild, honest woman with a heart full of fire," he said. "You're made of the stars, and you came here to love as wild as you can. Not in a way that you *think* is good. In a way that *feels* good. Can't you feel that? Can't you?"

She blinked hard, trying to see if she could feel something besides tipsy. Blinking didn't help. She closed her eyes, and tried to feel something in the dark behind her eyelids. Was it true, what he was saying? That she was wild, and afraid? She felt something stirring in her, not unpleasant, but not immediately familiar either. As if she remembered it from a long time ago. A memory of a feeling. It frightened her and she didn't know how to get past that fear. She needed something. A giant trust fall. That moment between deciding to fall and being caught.

She opened her eyes.

"I want you to throw me into the pond," she said.

"You—what?"

"Throw me in," she said, holding her arms out. "Just do it."

"But—why?"

"I don't know, but if you stop to talk about it I won't want you to and it'll be over, and I'll never get it back."

Carla was right. He was a good man. He didn't hesitate.

He scooped her up in his arms, and carried her to the edge of the pond, then stopped.

"Ready?" he asked.

"No," she said. "But go ahead."

She felt him swinging her back. "Shit," she said, feeling suddenly sober. Then, as if she were a stone, he tossed her.

She rose, and then she fell, obeying all the laws of gravity. She knew it must be happening very fast, but like the trust fall, it felt very slow. On the way up, she realized she was now completely sober, and exhilarated by a pure sense of motion. On the way down, she realized that she didn't believe the water would open up to receive her. That she'd never believed something that simple, even though all her knowledge told her it was true. Knowledge didn't matter, though. Something deeper than that did. Belief. Feeling. The sure and pure sense of being. She floated through all of it, toward the murky water.

She had time to worry briefly about the turtles, hoping she wouldn't land on one and hurt it. As she hit the water and felt herself sink down into it, she saw an image of herself as a meteor, coursing across the sky and falling into water to become part of the land, emerging from land and water as a human, knowing she was sent here to learn to love. Only that, and nothing more.

Then, she hit, and went under and felt the silencing quality of water.

It muffled all sound, including words. Even the words in her head were gone, and she was left with the perception of water against skin, the way it slowed her, the way it would carry her if she let it. There was only perception, and the felt presence of all the creatures that lived here, and she thought of how much she loved them for no reason other than that they existed. All the turtles and the frogs and herons and little fish and the land that held the water and held her. She loved them all, with an inordinate, inexplicable love.

It was good to be there, in this silence, feeling all that. She opened her eyes and couldn't see a damn thing except murk, but that didn't matter. She didn't want to rise to the surface yet. She just wanted to stay there, where she could feel all this, at last.

She prolonged the moment a bit too long, because the next thing she heard was a splash, and then she felt an arm wrapping around her and dragging her to the surface. She rose as she'd fallen—without volition or fear.

When she came sputtering to the surface, Jack was pulling her to the shore, and she was pissed off at being so rudely dragged from her reverie. They stumbled onto the grass and she fell down onto her knees, coughing, while he squatted behind her, slapping her back.

"Stop that, you shit," she yelled, trying to pull away. "You unmitigated shit. You did that on purpose."

The clarity of her observations stopped him cold. For a moment, he said nothing, obviously, she thought, stunned by the quality of her mind. When he could find words again, he spoke.

"Of course I did," he said. "You were under too long. Delilah, you can't stay under the water."

"But I *wanted* to," she said. Unexpectedly, her anger was turning to sorrow, and she felt a sob creeping into her voice. Embarrassed, she kept her back to him and buried her face in her hands. "I liked it under there."

She rocked back on her heels and kept her face from him so he wouldn't see the water falling out of her, as if she'd taken in the pond and it was coming out of her as tears. He would know she was crying. How could he not? But she didn't want him to see. They were her tears, and she had a right to them. Hadn't she gone into the pond just to find them, reclaim them for herself?

He didn't say anything, just occasionally put a hand on her back and rubbed. When it seemed like there weren't any tears left, she sat down hard on the ground and rubbed at her eyes. "Oh, God," she said. "I'm a basket case."

"Not too bad," he said calmly. "Sounds like you were due for a blowout. Did it help?"

"I guess so," she said.

"That's good," he said. "Are you sober?"

She held a hand up and blinked at it. It remained stationary and singular. "Yes," she said.

"That's good, too."

"Why? Maybe I want to be drunk."

"The way things were going, I was worried you'd get naked with me tonight, and hate me in the morning."

"What—the force of my attraction is that way over the top for you, you couldn't just say no?" She started to wring out the bottom of her dress.

"That's right," he said quietly.

She was sure she heard him right. She just couldn't believe it. "What?" she asked.

"The force of your attraction," he said. "It's way over the top for me. Way over. I've just been too much of a coward to tell you."

She sat there, hearing him breathe behind her, feeling him not move toward her, and let the words sink in. He was making a declaration, and she had to think about what that meant, understand it.

"Stop it," he said softly. "You're trying to figure it out. Stop it, and just—just—know what you want."

What she wanted. Romance? Love? To save the world? Something profound enough to wake her up in the morning. Something a little wild to toss her into the water now and then. Something real. Something true. Something wild about her heart.

She twisted around, wanting to see his face, wanting to question him, know more about it. But when she saw him, she couldn't get a word out of her mouth.

He wasn't wearing his eye patch. It was the first time she'd seen him without it, and he might as well have been naked.

"What's wrong?" he asked, then saw where she looked. He raised a hand to his injured eye and shrugged. "It came off in the water," he said. "Sorry."

"No," she whispered, raising her hand to his, and pulling his down, away from his eye. "I want to see."

He opened his mouth to say something, then closed it again and just let her look.

The eye itself looked normal, except for a sort of white cloud over half of it. But all around the eye were lines of scar tissue, spiraling out like the arms of the Milky Way. It was complex and beautiful. She lifted a hand to touch it. The scars were smooth and fine, like threads pressed into his flesh.

"Golden spiral," she murmured.

"What?" he asked.

It was something she learned about in an astronomy class. Golden spiral. It came from a certain type of rectangle that could be squared infinitely but still have the same ratio. If you connected a curve through the corners of these infinite rectangles, a golden spiral would form, infinite and perfect and ubiquitous, because it existed not only in geometry, but everywhere in nature. It was in milk stirred into coffee, in seashells, in fingerprints and DNA, in the face of a sunflower, in the Milky Way. It was a reflection of eternity, mapped in the skin and the sky.

And mapped in the scars around Jack's eyes.

She shook her head, unable to explain all this or what it meant to her. It was nothing. It was everything.

"It's beautiful," she whispered. "You didn't tell me it was beautiful."

"No," he said. "It's you. You're beautiful."

He put a hand on her shoulder and drew her close, and then they were kissing, and it felt even better than the first time, because now she could kiss him back, and press against him without restraint. He kept on kissing her, and she hadn't felt such unqualified intent in a kiss in a long time. Maybe never.

"God, you feel so good," he murmured into her hair. "Are you sure you're sober?"

"Sober enough to know this is a bad idea," she murmured back, her arms wrapped around him.

"How bad?" he asked, kissing his way down the side of her neck.

"I just broke up with someone. Two people. I obviously have relationship issues."

"Small window of opportunity," he said, starting on the other side of her neck.

"And we don't know each other very well, do we? Not really. So anything could happen, and it might be bad."

"That's right, too," he agreed. "Does it feel good to you, Delilah?"

"Yes," she whispered. "Yes, Jack."

He moved her hair so he could kiss the back of her neck. "Tell me another reason," he said.

"I'm cold," she said. "Wet and cold."

He stopped kissing and pulled back from her. "Take off your clothes," he suggested.

"What?"

"They're wet. You'll be warmer with them off."

Okay, she thought, so it was the old "you'll be warmer with your clothes off" trick. She tumbled to that right away. But he was right. Without the damp dress sticking to her skin, the night breeze felt just right. And his hands, that seemed to want to touch her everywhere, all at once, were soft and brought heat into her skin wherever he touched.

It was even better when he took his shirt off, holding her to him so that the heat of his body began to warm her. Somehow, Delilah thought as he pressed her back into the earth, the Taconic orogeny didn't seem made of clay and shale. It seemed soft, and still warm from the day.

And she didn't care if it was right or wrong. Stupid or smart. It just was, and it was what she wanted very much.

Looking over his shoulder into the sky, she could see the Milky Way, but it didn't seem half as interesting as the golden spiral of scar tissue around his eye.

She noticed, too, that he didn't stop looking at her the whole time. Not for a moment.

combined elements:
fire and earth

When Delilah woke in the morning, she was immediately aware of two things. First, the air was redolent with the smell of frying bacon, and she was hungry. Second, she was naked, and not alone.

"Jack?" she asked. He mumbled something, rolled over, and put an arm around her.

"Jack," she said with more conviction. "It's morning. Someone's cooking breakfast."

"Impossible," he muttered.

"No. Really."

"Then—Jesus." He sat up fast and looked at her hard. "Delilah?"

"At least you remembered my name," she noted.

His expression shifted from confusion to happiness. He still wasn't wearing the eye patch, and she got to see the fineness of scar in the light now, and how his eye seemed to have a half-moon etched over the dark iris. He reached down and stroked her face.

"You're naked."

"I know. I can't find my clothes. What if Kootch comes out? Stan the septic man shows up? Or Eleanor."

Her dress was under them. With some effort, she got it sorted out from her legs and the ground. It was still damp. "I've got to find my bra," she said.

"Over there." He gestured. Then he sniffed the air. "Is that bacon?"

"I think so. Hungry?"

"Starving," he said, struggling with his own clothes. "Carla's not that bad with breakfast, actually. She can fry an egg, at least. Let's go inside."

Delilah was on all fours, crawling around, feeling successful that she'd found both bra and underwear and was getting them back on her body. "I can't go in there like this. You can't go in there like that. You can't go in there at all."

"Why not?"

"Well, she'll know."

"So what?"

"So what? She'll—she'll— I'll be embarrassed."

"About me?"

"About this. Having sex."

He put a hand on her shoulder. "I hate to break it to you, Delilah, but Carla knows about sex. In all probability, that is. Of course, there's the odd chance that . . . hell."

"What?" she asked. "Hell?"

"It's six o'clock," he said, glancing at his watch to confirm that this was true. "I have to be at the clinic this morning. Hell."

"You can't leave me here like this. To go in there alone?" she protested.

"I thought you didn't want me in there."

"I don't. But I don't want to go in alone, either."

"Delilah, I have to go. Listen, I'll call you later. Tonight. Will you be here?"

"Yes. Later. I'm supposed to have dinner with Monica. After that."

"Okay. I'll call you," he repeated. He kissed her once, and started to leave. She grabbed his arm.

"Wait," she said. "Wait. You're not going to go have sex with someone else, are you? When you leave here?"

He laughed. "Looking at it objectively, I've got more to worry about than you do. Will you run back to Michael when he calls to apologize?"

"No," she said. "Definitely no. But a week from now, or a month, will I find you in bed with someone else?"

"No, Delilah. I don't do that."

"Will you make me get in a tub of blue Jell-O cubes?"

He frowned. "I tend to doubt it," he said. Then, "Look, Delilah. I'm a monogamous kind of person. I just don't spread myself that thin, okay? You'll have to get used to it. And you'll have to be monogamous, too, if you want me around."

"Huh," she said. "A possessive man."

"Yeah," he said. "Sorry about that. It's the way I am."

He kissed her again, briefly, and left her with his shirt, which was too damp to wear, he said. It was all the comfort she was going to get. She went inside.

Carla was standing at the stove humming something that sounded like the wedding waltz. She turned when Delilah entered and smiled, then made a face. "You're alone?" she asked.

"Yes," Delilah said. "Of course. You expected the army?"

"Wasn't . . . somebody else here?"

"Of course not," she said, too loudly. "You can see I'm alone."

Carla looked her up and down, and stopped at Jack's shirt, which she was clutching in one hand like a security blanket. "Mm-hmm," she said, and went back to frying and humming. "Bet you're hungry."

"Starving, actually."

"Mm-hmm," she said again.

"Sleeping out in the air does that to you," Delilah said, again too loudly. "I guess I dozed off out there."

"Yup," Carla said, flipping an egg. "Some good night air, and a few orgasms work up an appetite."

Delilah stared at her back. She saw that it was shaking a little, then noticed Carla was chuckling.

"You know something," she said, her back still to Delilah. "I didn't have an orgasm 'til I was thirty-six. I didn't know what it was. Thought I was dying or something. Then, the man I was with, he told me. Said it was about time. I took to it real good after that."

Delilah sat at the table. Carla grabbed a plate and slid an egg onto it, and bacon and home fries, and some toast that was waiting on the counter.

"Orange juice?" she asked when she brought Delilah the plate.

"Um—yeah. That'd be great."

She got it, and brought it over.

"Um—Carla?" Delilah asked.

"Yes, dolly?" she said.

"Why are you being so nice to me?"

"I don't know," she said. "I guess I just feel good about things today. About the world. And my place in it."

Delilah narrowed her eyes. "Did you call Jack last night because you knew I was down here getting drunk?"

"I didn't call Jack last night," she said, eyes wide with innocence. "Did I?"

"He said you did."

"Old people are so forgetful. He tell you that last night, or this morning?" she asked.

"Last night," she said. "This morning he told me he'd call me later."

Carla's grin spread as wide as Delilah had ever seen it, her face filled with triumph.

"Jeez, Carla, I don't have a clue what you're enjoying so much."

Carla pointed a thin finger at her. "Being right," she said.

Delilah thought about arguing with her, then gave it up and laughed instead. Carla deserved her pleasure, she thought. What the hell. God knows, she'd had hers.

"Okay," Delilah said. "But when he comes to visit, I'm not going to make him stay in another room."

Carla chuckled some more, and shook her head. "You know what I think you should do," she said.

"No," Delilah said. "I don't."

"I think you should call your mother, and tell her to come for a visit."

Delilah gulped at the orange juice, and it went down the wrong way. "You do?" she sputtered.

"Yes. Call her today. Tell her," Carla said. She pushed herself up from the table and left the room.

When she was gone, Delilah noticed the burning smell. The stove was still on. She caught it just before it curled all the Teflon off the pan.

After breakfast, Carla went to do whatever mysterious things she did when she wasn't visible, and Chaos, of course, came to visit for a while. Delilah was getting used to it. Either you saw Carla, or you saw Chaos, and there was no explanation for these things. That's just the way it was.

Kootch appeared and made himself a sandwich, and when she greeted him brightly, he narrowed his eyes at her, shook his head, and took his sandwich elsewhere. She cleaned up and then got on the phone and called her mother.

"Delilah? It's you?" she asked.

"In the flesh. At least, I am here. Not there."

"What?"

"Nothing."

"Delilah, Thomas says you broke up with him."

"That's right."

"He said—um—you're sleeping with Michael?"

"I don't think you needed to know that, Mom," she said. "Anyway, it's not true. Not anymore. I'm sleeping with Jack."

"What? I think my cordless isn't working. Did you say you're coming back?"

"No, Mom," she said. "Listen. Carla said she wants you to come visit. She said she'd like to see you."

"Oh," her mother said. "Oh my. When?"

"Anytime. Tomorrow?"

"Well," she said, and Delilah could hear her backpedaling. "I've got the Save the Reef benefit on Thursday. Maybe I could come after that. Oh no. Then there's the—"

"Mom," Delilah said. "Here's some advice. Show up before she changes her mind. This weekend. Saturday."

Her mother made a twittering sound. "I'm a little nervous about it," she said.

"Don't be. She—she loves you, Mom."

"What? What did you say?"

"Nothing. I'll tell you when you get here. Saturday. Call and let me know when you're getting in as soon as you know, okay?"

"I—I guess I will, darling. See you soon."

That done, and Delilah's feeling of satisfaction about it only adding to the satisfaction of the day, she called Monica at work, and miraculously, got her on the line.

"Hey," Delilah said. "We're still on for dinner, right?"

"Absolutely. Did we pick a place?"

"Not yet. That's why I'm calling. Provence?" she suggested. It was a nice little place nearby with good food and high prices. She felt celebratory, and she had a credit card.

"Oh my," Monica said. "Are we celebrating?"

"Sure," Delilah replied.

"What are we celebrating?"

"I'll tell you tonight," she said.

"You know I can't wait that long to hear," Monica protested.

"You'll have to. See you at seven. Ta ta."

Delilah distinctly heard her say "bitch" before she hung up.

While her hand was still on the receiver, the phone rang again. She picked it up, and said hello.

"Delilah," a voice said. Michael's voice.

She hung up.

At *seven that evening,* she was sticking her fork into a thick piece of lobster. Provence had the best *fruits de mer* she'd ever tasted, bar none. Delilah enjoyed it, having already filled Monica in on the developments of the night before.

"It can be a nice small wedding," Monica said as she ate. "Very tastefully done. I hear this restaurant caters as well. I'll wear something in a deep blue. Such a nice color for me."

"You'll wear a cream-colored pantsuit from Ann Taylor. And I'll wear red," Delilah said. "Or green. Anything but white. But don't order the flowers yet. It's early days."

"Oh," Monica said. "You might as well put his initials on the towels."

"Jeez, Monica. I haven't known him that long, first of all.

Second of all, he hasn't said anything about commitment. Well, not per se."

Monica reached over into her purse and pulled out a napkin, which was a little worse for wear. Her scrawl was all over it. She waved it in Delilah's face. "Remember?" she said. "What I was writing that night you came over?"

"The Foundation tabled it and moved on in the agenda."

"Time to take it back out. Look at that."

Delilah did, but as usual she couldn't read Monica's writing. "It says something about peace in the Middle East, I think. Is the Foundation working on that now?"

"Give me that," Monica said, and grabbed it back. "It says that the reason I didn't stay at the powwow is because Jack had already made his choice, and it wasn't me."

"What?" Delilah said. "It says that?"

"Very clearly. You see, that's what I sensed about him. He's a man who makes up his mind and then stays. When he kissed you, he obviously meant it, and once he means something, it's all over. And you better pay attention to that quality in him. You're not accustomed to it."

Delilah was suddenly a little nervous. Love was all very well and good. As was romance. Even monogamy. But Monica was talking staying. "You mean it, don't you?" she said.

"Most seriously," she said. "Delilah, this man is different than the other men you've been with. He's a—what's the word"—she said something in Spanish. "He's substantial. He's not like Thomas, who you can ignore. Or Michael, who you know is going to disappear sooner or later so you don't have to worry about it. He knows what he wants. At the powwow, that was you."

"Well, how come I didn't pick up on it?" Delilah asked. "I'm the one he kissed."

"You didn't pick up on it because you had a head full of revenge."

"Revenge?"

"Not revenge. Avenging. Avenging your past mistakes. With Michael."

"Yeah," she admitted. "I kind of came to that conclusion myself."

"I knew you would sooner or later. You usually see the light, once you open your eyes. You and Michael were never going in the same direction, anyway. It just looked that way because you were both in flight."

Delilah nodded. "Am I still? In flight?"

"No. Just scared shitless."

"Not shitless," she said. "Just scared."

"Good. You should be. This is a for-keeps kind of guy. And not just about you. Once he makes a commitment to something, he sticks by it. He's going to take you seriously, Delilah. It will be a new experience for the Foundation."

"Yeah," Delilah said. "Me, too."

Carla sat in her room smoking and watching the moon. It was near full, its light pouring down over the expanse of the land Carla could see from where she sat.

Jack had told her something about the moon. Something about how you thanked it, because it was responsible for all things relating to women. The menstrual cycle, the bearing of children. At the time, she'd laughed, because she still remembered how full the moon was when she had her baby.

But she was long past that now. She lifted her face, and let moonlight pour down on it, not thinking, just being part of the motion of light as it moved over the face of the earth.

It was like the blue tube she'd ridden down. Just like sliding down the blue tube.

She breathed in smoke, and let it out. The curling motion of it was the same as the moonlight, the same as the motion of her soul as she watched it become part of the moonlight, part of the smoke, part of whatever it would become.

It would feel like that, she hoped. When the time came, if it felt like anything, she hoped it would feel like curling smoke, like moonlight, like sliding down the blue tube.

When she was in the circus, she did trapeze work for a while. She didn't have a talent for it—the tigers felt more natural to her—but while she did it, she remembered the wind moving through her hair, which was long and dark, and she was very proud of at the time.

There was a perfect freedom in that motion, which was only disturbed by the knowledge that she had to leave the trapeze, and leap into the waiting hands of whoever was catching her. That was the part she didn't do well. She knew the man who was catching her was a drunk, and how could she give herself to that? But the moments before, when the trapeze moved back and forth and she moved with it, held securely in her seat, the wind moved through her hair. She hadn't felt anything like it since, until she tried the blue tube with her granddaughter.

And now, sitting in the moonlight.

She remembered what Jack told her. He said—now we thank our grandmother the moon, who is responsible for all things relating to women.

Delilah would be alright now. The moon would see to it. The land would hold her like a mother, and show her where to go, what to do.

She lifted her cigarette in silent salute to that body of light. She drew in smoke, and breathed it out again.

TWENTY

combined elements:
water, earth, and fire

Jack was true to his word and called that night. Delilah thought that was a good sign.

They talked in whispers while Carla watched the Discovery Channel in the other room—Delilah had taught her to like it, and felt proud of that, though she did seem to prefer the shows on murders to the warthogs and cheetahs. Everyone has his preferences in predation, however.

"Why are we whispering?" Jack asked at one point.

"I don't want Carla to hear," Delilah said.

"Why not?" he asked.

"I don't know," she said.

"Oh," he said. "As long as you're clear about it."

She laughed, and stopped whispering. He was right. It was ridiculous.

"Listen, I have to work at the clinic tomorrow night, but I'm done at ten. I can come over after, okay?"

"Okay," she said. "You're sure you want to? Won't you be tired?"

"Not that tired," he said. "See you then."

"See you then," she agreed.

She slept well, having only one strange dream about getting married to three men at once while wearing her pajamas, and woke the next morning to hear Carla in the kitchen, cursing soundly. She clambered down the stairs to see if the roof was falling in around them, or there was a fire or earthquake, and found Carla in the laundry room, water curling around her feet.

"Shit," she said. "Shit and damnation and hell and—and cock-sucker."

"Carla!" Delilah gasped. "Cursing in the house?"

"Why not?" she shouted. "You do. Everyone else does. What the hell is my problem, trying not to?"

Delilah had a feeling she'd been a bad influence. "I don't know," she shouted back. "What the hell is your problem?"

"Nothing. I don't have any goddamn problem except this f-f-fucking washing machine. It's leaking."

"It's fucking leaking," Delilah said emphatically. "Is it the fucking machine, or the pipes?"

"The fucking machine," Carla said. "Get a fucking towel."

Delilah got a few, and helped her wipe up the mess. Carla grumbled as they were going along, but seemed to calm down by the time they had it all mopped up and the towels were in a bag to go to the Laundromat.

"Carla," Delilah said, "did you ever think maybe it's time to retire this old place? I mean, we've got plenty of room in Key West. You could live there with us."

Carla fixed her with a cold eye. "This is my home," she said. "I'll never leave it, alive or dead."

"Maybe," Delilah suggested, "there's a time to leave things. To—let them go."

"No," she said, and raised a finger to point in her face. "Listen, young lady. You're the youngest person besides Jack I've had around here in a long time, and more than once all I could do is look at you and wish I had your arms and your legs and your heart and lungs and—and pancreas. And you know why?"

Delilah shook her head.

"Because if I did, I could take care of this land the way it ought to be cared for. I could—tend it. I could fix it. You don't have a clue what it means to take care. Neither did I when I was your age, which is why your mother went somewhere else to grow up. But I know now, and I'm telling you, I will not leave this house. When I'm dead you can bring me to Macintyre's Funeral Home and cremate me, and put my ashes right back up there on that hill. I stay here. Do you understand?"

Delilah understood. At least, she understood when a force of nature was confronting her, and knew better than to argue. You just listen to it, or get the hell out of the way.

Carla stomped out of the laundry room. After a while, Delilah heard the car start, and said a silent prayer that, wherever she went, nobody would get in Carla's way.

When all was quiet again, Delilah made a radical decision. She went to the mall and spent a long time looking at washing machines at Sears, ordering an expensive, energy-efficient one for Carla, which they'd deliver later in the week. She had a credit card and she knew how to use it. And if there were problems with the pipes as well as the machine, they'd let her know when they got here. While she was there, she went shopping for new underwear—new lover, new underwear, she thought. That's the rules.

Then she made a trip to the Laundromat with the towels and wet clothes, and sat reading magazine articles about sex and dieting while she watched them tumble around and around in the soapy water. She had either a quiet or taciturn or sullen supper with Carla, depending on how generous she was feeling with her adjectives, and stalked around nervously, waiting for Jack to arrive.

Which he did.

She was in her room, as it happened, and he just opened the door and walked in.

"Hi," she said, feeling a little shy of him suddenly.

"Hi," he said, and looked around. "Your room, huh?"

"Big Bertha's room. I get to use it in her absence."

"That explains the art," he noted. "I stopped and said hi to Carla. She told me about the washing machine."

"It's okay," Delilah said. "I bought her a new one."

Jack's eyebrow lifted over his patch. "Brand new? Does she know that?"

"Not yet. She'll know when it gets here."

"She won't buy brand new, y'know. Doesn't want anything that'll last longer than she will. That's what she says."

"I didn't hear anyone giving her a choice this time," Delilah noted.

Jack grinned. Took a step toward her.

"Uh-oh," she said. "You're going to kiss me again, aren't you?"

"I think so," he said. "Is that a problem?"

"I don't know. Do you think we should?"

"Give me reasons why not?"

"Um . . . I'm scared?"

He stopped walking. "You, who dares to buy Carla a new washer? You're scared? Of what?"

"Of . . . I guess I wasn't expecting anything like this. Like us."

"I thought you liked unexpected things."

"I do. Only, they scare me sometimes."

"Then we'll go slow," he said, walking toward her in slow

motion. She giggled, and took a step toward him. Sure enough, he kissed her. Then he kept walking, until they both fell on the bed, which creaked loudly.

"Shh," Delilah said. "Carla'll hear you. No creaking in the house."

"She doesn't care. No. That's not what I mean. I mean, I have special dispensation to creak. She said I should ask you out."

"Ooh, I knew it. A plot. A conspiracy."

"Shh," he said.

To avoid noise, they used the chair instead. And then the floor. Then the windowsill, which was a little dicey but nobody got hurt. "You like sex, don't you?" Delilah noted.

"Yeah," he said. "I do. A lot. And it's been a while. It's particularly good with you, too. With us. Don't you think so?"

She did, and proved it with her actions.

He was pretty tired after that, so they went to sleep, curled against each other like two leaves folding against the night. Before they fell asleep, Delilah said, "Jack?"

"Mm?" he replied.

"I want to ask you something."

"Go ahead," he said, sounding awake now. "But if it's about STDs, first of all you should've asked before, and second of all, I've been tested for everything."

"No," she said. "It's—" she stopped.

"What is it?"

"Your eye. Does it—bother you? I mean, the way it looks, not the way it feels."

"Not unless I'm aware that it's bothering other people," he said. "Some people are funny about it. They stare, but they don't know what to say, and it makes them nervous."

"Praised are you, Creator of the Universe, who varies the forms of your creatures."

"What?"

"That's what you say when you see unusual things. At least, that's what my father taught me. You couldn't ever have it fixed?"

"When it happened, no. No money, and no real procedures. In the last few years, with laser surgery, there's possibilities."

"But you haven't looked into them," she noted.

He ran a finger contemplatively in little circles over the skin of her arm. "You get used to your scars," he said. "They become a part of you. And in some ways, I think it makes me a better doctor. My patients see the patch, or the scar, and know I'm someone who understands pain. Makes them trust me more." He shrugged. "Maybe I'm a little afraid to get it fixed. What would I be like then?"

He leaned on his elbow and looked down at her. "Does it bother you? Is it painful to look at?"

"No. It's kind of intricate and beautiful, actually. I was just wondering."

She lay there and felt the warmth of his body next to hers, thinking about how fragile it all was. Their skin permeable to all kinds of dangers, their bodies subject to scarring and burning and disease and age. Yet, they continued to love them, scars and all. Continued to live with the knowledge that they'd have to give it all up someday, and loved in spite of that. Or maybe because of it. Maybe it was only the limits of time that made them learn to love as foolishly and passionately as they did.

"First time anyone said that about it," Jack murmured. "Maybe that's why I'm in love with you."

"You—love me?" she asked softly.

"I do. I've been crazy for you ever since you pointed that pitchfork at me. Very sexy," he said. "Pitchforks are very sexy."

"You mean, you're infatuated with me."

He sat up and hovered over her. "I'm infatuated with Britney Spears. I love you."

"But—you hardly know me."

"I don't believe love is about what you know," he said. "It's about what you feel, and your willingness to stay with that. I'm pretty clear on both."

Delilah thought about this, letting the words roll around inside her to see if they made sense. The first half was easy, she thought. It was the second half that got tricky. The willingness to stay. Because how could you predict that, if you didn't have enough information to judge what staying might mean?

"But I've never been to your apartment," she protested. "How can we be in love if I've never been to your apartment?"

"I don't think," he said, "that necessarily counts for much. But if you want, you can come over tomorrow. I'll cook dinner for you."

"You cook?"

"Somebody's got to feed me. I'm usually the one who's home to do it."

"Is that why I'm in love with you?" she asked. "Because you're the one who's home?"

He stroked her face. "Seems like a pretty good reason to me."

He left early in the morning. When Delilah went downstairs, Carla was humming again, making bacon and eggs.

air

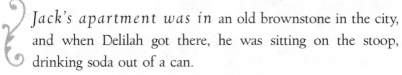 *Jack's apartment was in* an old brownstone in the city, and when Delilah got there, he was sitting on the stoop, drinking soda out of a can.

"Hey," he said, holding out the can. "Lady. Spare a dime for an old soldier?"

"I'm sorry," she said. "You look more like a pirate, and I don't give money to pirates."

"Then how about a kiss?" he said, grabbing for her hand.

"Oh," she said. "That. I *only* give those to pirates."

"My lucky day," he murmured as he drew her to his lap and kissed her.

The kiss went on for some time, and she was aware of people passing by, whispering to each other.

"Maybe," she suggested, "we ought to take this inside."

They did, and spent some time working up an appetite before

he served her something with scallops and lime that was really good. She accused him of trying to impress her.

"Absolutely," he said. "Usually, I live on baloney sandwiches and Oreos. All us bachelor men are like that, you know."

After dinner, they were tired and went back to his room to lie down. He had a water bed, which was warm and accommodated the body in some ways that regular beds didn't. Delilah felt herself rocked gently within it as if in a womb, and was in danger of falling asleep there, which she didn't want to do. There was the question of Carla, and letting her spend a night alone.

"Not that she hasn't spent plenty of nights there on her own," Jack said. "She'd actually hate the idea of you going back just to look after her. She hates the idea of being looked after."

"I know," Delilah said, "She hisses and spits at me when I check her feet."

"You've been doing that?"

"I said I would."

"I know. I just wasn't sure how comfortable you were with it."

"It's fine. And she seems to be doing okay. But . . ."

". . . But your parents are coming, and you don't want her to set the house on fire before they get there, because you'd have to explain that it happened while you were out having sex with—with—"

"A minor deity," she finished for him.

"Come here, human chattel," he said. "And worship."

She didn't leave as early as she planned, but she thought there were some forms of prayer that were rather compelling. And even though it was almost midnight by the time she pulled into the driveway, when she got in the house, Carla was still awake, watching TV. She went into the room, and Carla blinked at her, then rubbed her eyes.

"Eleanor?" she asked.

"It's me. Delilah."

"You," Carla said. " I knew that."

"You okay?" Delilah asked.

She waved a gnarled hand. "Fine," she said. "My eyes bother me at night. And don't start on it, okay? Everybody's eyes bother them at night sometimes. Sit down and tell me how Jack's doing."

"How do you know that's where I was?" Delilah asked.

"Because your face is flushed, and you got a mark on your neck."

She put a hand to it. "Oh," she said. "Huh. How'd that happen."

"I don't want to know," Carla said distinctly, then softened some. "I'm glad you're enjoying yourself."

Delilah sat down. "Carla, how come you like him so much?"

She shrugged. "What's not to like? He's handsome. He's smart. He's a good man. And a doctor. Anybody'd be glad to have him, and I hope you appreciate that."

"No, I mean how come you're so glad about me and him? I mean, what's it to you?"

"Like I told you," Carla said. "It's good being right. You losing your memory?"

Delilah persisted. She'd learned that was the only way with Carla. "But—I mean, you really thought it was right, from when I first got here?"

Carla leaned back in the chair and closed her eyes. She was quiet for some time, and Delilah was just beginning to think she'd fallen asleep when she spoke.

"No," she said. "Before that. Before you got here."

"Before?" Delilah asked. "Carla, you take your shot yet?"

"I told you, I'm fine. Turn that damn TV off. I can't hear myself think."

Delilah picked up the remote and hit the power button. The room got quiet.

Carla sighed. "Go to the living room closet. There's a box in there. A shoe box. Payless Shoes. Bring it in here."

Delilah did as she was told. When she came back and tried to hand Carla the box, she waved it back. "Open it," she said.

Delilah did, and looked inside. It was filled with papers, some of them news clippings, some of them letters. She picked one up and read. It was the announcement of her mother and father's wedding. She put it back and picked up another one. It was the newspaper announcement of her birth, and Joshua's. Then, another, which was his obituary.

"How—how did you get this?" Delilah asked. It didn't make any sense, didn't fit into any context she knew or could create.

"Kootch," Carla said. "He's a private detective. Retired now, but he keeps on top of this for me."

"I—thought he was in the circus."

"Kootch? Not him. He was a friend of Big Bertha's. You know."

Delilah didn't want to think about it. She had other concerns. "But he—what—tracked us?"

Carla pierced her with her dark eyes. "Did you think I'd just give my baby away and not check up? Not make sure it was all okay? That she was with good people, and her life went well?"

"I thought there were laws against that kind of thing."

"Not back then," she said. "Or at least, it was easier to get around them. I knew who took her. I stayed out of their way, but had Kootch keep track. He even managed to get me some copies of your mother's report cards. They're in there. You can look."

Delilah rummaged through paper and saw that Carla was

telling the truth. Report cards, and even a funny drawing of a chicken were there. Under that, she found a copy of Margo's wedding announcement, and her own standardized test report from high school.

"Carla," she said. "This is mine."

She wasn't sure if she was horrified, or pleased. There was something eerie about having been watched all that time, without permission. But there was also something flattering about it. She did matter, after all. Her life was a story that interested someone she didn't even know.

"Sure," Carla said. "I checked up on you, too. And your sister. And your brother." She shook her head. "That was sad," she said. "I wished I could see you then. But I didn't think it'd be right. Anyway, I knew all about you. Going to school to study rocks. I knew you were around here."

"But you never tried to—to talk to me?" Delilah asked.

"Are you deaf, child? I said I didn't think it was right." She looked around, as if someone might be eavesdropping nearby, and lowered her voice. "I did see you, though. You didn't know about it."

"Where? How?"

"At a bar. Kootch told me the bars all the kids at the University went to, so I went and hung out at them. One night, you showed up. Had this guy with you looked like a real snake-oil salesman."

"That would be Michael," Delilah murmured.

"I heard you call him that. Didn't like him much."

"I wish," Delilah said, "you told me that at the time."

"You wouldn't have listened. I could see the look on your face. Didn't listen this time, either, did you?"

"No," she admitted. "I didn't."

"Water under the bridge," Carla said. "Anyway, I knew about

you. And I knew about Jack. I picked him for you a long time ago, when I met him at the clinic. I was saving him for you, trying to figure out a way for you to meet him, but then you went away," she said.

"And I came back, because my mother got the wrong information."

"And I was right, wasn't I?" Carla said.

"So far," Delilah said. "But it's a ways to go yet."

"Hmmph," Carla said. "You're already there and you don't even know it."

She pushed herself out of her chair, and started to hobble out of the room. At the door, she stopped and put a hand on the wall. "You be good to him," she admonished. "And make sure he's good to you."

She didn't wait for Delilah to say anything, but continued her journey.

"Carla," Delilah called after her. She stopped, but didn't turn around.

"Thanks," she said. "For Jack, and for everything. I'm glad I found you."

Carla was still for quite some time. Then, very softly, she said, "Me, too, dolly."

"Carla?" Delilah asked.

"What, dolly?"

"You put the lotion on your feet?"

Carla was still, and then she chuckled softly. "Damn kids," she said. "Go to sleep." And she made her way up to her room.

Delilah would like to have been able to say that she knew something was wrong. That she had a dream, or a premonition, or even an instinct. But she didn't know until she knew. The only thing different she observed, and that only in looking back, was that

Chaos wasn't in her room that night. But who can ever fathom cat behavior fully? She thought nothing of it.

In the morning, she got up and saw that nobody was in the kitchen. She went out in the yard and saw that nobody was out there, except the turtles in the pond, and the heron, who stood contemplatively in the water, peering down.

"Hey, kids," she said to everybody in general. "How's it going? Pretty day, huh?"

And it was. The sun was shining, and her parents would arrive around noon. They were going to rent a car, so she didn't even have to go pick them up. Margo wasn't coming. They didn't want to overwhelm Carla, so she would show up in a couple of days.

Delilah lingered by the pond and watched the heron, watched the turtles stick their butts up, then float back down into the water. The heron made a dive for one of the turtles, and they all quickly receded. She came up empty.

Delilah was glad. She knew it was nature for heron to eat turtle, but she didn't necessarily want to watch. Not today. Soon, the turtles reappeared. They didn't seem afraid of being eaten, she noticed. They didn't make themselves invisible, or cease floating at the surface of the water because the heron was there. Apparently they'd all adjusted to each other's presence, and accepted it. It reminded her of a cat she had when she was little, who would sit in the yard near the bird feeder. The birds came to the feeder anyway, and sometimes the cat would just sit there and lick her paws while cardinals and chickadees fed within a foot of her. Other times, she would leap up and grab one.

Still the birds came to the feeder, and most went away alive.

Delilah turned her face up and let the sun warm it as she listened to the soft buzzings of insects in the grass, and the motion of air through the leaves of the trees.

The land speaks for itself, she thought. It didn't need her to say anything about it, though for all she knew it might listen to her the same way it listened to the rain and the wind, the forks of lightning and the undulating clouds that roll above it. She spent a moment wondering how it might perceive her. What she looked like, sounded like, felt like to it. She thought of the pond, and imagining herself as a star, falling into water to become a fish, and then bones that become land and grow humans, so that she might be a human on the land.

Maybe her drunken perception as she fell into the water was the right one. Maybe the land made humans to love. Just for that. To take care. To love. Maybe that energy of love fed the land in ways they would never know, and that was all the earth perceived of humans. The way they love, and the stories they told of loving each other in so many different ways.

She thought, I am human. Small. Brief. A rain of words and emotions. Maybe that's what she was here for. Maybe, she thought, that was enough.

She went inside, but Carla still wasn't up. She went upstairs, and saw that the door to her room was closed. She decided to go knock on it. God knows, Carla had woken her up often enough that Delilah could return the favor.

"Carla?" she called softly, after knocking. No answer. Delilah opened the door.

She saw that Carla was still in bed, her eyes closed. Her face had a sort of smile on it. "Carla?" Delilah asked. No answer.

She went closer to the bed, still not thinking anything much. Still in a heronlike state of contemplation. "Carla?" she asked again.

Still no answer. Delilah put a hand down and touched her shoulder. It was cool, her skin papery and dry. She had one more brief moment of not knowing, then she saw that Carla wasn't breathing.

"Carla?" she asked one more time, but it didn't come all the way out because she started to cry. She cried fast, and hard, not knowing she'd do that, not expecting that of herself. She sat down on the bed and kept crying for some time. "Oh, God," she cried. "Carla? Carla?"

But of course Carla didn't answer. She was dead.

TWENTY-TWO

earth

Delilah stayed in Carla's room, crying, for some time. When the tears subsided, she looked around to see if there was any evidence of what caused her death, and she saw none. Carla was old. She died. That was all.

Delilah noticed a sheaf of papers on the table next to Carla's bed, which looked as if she'd been reading them. Delilah opened them, and saw the word "will" and wondered if Carla had some kind of premonition, and wanted to make sure everything was in order. She would, Delilah thought.

Then, she remembered that the order of the day included the arrival of her parents. She had no idea what to do next. There were things you had to do when someone died, weren't there? But what? She tried to think. She asked herself what Carla would like. She looked down and saw that she was wearing a decent nightgown, which was good. She wouldn't want to be caught dead in a bad one, Delilah thought. Then again, she might want to have real clothes on. Delilah went to her closet and got some out, thinking she would dress her. But there were legalities to attend to. Didn't a doctor have to say she was dead? Say she wasn't murdered? Did she have to leave everything the way it was? It didn't seem right to call in some stranger for permission to change Carla's clothes.

Then she remembered that she knew a doctor who wasn't a stranger. She went to the phone and called Jack.

"What?" he asked. Not hello, or who is this. What.

"Did I wake you up?" she asked.

"Clinic called me in," he said. "Late. Three emergencies at midnight."

"I'm sorry," she said. "It's Delilah."

"I know," he said.

"Listen, I think you have to wake up, or tell me what to do or something."

"Do? About what?"

"It's Carla," Delilah said. "She's—Jack, she's dead."

There was a long silence.

"Are you sure?" he said at last. "Sometimes a diabetic coma . . ."

"She's not breathing," Delilah said. "There's no heartbeat. And—she's cold."

He breathed in and out. "Okay. I'll come over."

"Jack—wait. She's in her nightgown. I thought I should dress her. Is that okay?"

"Any sign that Kootch came in and killed her for her money?"

"No," Delilah said, a little shocked. "Of course not."

"It was a small, sick joke, Delilah. It's okay to dress her. I'll get there as fast as I can."

Undressing and dressing a dead body wasn't as easy as she thought it would be. It didn't work with her. Of course, with Carla, at least dead she wasn't working against her.

Delilah was surprised that it didn't feel creepy. It felt like the kind of intimacy women had shared since the beginning of time. Dealing with the dead. Being kind to the body, even after it was no longer in use. Respecting that fundamental tool that walked us through our days.

Delilah talked to her as she went along, telling her what she was doing next, and why. Then, she stopped talking, and started to sing. She didn't know any religious songs, so she sang a Pretenders' song called "Hymn to Her." Then she cried some more.

The body, she thought, was a wonderful and terrible thing. It brought so much pleasure, and so much awareness that the pleasure was fleeting. Small and brief. It was a terrifying thing, being human. It took courage just to be, and accept not being as an end.

It seemed odd, when she thought about it, to dress someone for decomposition. Or cremation, which Carla had asked for. She didn't know if she believed in any kind of afterlife, though she did believe in infinity in a scientific sense, and she believed in ghosts, which was one way of saying of course there's something else. Maybe she just didn't know what she believed an afterlife would be like. Reincarnation? That was the basic law of the universe, it seemed. Energy can neither be created nor destroyed. It was all just the same old stuff, popping up in different forms.

She imagined Carla, in the ground, the earth consuming her and sending her back as a place to plant flowers or vegetables, as little tiny creatures that crawled invisibly between layers of earth that were then eaten by bigger creatures, which were eaten by bigger ones, until perhaps Carla would be, in some measure, a deer, or a coyote, or even a wolf. Knowing her, if she had a choice, she'd pick the wolf.

And if there was no consciousness during the process, perhaps you became part of the consciousness that consumed you. Delilah could imagine being a part of this beautiful blue planet spinning in space, pulsing with life and life and more life. It was everywhere, and no matter where they put you in the earth, you were bound to be part of it.

She wondered if Joshua, who had been cremated and his ashes scattered at his favorite lake, was part of it now, and if so where she might look for him. In the pine trees around the lake? In blades of grass at the edge of the water? In the pulsing of a firefly that sat on the blade of grass, seeking a mate, a mate, a mate? Or in herself, because she had breathed him in, after the trees breathed him out?

He could be anywhere. Everyone was everywhere. Carla would be, too.

The largeness of life that ate death and spit it back out as life again filled her, and came out of her eyes as more tears, which would water who knew what little specimen of microscopic life crawling across her skin, or the floor, or Carla's face.

When Jack arrived, she was still crying. He came into the room and put his bag down and held her for a while.

"I'm sorry you were alone with this," he said. "Are you okay?"

"I'm better than Carla," she said.

"We don't know that, do we?" he said. "Not for sure. Listen, you want to go downstairs and let me do my thing with death certificates and so on?"

"I've been here all along," she said. "I might as well stay."

"Okay," he said.

He took out a stethoscope and listened to Carla's heart, which was silent. Then he put a hand on her pulse, which was also silent. He wrote things on a piece of paper, and then opened her eyes and looked into them.

"Is that weird?" she asked.

"It's my job. Or part of it. Not the part I like best, I'll admit."

"But is it weird? I mean, to sort of treat her like a thing? Like—like not Carla."

"I hope," he said, smoothing a hand over her cheek, "I'm not doing that."

"No," Delilah said. "You're not. Only—sometimes you have to see bodies like they're machines, don't you? Fix the broken parts."

"Sometimes," he said. "I guess I do. Did you check her meds?"

"No. Should I?"

"I just wonder . . ." He let the words trail off, and opened Carla's nightstand. Delilah saw his hand moving, his lips moving as he counted. He closed his eyes and seemed to have a conversation with himself, then turned to her.

"Delilah," he said, a question in his voice. "Was Carla—was there anything—did she act strange last night at all?"

"She showed me this box. It had clippings in it about me, and my mother."

"What?"

Delilah explained it to him, even the part where Carla had said how she'd picked Jack for her, long ago. He listened, little wrinkles forming on his forehead as he absorbed it all.

"Hell," he said. "Carla, you didn't."

"Didn't what?" Delilah asked.

He seemed to think hard for a moment, then said, "To hell with it." He wrote something on the paper, which Delilah guessed was the death certificate, then took her arm. "Let's get out of here. We've got some things to attend to."

"Jack," she said. "What is it?"

"Nothing," he said. "I'm just—a little shook up."

"No," she insisted. "Tell me."

He ran a hand over his face. "I can't tell if she took too much insulin. There's no way to tell. She could've been hoarding it, saving it up. I just—I can't tell."

"Would she do that? Deliberately?" Delilah asked.

"It's possible," he said. "She knew her kidneys were going. She was facing dialysis. She wasn't afraid to die, but she was terrified she'd have to leave this house. No. Not terrified. She just knew how much it would hurt, and that was a pain she couldn't bear. So maybe she solved the problem herself. The thing is," he continued, "even if we autopsy, we'd never be able to say if it was an accident or not. Especially the way she's been forgetful lately."

Delilah didn't know what to make of this, or how to feel about it. Carla was dead, one way or the other. Through forgetfulness, accident, deliberation, or just the workings of nature.

"Does it matter?" she asked quietly.

"Only for insurance purposes," Jack said. He shook his head. "It doesn't matter, Delilah. Not one little goddamn bit."

"No cursing in the house," she said. "Let's go downstairs."

After that there was all the business of death to attend to. They had to pick a funeral home, and Delilah knew the right one.

"She told me Macintyre's," she said.

"She did? When?"

"When the washing machine broke. She said— Jack, should I have known something was wrong? Should I have done something about it?"

"Like what? It's just—what happens."

How do we ever learn that lesson, Delilah wondered. Do we ever? Maybe not. Maybe we shouldn't. Do not go gentle into that good night.

They called Macintyre's, and continued taking care of this and that. Kootch appeared in the kitchen to make coffee, and was told the news. Jack called Big Bertha, who said she'd get in touch with Carla's friends. They called the paper to put the obituary in, writing it out on napkins at the kitchen table. They had enough to do that Delilah didn't even think about her parents until the hearse arrived and Carla was being taken away from the house.

Then, she became aware of another car pulling into the driveway.

"Jack," she said, as they were walking the body, on a stretcher and covered in a blanket, out the door.

"Who's that?" he asked, looking at the strange car.

"Well, there you are, Delilah," her mother said brightly as she exited the passenger's side. Her father got out after her, but he took in the scene, and the possibility began to register on his face, while her mother merely walked up to Delilah and kissed her cheek.

"Delilah," she said. "I've missed you."

The stretcher went right past her, and she didn't even see. "Mom," Delilah said, indicating Jack, "this is Jack. Jack, this is my mom. And that," she said, pointing toward the stretcher, "was your mother."

For the first time in her life, Delilah heard her father use the "f" word. Even Carla would have understood.

air

Delilah wasn't surprised that Carla's funeral was interesting, nor that it was odd. She was surprised, however, at how crowded it got. Between the circus people who were still alive, neighbors, and all the workmen who at one time or another had to fix something at her house, they had enough occupants for all the seats at Macintyre's. Then, young people started showing up, and it was standing room only.

There were cashiers from the local supermarket, who said Carla always told them what to do about their love lives. There was a group of young and middle-aged women, who Carla played gin rummy with at the hairdressers on a regular basis. And there was the hairdresser, who said Carla told the best stories about being in the circus. People from the nearby village showed up, saying they were grateful to her because she could have sold her land for a lot of money, and it would have changed the whole area, but she hung in there. She didn't sell out.

And a young man who met her at the clinic showed up. He said she loaned him fifty dollars. He used it for drugs and Carla probably knew that, but she gave it to him anyway. It weighed on him so much he got clean and sober. So he was here to thank her.

Huh, Delilah thought. Who knew?

In fact, the only one Delilah expected to see who didn't show up was Chaos. She had absolutely disappeared.

The minister at the funeral was old and said something bland about the rewards of heaven and a good life. He let other people get up and say things about Carla when he was done, and Delilah thought that was better. She got to hear some stories, and she even got up and talked about Waterslide World, and the way Carla made her eat those awful cakes. Some people there groaned when she mentioned it, so she knew she wasn't the only one.

Her mother and father were introduced, and nobody took it as odd that Carla's daughter and granddaughter should suddenly appear out of nowhere. They were the kind of people who took irregularity for granted, and Delilah appreciated that about them.

After the funeral, a lot of people came to the house for sandwiches. Kootch was there, of course, and Big Bertha, and Eleanor, who got back just in time for the funeral. They stayed on after the others had left, hanging around the kitchen, and the talk turned to what might happen next.

Eleanor sighed and said, "I wonder what'll happen to this old house now."

"Probate," Big Bertha said. "For sure. End up with some bank or something, and yuppies'll buy it. Make it into a bread-and-breakfast."

"Isn't that bread-and-circus?" her mother said. "Like the Romans had?"

"I think she means bed-and-breakfast," Delilah said.

"No," Eleanor said. "It won't take CEP but a minute to find out and come clamoring for it."

"Bread-and-breakfast," Big Bertha repeated, making sure everyone heard.

"Carla had a will," Kootch said. "It won't probate. There's a will."

"Are you sure?" Eleanor asked. "You know how she was."

"I know she had a will, because I made her go get one. And I witnessed it."

There was a silence. After a while, Delilah's father cleared his throat. "Does anyone know," he asked, "where this will might be?"

"With her lawyer," Kootch said. "Jimmy Duran. I know him, too. He was at the funeral last night."

"No," Delilah said. "I mean, maybe it is, but there's a copy upstairs. I—I saw it by her bed. At least, I saw something by her bed that said will."

Everyone turned to look at her. "Well," Kootch said. "Go get it."

Both her father and Jack spoke at once. "I'll go," they said, and both put their hands on the table to push themselves up. Delilah bit back a giggle. Jack and her father looked at each other.

"It's okay," Jack said. "I know my way around better."

Kootch snickered. Delilah glared at him, and he was silent. "Sorry," he said. "House of mourning and all that."

Jack left and came back before anyone else had a chance to embarrass themselves. He had the sheaf of papers in his hand. He handed them to Delilah's mother, but she waved them to her husband. "He understands the language," she said. "Let him."

Delilah's father got his reading glasses out of his pocket and put them on, opened up the sheaf of papers, and read.

"What's it say?" Bertha shouted after the suspense became too much for her.

Delilah's father looked at her over the rim of his glasses. "You get the linens in the front closet, the—um—rooster china in the back room, and the Orange Moon Face picture, along with any other contents of the room that are rightfully yours."

"The rooster china?" she asked, and sniffed into her sleeve. "That Carla. The rooster china."

"What about me?" Kootch asked.

"There are," Delilah's father said, "some volumes on the topic of penguins that are yours, and—well, it says here you have the right to stay in the house during the months of August and September, in perpetuity. I'm not quite sure . . ." He rifled ahead in the will. "Anyway, that's what it says. Oh, and the silverware in the front closet, next to the rooster china. She said you admired it."

"I did," he said. "I really did. Funny she remembered that."

There were similar bequeathments for Eleanor, for names of people Delilah didn't know who Kootch said were dead. "She made it a while ago," he pointed out. "Not everyone could hang on that long."

"Yes," her father said. "Of course. But there's a recent addendum. Added—well, just a month ago. Here," he said, pointing to it. "To Jack Brown. It seems she left you a life insurance policy." He squinted at the paper. "Been around for some time, so it might be worth something. And then—huh. That's odd."

"What, Dad?" Delilah asked, leaning to look over his shoulder.

"It says, 'And to Jack Brown, who has been as kind as any son, and kinder than many, I leave what I love best in the house.'"

Delilah squeezed Jack's hand, and felt him squeeze hers in return.

They waited.

"Well," Bertha asked, "what is it?"

He turned a hand palm up. "It doesn't say. Just that. What I love best in the house."

"Maybe it's me," Kootch said. "She said I could stay here."

"Yes," Delilah's father agreed, "she did. But we have yet to see how she plans to dispose of her real property. He shuffled ahead and read silently. Then, he looked up and stopped reading. He cleared his throat a number of times. He pulled a pack of Tums out of his pocket and ate one.

"Dad," Delilah said. "What is it?"

"Delilah," he said. "She left the house to you."

She stood up. "Excuse me," she said to all concerned. Jack started to rise with her. "No," she said. "Excuse me. I need to be alone."

And she left the house.

TWENTY-FOUR

combined elements: water, air, and earth

She walked out the sliding glass doors, and kept walking beyond the pond and up the ridge. She walked to where the ridge became woods, and then walked into the woods until she could see only trees. She found a tree and slumped at its base.

She asked herself what she felt, and the only word she could come up with at first was bad. She felt bad. Bad refined itself into a sensation of weightiness, as if the world rested on the back of her neck. This feeling became a sharp sense of anger, because it was too much to carry the world. Too much, and she hadn't asked for it, and she didn't know what to do with it. It simply pissed her off.

She picked up a stick and started thrashing around at trees and things. "The old witch," she muttered. "Witch. She-devil. God*dammit.*"

Less than two months had passed since she left Key West,

where she was living the high life in a mansion, without a responsibility to her name. Now she was owner of a house she hadn't picked, that Carla had perhaps killed herself to give to her. And it was a house that would own her. Carla had basically decided her life for her, doing it in such a way that she'd feel guilty as shit if she refused the gift.

Hadn't she left Key West because it seemed like a good idea to choose her own life? To find something worth doing and do it? Maybe not save the world, but something important and worthwhile. Hadn't she come here to make her own choices about that? She didn't choose that old house. She didn't choose for Carla to die. In fact, she was trying to keep Carla alive. What right did Carla have to take that away from her, make her choices for her? What goddamn right?

She hit vigorously at the trees with her stick, and started making guttural noises. "Goddammit," she repeated. "Can't swear in the house. Fuck that. Fuck that shit. Fuck it all." It felt good to do that, so she kept it up, getting louder and louder, until her throat began to feel hoarse, and she heard someone behind her, and whirled around.

It was her father.

She stopped thrashing and stood there, getting her breath back. "Was I loud?" she asked.

"Sound carries from a hill. Kootch was concerned," he said. "Jack wanted to come, but I said I wanted to talk to you anyway. Come and sit down . . ." he looked around. "Somewhere."

Delilah picked a tree and put her back against it. Her father lowered himself next to her, and they sat staring into the woods.

"I like Jack," her father said at last. "He's a good man."

"Yes," she agreed. "He is."

They were silent for a while longer.

"You don't have to keep the house, you know. You can sell it."

Delilah thought about that. It hadn't occurred to her. Carla gave, she had to take.

"I can, can't I?" she said, feeling better already.

"You may not want to, of course."

"No," she said. "I do. Of course I do. I mean, first of all, what the hell would I do with it? Live here? I don't want to live here. And second of all, I really, *really* resent Carla deciding my life for me, posthumously no less. Like I have to be her, and stay here and get old and cranky and—and damp."

"I'm sure there's solutions for the damp," her father noted. "Sump pumps and so on."

Delilah sighed. "Do you think I should keep it?"

"I think," he said, "you should be aware of all your options, and pick the one that's best for you."

All her options. Choices. What she wanted. And she had all she could possibly use, when she thought about it. She could go back to Key West and waitress. Jack might enjoy Key West. She might enjoy it more with him there.

Or she could call the man at CEP about that job. Michael would feel guilty enough now to do all he could to help her get it. She wasn't sure if Jack would be as amenable to that as he was to Key West, but she wouldn't know unless she asked. And she was willing to compromise. Work there only for a year, then look for something else. Relationships were about compromise, after all.

"I've got a lead on a job possibility," Delilah said. "Working for a petrochemical. It might not come to anything, but if it did, maybe I could do something good there. Make a difference, you know."

"If anyone can, Lilah," her father said, "you can. You always make a difference."

"I do?" she asked.

"You made a difference here already. You know, if you want to stay, your mother and I will help get the place fixed up. After all, it's her family property."

Delilah shook her head. "I don't want to be dependent on you two anymore. I'm thirty-one. I really should get a life of my own."

"Maybe," her father suggested, "this is your life. Only you can't see it because you're so angry at Carla for dying."

"Is that why I'm angry at her?"

"I would imagine so. You were angry at Joshua. Besides, death always makes you angry," her father continued. "It's a slap in the face, some bigger than others, but always a slap because it reminds us we all die."

He was right. She was angry at Carla, and not just for leaving her the house. "Jack's not sure if she killed herself. Did you know that? She may have taken a deliberate overdose of insulin."

"Oh. But—why would she do that?"

"She was getting sicker. Her kidneys, Jack said. She told me she'd pick her own way and her own time out."

"Well," her father said, "more power to her."

That surprised her. "Dad, how can you say that?"

"Wait until you're eighty-one, and then ask me. Or, no, ask yourself. I'll already be gone."

The thought of a world without her father in it was more than she could bear in the moment. But then, so had the thought of a world without Joshua. And lately, she'd begun to think Carla would be around forever, too. Maybe she didn't like change or the unexpected as much as she claimed to. Not that death was something unexpected. It was the great inevitable, along with taxes, and Michael Jackson's continued plastic surgery. Still, it always came as a shock. A slap in the face, as her father said.

"Dad," she asked quietly. "Why did Joshua die?"

Her father was quiet for a moment, then said very gently, "He had leukemia, Delilah."

"No," she said. "That's how. I want to know why."

"That," her father said, "I can't tell you, except it's what happens."

"But—how do you live with that? How do you just go on, knowing that?"

"You just—" He paused for some time, and Delilah was beginning to think that she'd asked too much of him. It couldn't be easy for him to probe this wound. Surely he had scars, too, though not as visible as Jack's. A sort of golden spiral around his heart. She wasn't even sure why she asked it, except that it was the question she never asked before, and she was tired of holding it in her heart.

"I don't know if I can answer that," he said at last. "I know I went on because there was you, and Margo and your mother. And maybe they went on because there was me, and so on. I'm not a religious man, Delilah. You know that. But I do think it's important to—to add to the store of joy and love in the world. And if we let our pain or fear keep us from doing that, well, maybe that's the only kind of sin there really is."

As answers went, it wasn't a bad one, though it really didn't matter what he said. What was important was that she asked, and in doing so, released a sorrow she'd held close and quiet for too long.

"Well," her father said when she remained silent, "give it some time. Don't decide based on your anger. Wait until that passes. As I said, we'll help if you need it—and don't worry about being dependent. After all, if you take a job with a petrochemical company, you'll be dependent on them. We're never as independent as we'd like to be."

"Maybe not," she murmured.

"The important thing is to find what it is you really love, and stick with that." He patted her hand, then pushed himself up.

"Your mother and I are going back to our hotel to get some sleep. We're leaving tomorrow, unless you need us to stay longer."

"No," she said. "I'll be okay here. After all, I'll have Kootch to keep me company."

"Yes. Kootch. I don't know if there's anything we can do about that, except hope he doesn't feel comfortable with it."

"You met him," she said, pushing herself up and standing beside him. "You know better."

They made their way back down the ridge.

When they returned to the house, everyone was gone except for Kootch, who had disappeared to some unknown part of the house, and Jack, who sat in the kitchen staring out the sliders. Her mother and father helped clean up, and then said their good-byes. When they were gone, the house was quiet. Delilah looked at Jack. He looked at her.

"Well," she said.

"Well," he agreed. He looked around. "There'll be a lot to do here," he said.

"If I want to get it ready for the market before winter," she agreed.

He turned back to look at her. "Market?"

"I'll bet it'd bring a pretty penny if it was spiffed up."

"You'll—sell it?" he asked.

"It's mine," she said defensively. "I get to decide, don't I?"

"Of course," he said. "Of course you do. It just—didn't occur to me."

"Come on, Jack. What do you think, that I'd live here?"

"I—I guess I thought you loved the place."

"Love this tumbled down piece of shit? I said shit, Carla," she shouted. "It's old, and it's broken beyond repair."

"So was Carla," Jack pointed out, "but you loved her."

"She was alive," Delilah said. They were still smiling at each other, but their smiles were getting strained.

"So is this," Jack said, sounding perplexed now. "The land and—everything. It's all alive. You know that."

She didn't want to go there. If she did, she'd lose her head. "There's other land. There's Key West. And Alabama. Or Georgia."

"Alabama? Georgia?"

"Two beautiful states," she said.

"Alabama?" he repeated.

She turned and walked toward the sliding glass doors, looked out on the pond. The heron was there. She turned away. "I'm just thinking it through. Weighing my options."

"Jesus," Jack said.

"What?"

"What? You know what. You take care of this house when it's not yours because then you don't have to really be attached to it. But when it's yours for real, you walk away because you're too scared."

"Sometimes, the smartest thing you can do is be scared," she noted.

"Not if it means you can't look at what you love best and say okay, I love this. Hell or high water, it's mine. You can't say it about a man, or a job, or even your own body, which you think betrays you at every turn."

"Dammit, Jack, it does. We all die, don't we? Everything dies. People. Houses."

"That doesn't mean you don't love the thing anyway. If that's what you love, then you just go ahead and do that."

"What for?" she spit out.

"Because that's what humans do best," he said. "It's the best thing we do."

"Those are two different statements," she said. "The first one implies some talent on our part. The second implies an ethical stance that—"

"Fuck that bullshit," Jack said.

She stopped cold and stared at him hard. "What did you say?"

"You heard me," he said. "I said fuck that bullshit. This is not an abstract philosophical moment. This is—important. It has consequences. Real ones. Who'll you sell it to? CEP? Since you want to work for them, you might as well."

"That," she said, "is not fair. You know I wouldn't do that."

"Do I?"

"Oh, you're gonna start on that integrity thing again, are you? Well, how about this—I'm Carla's granddaughter. She kept an eye on her own needs. So will I."

"She didn't sell her soul to do it."

"She gave up her baby, didn't she? And this house is not my soul."

"CEP is? I don't think—" he started, but she cut him off.

"I don't think," she said, "that I heard you say the pertinent words here. Like, whatever choice you make, I'll back you on it. If you stay here, I'm with you. If you don't, I'm still with you. Because *you're* what's important, Delilah. Not any damn old house. I love you and I'm with you, regardless. I don't hear you saying that, do I?"

And that was the heart of the matter for her. Carla left him what she loved best in the house, but what if Delilah wasn't in the house? Would he still love her? And if not, what kind of love was that, anyway?

"Or maybe you're just pissed because she didn't leave the house to you," she concluded more quietly.

His face went through a lot of motions, and then got still.

"I'm right, aren't I?" she said, calm now. "You're not in charge of it anymore, and that bugs the hell out of you. Tough, being only a minor deity, isn't it?"

"That's not fair," he said.

"But it's true, isn't it? I'll tell you what. You want the house? Make me an offer. How's that? Or does that prick your pride too much?"

He was silent, glowering at her.

"Oh, great," she said. "And you say I can't face myself. You can't even make an offer for what you love. I'm not surprised. After all, you married a lesbian."

"What the hell does that have to do with anything?"

"Well, there must've been some hint about it. But you picked her anyway. And you thought I was a lesbian, but you fell for me, too. You don't have to be afraid of failing because you front-load the failure, and walk away a good guy, just like you're doing now. But then again," she said, her voice like ice, "you can't even give up your own scars."

She was sorry as soon as she said it, but the words would not retreat back into her mind where they could do no harm. Instead, she saw them written all over the pain in his face, and heard them in the tight control of his voice when he spoke next.

"What do you want?" he asked. "What is it?"

"Choices," she said, hoping she sounded more mature and deliberate than she felt. "Not yours, and not Carla's. My own."

He opened his mouth to say something, but it never came out. The phone rang, interrupting him. It rang once. Twice. They stood listening in silence, and then Jack stomped over to it and picked it up.

"Hello," he said. Then, "Yes. She's here. Can I tell her who's calling?" He held the phone out. "It's for you," he said. "It's Michael."

She stood still. "Michael?"

"Do you want it?" he asked, with a dare in the words. "It's your choice."

Delilah felt fury rise in her again. How dare he do this, use Michael to hurt her when he knew. He knew. But then, she knew, too, about his scar, about how to hurt him. Love was hopeless, she thought. It's a weapon in our hands, and we always use it. Her fury turned to defeat.

"I might as well talk to him as to you," she said, and took the receiver from his hands.

Jack stood looking at her a moment, then he turned around and walked out of the room.

"Hi, Michael," she said into the receiver. "Listen, that job you were telling me about. Is it still available?"

She heard Jack leave the house, slamming the door hard behind him.

TWENTY-FIVE

water

She stayed for another week, cleaning up, sorting stuff out. There were boxes and boxes to deal with, and she began to understand Carla's urge to burn. But she couldn't do that. Some of what she found she sent to the Salvation Army. Some, she had shipped to her mother, who might find it interesting. The rest she would store, or throw out.

She talked to a realtor, who asked her to describe the place, and tell him where it was, and so on. When she gave him the address, he said, "Oh. That property."

"What?" she asked. "Is there a problem?"

"Not at all," he said. "We could get you a sale on that right away. A very good one."

"You can?"

"There was a corporate interest in the property. Twenty acres, right?"

"Right. What corporate interest?"

"A few years back. I deal with the company on other properties."

"What corporate interest?" she repeated.

"CEP. That's—"

"I know what it is. I'm not selling to them."

He was silent for a moment, and when he spoke, his voice was soothing, reasonable, and a little oily.

"To be honest with you, I think you'll have a hard time selling the place for any decent price to a private buyer. I remember it well, and it's not in very good condition. If you like, I could just inquire."

"No," she said. "You could not."

She hung up, and got another realtor, who didn't mention corporate interest. She just said she'd come over and look around in a few days.

Delilah continued sorting, packing, and cleaning up.

During this time, she was mostly alone. Kootch was on the premises, but didn't make himself apparent except at mealtimes, when he'd appear to startle her, then disappear just as quickly. Jack didn't come around or call. Eleanor stopped by now and then, and Monica came over to help her sort things out.

"It's such a lovely place," Monica said. "It has such a nice feel to it. Are you sure you want to sell it?"

"You like the feel of it?" Delilah asked, surprised.

"It feels lived in. I mean, really lived in. Like real people lived here, and loved here, and died here." She shuddered a little. "Are there ghosts?"

"Not too bad," Delilah said. "Kind of like everyone else here. They come and go."

"We all do, Delilah. We all do. Such a lovely house."

"Yeah," Delilah said. "And you thought Jack was a lovely person."

"He is," Monica said. "Just because he has issues doesn't change that. Find me somebody without issues, will you?"

"His issues mean he's not here."

"Not right now," she said. "Maybe he has to think it through."

"Maybe he does. But I'm not waiting around to find out."

Monica sighed. "I was looking forward to a wedding. When do you leave?"

"A few days. I have to talk to the realtor."

"Where are you going?"

"I'm not sure. I have an interview in Alabama, with CEP. If that doesn't work out, I guess I'll go back to Key West. Maybe when the house sells, I'll try school again."

Monica patted her shoulder. "I have absolute faith in you, Delilah. You have issues, but you're like Jack. A lovely person. You'll make a lovely choice."

The realtor came and said that although the house itself wasn't worth much, given the location and the acreage, Delilah could get more than a hundred thousand for it. "An investor would pay that much," she said. "Of course, they'd resell it, but that wouldn't matter to you, would it?"

"Who would they resell it to?" she asked.

"A developer, perhaps. Or I seem to remember there was a company that was interested in developing this area commercially."

She felt the weight of Jack's stare at the back of her head. The weight of Carla's finger pointing at her. The weight of the turtles in the pond, and the heron.

In her mind, she whirled around and swore at all of them. Fuck you, she said. I did not ask to be responsible for any of this. You eat each other on a regular basis, anyway, and how will I save the world in my own damn way if I have to worry about all of you?

In her mind, they didn't have an answer.

"Put it on the market," she said to the realtor. "Sell it, and send me a check. I'll have a lawyer take care of the paperwork for me."

The realtor said she could put the sign up later today.

All that arranged, Delilah packed her bags, put them in the car, and drove away. She didn't go out to the pond to say good-bye, or turn back to look at the house one last time. She knew what happened when you turned around.

Once on the road, she felt better. A little lighter. She'd shed her burden, and what happened next wasn't entirely up to her. She didn't have to worry about it anymore.

She took a road out of the city that led past the river, because it was pretty with the sun just beginning to go gold over the water. The road was lightly traveled, and wound by the bike path that the state of New York had had the good sense to put in. She was driving along, feeling better by the minute, when she saw something in the road.

She drove past, then pulled over to the side and looked back.

It was a turtle, sitting in the middle of the road, looking around.

"Damn turtles," she muttered. "Damn fucking turtles." She decided to start the car and drive away, let it fend for itself. But she couldn't.

She got out of the car and went to it. She stood in the road, staring at it. It stared back. It was a snapper, as big around as a pizza, which she thought it would become if it stayed in the road for too long.

But she knew about snapping turtles. They were slow and not particularly bright, but once they latched onto something like a hand, they don't let go. They just don't know how. And once they set a course, they stayed on it.

She suspected that this one wanted to get back to the river, though she wasn't sure why it had left. She wanted to help it, but she didn't feel good about picking it up. It was still a snapping turtle. A car came down the road, and she waved it around. The driver craned his neck, then drove on. She looked around and saw that part of the road was treed, and there were sticks under the trees. She grabbed one, went back to the turtle, and started pushing its butt across the road.

"Damn turtle butts," she muttered.

Their progress was slow and laborious, because it kept turning around to snap at the stick. More cars went by, some of them fast, and she began to get concerned about becoming road pizza herself.

"Okay," she said. "We'll try it your way." She went around to the front of it and teased it with the stick. It turned its head away, and tried to walk in the other direction. "*Fucking* turtle," she said, good and loud. "Don't you get it? I'm trying to save your stupid turtle life."

Another car whizzed by. This one didn't even slow down to look. Just flicked a cigarette out the window as he passed.

"Asshole," she screamed. "It's his road, too, isn't it? Isn't it, asshole?"

Somehow, that made her think of the baby turtles in Carla's pond, and how it was their house too. Not just Carla's. Not just hers. Not something she could just sell out from under them. Her house, but their home.

"Stop it," she told herself. "Fuck that shit. And fuck you, too, turtle." She tried to turn to leave, go back to her car, but she couldn't do it. She could stand there and curse herself and fight with herself all she wanted, but she couldn't get back in the car until that snapper was on the other side of the road. Dammit.

She got behind it again, and started pushing hard with her

hands, muttering to it as it kept trying to reach around and snap at her. In this position, she realized she was even more likely to become a casualty, but she was determined now. That damn turtle was going across one way or the other.

She heard the sound of a car approaching, but it slowed and then stopped. She ignored it, and kept pushing.

"Turtle?" a voice said.

"That would be it," she said without pausing in her efforts. They were making progress, and she didn't want to lose the momentum. She kept pushing, turning only briefly to make sure it wasn't a cop. It wasn't. It was a middle-aged woman in an SUV, with a baseball cap on her head, turned backward.

"I don't know why they do that," she said. "This is the third one I saw this week."

"Yeah," Delilah said, and kept pushing and dodging. Little by little, with the woman watching, they made it all the way to the side of the road. She gave it one more good shove to make sure. It gave one more snap to make sure, and then it ambled off toward the river.

Delilah felt triumphant. Saving the world, one turtle at a time. She turned to smile at the woman, who was grinning in a lopsided way.

"You must be one of them decent people," she said.

"Saving the world," Delilah quipped, "one turtle at a time."

Then, she burst into tears.

The woman's mouth opened and she gaped at Delilah, who fled to her car, where she sat, sobbing.

She wasn't a decent person, she thought. Not even close. She wanted to save the world, but she wasn't even willing to take care of a few turtles, a heron, a home, herself.

She felt Jack's shock at the idea of selling the house, selling out. She saw all those baby turtle faces staring at her from the pond, asking her what would happen to their home, their home, their home. And she loved them, the way they turned their little butts up and dove into the murky green bottom. She loved them and the land itself, the way it whispered to her, and how soft the grass was in some places, how prickly in others, and the places where the deer bedded down at night. She loved it all, and felt like shit about it. Their home. Their home. Their home. A real home, not just Anyplace, USA.

And then, there was the snapping turtle, snapping at her, not knowing she was trying to help. Something about the way she helped it anyway. Something about Carla, pushing her into herself, her life, her home, her home, her home.

All of this was in her tears, as was the thought that maybe the way to save the world was one turtle at a time. Or one pond of turtles. A few acres. An old house and two hearts that yearned for each other.

And yes, it was impossible and pointless. The world couldn't be saved. She couldn't even save a turtle, really, because the heron might eat it, or she might eat it, being fond of turtle soup. But that didn't matter, because everything was pointless and impossible.

Turtles themselves were impossible and pointless. And so was she, and everybody in the world. And so was the whole damn planet, filled with turtles and herons, and lightning and fireflies and tarsiers, with those huge eyes, grabbing for bugs in the dark. Hedgehogs, and tornadoes, too, and all the funny little white flowers that popped up in Carla's grass, and all the bugs that lived in the grass—bugs that glow and bugs that look like sticks and leaves. And how about dwarves and Carla and Jack and Monica and herself. Most of all, herself.

It was all pointless and impossible, but that didn't stop the heart from loving anyway.

And in knowing that, she was no longer sure if she was saving the turtle, or the turtle was saving her.

"Praised are you, Creator of the Universe," she sobbed out, "who varies the forms of your creatures. Oh hell."

Then, she turned the car around, and went back to the house on Settles Hill.

combined elements: water, earth, air, and fire

Her father always told her that if she tried to do the right thing, in all likelihood the right thing would happen. When she became a cynical teenager, she asked him how that fit in with Dachau, and he said that was an anomaly. A breakdown of the working order. It was a statistical error, and shouldn't be used as a measure of normalcy.

She didn't believe him one hundred percent, but she found that what he said was often true, and when it was, it felt damn good.

She got back to the house before dark, and slept there quietly, better than she had in a while. She'd decided to call the realtor in the morning and take the house off the market. She'd get help from her parents, and do what she could to keep the place. She also thought she might go back to school, take some courses in environmental studies. It seemed like something that would suit her. In the meantime, she would waitress, and work on the house.

She was a little worried about what it would be like to be in the house alone, but then again, it was the kind of house you were never really alone in. Too much life around it. Besides, it seemed to fill up pretty fast on its own. Maybe that would continue.

First thing in the morning, when she woke up and heard a car crunch into the driveway, she guessed it would.

Somebody jiggled the handle, and she realized whoever it was expected the door to be open, and she'd locked it. She went padding to the door and opened it.

She saw two things. The first was Chaos, who shot into the house like a shadow on the move, stopping briefly to curl around her leg and purr before padding away. The second was Jack, who stood there gaping, as bleached as one of Carla's linen sheets.

"Jesus," he said. "Mary and Joseph."

"No," she said. "Just a minor goddess."

He put a hand over his face, then removed it and gaped at her some more.

"Still here," she said. She stepped back and waved him in, and he entered. They walked toward the kitchen.

"You here to make an offer?" she asked. "List price is a hundred and twenty thousand, as is. Realtor's number is on the sign."

"I came to get the realtor's phone number. I wanted to see if they had a number for you. I wanted to talk to you. Where's your car?" he asked. "There's no car."

"I put it *in* the garage instead of parking it outside the garage. Radical, huh?"

"Carla would be reeling," he said.

"It's not her house anymore," she said. "It's mine."

He stopped walking. "Yours?"

"Mine. And I get to do what I want with it. I was thinking of ripping up this stupid carpet," she said, poking at the stupid kitchen carpet with her toe. "Putting down a real floor. And the upstairs bathroom would be nice if you pushed it into that teeny tiny adjoining room, put in a real sink. A few mirrors even."

"You'll yuppify it," Jack said. "Bertha'll have a fit."

"It's not her house, either," Delilah said. "Not even Kootch's, though he can stay here because I can't stop him. And Bertha's certainly welcome to visit anytime."

"She is?"

"Of course. Friends are always welcome."

"Um," he said. "Does that include me?"

She stood in the kitchen, a few feet away from him, and shrugged.

He took a step toward her.

"Wait," he said. "Let me start over. Because there's this speech I've been rehearsing, in case I found you and you ever spoke to me again. Since you're here, I'd like to try it out. See if it plays."

"Shoot," she said.

He cleared his throat, and took another step toward her. "Delilah," he said, "what I meant to say before I got stupid is that you're right. You have to choose your own life. But I love you and I want to be part of that. Move to Alabama with you, if that's what you want. Fix up an old house with you, or buy a new one if you prefer. But be with you, regardless. That's what I want."

She let the words sink in a minute before she spoke.

"That offer's good if I sell the place and move back to Key West?" she asked.

"That offer is good if your address is the lower regions of hell," he said, his voice not a little husky. "It's you I love. You I want to marry."

Huh, she thought. He used the "m" word.

"Is that a proposal?" she asked.

"Yes," he said. "It most definitely is."

She took a step toward him, then stopped.

"Yes?" he asked. "No? You're not sure?"

She considered a minute. "Yes, I'm not sure," she said, and he scowled.

"I mean, I'm not *sure* that we'll do it well, or that it'll work, even," she continued. "Anything could happen, and often does. And I suppose we'll fight a lot, because we're both pretty stubborn. But I'm sure I love you. A lot. The way you laugh, and the way you understand about the turtle butts, and your scars and the way you're a pain in the ass. And I'm sure you're a good person to learn about love with. You don't drop people."

"So," he said, a little uncertainly. "That's a yes?"

"It's a big yes," she said.

And sure enough, he kissed her.

the hill

The old woman stood on the ridge, at the edge between the clearing and the trees, and listened to the land breathe in, and breathe out. It breathed slowly, she thought, and you had to learn to listen slowly in order to hear it.

Tonight was quiet enough to do so, and in the breathing, she imagined she could discern the echo of many voices that had been there before. People who stayed with Carla. People who stayed before Carla. The voices of her own children, Joshua and Cara. The voices of their children. The voices of all the people who stood on the ridge and witnessed her wedding, years before.

It had been a lovely wedding, she thought. Her maid of honor wore a beautiful cream-colored pantsuit, and she wore a green and gold dress. Her groom put on a suit jacket, but no tie. He preferred T-shirts.

The years they spent on the hill since then were just as beautiful, and just as busy. They always had something to do to fix the house, and after a while her husband got interested in landscaping, so that now the ridge bloomed with the fiery glow of red rhododendrons in the spring, the gold of chrysanthemums in the fall. All this while she went back to school, started work for an environmental agency, and they both fought the protracted battle necessary to make the 200 acres around the house forever wild.

Then the babies came, and grew, and had babies of their own.

She couldn't say it was always easy. Marriage had its tough parts, especially when the two people involved were as stubborn as they were. But they were just stubborn enough to keep at it. And the sex stayed great. The better the better, she remembered Monica saying. Monica was right.

But she wasn't surprised. She'd married someone who was like the land. He listened beyond words, and he called her beyond herself to that wordless place where all the wild things roam, and things were unpredictable at best.

Then again, she had come to learn that what was unpredictable *was* the best thing of all. At least, it worked out that way sometimes, though she'd be the last to say it would always be so. If it was, that would be, well, too predictable.

A light wind caressed the back of her neck, and she thought of her husband, kissing her there. She walked back down the ridge, and toward the house.

The hill breathed in, and out, and was silent.